The Protector

The Protector

MEREDITH WILD
MIA MICHELLE

PAGE
&
VINE

Page & Vine
An Imprint of Meredith Wild LLC

For Krystin, thank you for everything…
—Meredith

*For Emma, Braelyn, and Fuchsia—I am
so incredibly blessed to have you beautiful
ladies in my life. Thank you for always
believing in me, even when I didn't. I love
you with all my heart.*
—Mia

CHAPTER ONE

Every minute that passes, I seem to sink farther down into the couch. I'm smaller, heavier, less noticeable. I'm not sure I mind.

The room is noisy with music and people I don't want to talk to. I may be one of the most important people in the room, but I'm still new to the DC scene. Right now, there aren't that many friendly faces, though I'm sure that will change quickly. Our parents might run the world, but the rest of us just want to get fucked up and have our fun while no one's watching.

I take a gulp of tequila from my crystal tumbler and glance sideways toward the hallway. Zane stands there like a stone mountain, his body half-obscured behind the wall, the other half visibly squared toward me. His eyes are slate gray and seem to blacken when he's particularly pissed off. The rest of his features match his dark demeanor. His neatly trimmed chestnut hair does nothing to hide the earpiece he wears constantly. His skin is a natural olive. His typical black suit is tailored perfectly to his muscular frame, and my gaze lingers where it shouldn't—the apex of his thighs.

I return my focus to my drink and take another sip. My head is already buzzing with the effects of the alcohol, but I don't care. I've been living and breathing my father's election for almost two years. All eyes on us. All the right moves. Cameras, interviews, gossip, drama. At some point, my anxiety took over. And at some point, I started using whatever means I could to temper it.

The life of a politician's daughter was one I was used to, but nothing could have prepared me for the nationwide attention of the campaign. Months of brutal, relentless attention. As much as I wanted him to win, I dreaded the life we were signing on for. A new home in a new city, new friends, new everything. The only plus was no one was going to be looking at me under a microscope that way anymore. At least not until the next election.

Over the rim of the glass, one familiar face stands out among the group gathered in the large living area. Nate Christiansen's curly brown hair is tight to his scalp. He's tall with a pale complexion and a bright, practiced smile. The more I drink, the more attractive he becomes. He doesn't seem like a bad guy, either. This is the third time he's invited me over to his penthouse. Once for another party, and once for drinks that could have led to sex. But of course Zane was banging on the door, telling me I had to get back home.

Well, not tonight.

The inauguration buzz has died down, and my parents have settled into a routine that doesn't involve me. My mother's redecorating the Lincoln Bedroom, and my father has his finger on the pulse of the world. No room for me. No time for the daughter who only tried to be perfect for them.

I lift myself from the couch, steady myself on my heels, and move toward Nate. He turns away from the person he's talking to—another senator's son, no doubt—and the corner of his mouth lifts into a smug grin. I match it, and by the time I reach him, he's alone.

"Hey, stranger." I greet him in a sing-songy voice.

He trails his fingertip down my bare arm. "How's the party? I feel like we haven't talked all night."

"The party is great. But you know what?" I hand my empty glass to him. "Sometimes talking is overrated."

His lips part slightly as his gaze takes a journey from my lips to my tits and back up again. "You're absolutely right, Charlotte. I don't want to be inattentive to the needs of my guests. So tell me, how can I make this night everything you want it to be?"

The suggestion in his tone is heavy and obvious. Unquestionably, I'm heading down a path that will lead to his bedroom. And that's what I want. I want the tequila to numb the last of my inhibitions, and I want to get fucked out of my mind.

"Perhaps we could find a quiet spot," I say.

I glance back to Zane, who's crossed the threshold into the room and has me in his crosshairs, as usual. His intense gaze has my breath catching. Without a doubt he works out, and I'm guessing years of training has armed him with lethal skills that he'll never have to use following me around for the next four years.

I'm trouble, but I'm not that much trouble... Well, maybe

I am.

I turn back to Nate and keep my voice low. "Problem is, I have a hard time getting any privacy."

Nate's focus shifts to Zane and then back to me. His eyes are still and calculating. "Sure. Listen, the guest bathroom probably has a line. Why don't you use the one in the master at the end of the hall? It has a connecting room on the other side. I'll meet you there in a few minutes."

I smile easily, because the tequila is warming me, and I want a man's hands on me now at any cost. His plan sounds perfect.

Without another word, I spin and head back toward Zane, who is guarding the path I need to take. I don't bother acknowledging him or my plan in any way and slip past him. I'm almost to the door at the end of the hallway when he says my name.

It's low and clipped and sends a shiver down my spine. I spin toward him instantly, and he almost barrels into me. I brace my hands against his chest, but I'm off balance. He lassos my waist with his arm and straightens me before I fall.

"Sorry," he mutters, but there's no genuine feeling behind the word. He steps away, regaining a professional distance between us.

I blink a few times because I can't remember another time when he'd touched me that much. A subtle touch here or there to guide me through a crowd, but nothing that demonstrated his strength, his warmth... I'm probably just revved up in anticipation of being with Nate, but I feel like all the blood in my body just rushed between my legs.

"It's no problem," I say wistfully. God, I'm ready to fuck anything with a third leg right now.

"Where are you going?" His unfeeling tone brings me back to reality. He's only here to protect me and kill every chance I have at fun.

I take another step back. "I'm going to the bathroom. There's a line at the other one."

"I don't think you're supposed to be in there." He nods toward Nate's bedroom door.

I roll my eyes. "Zane, I've been here before at Nate's invitation, as you well know. I don't think he cares if I use his bathroom."

Zane's jaw hardens, and he resumes his normal posture. Legs wide, hands clasped together. Cold, silent eyes. "Fine."

I exhale with relief and hurry away before he changes his mind. I'm so horny now I can barely see straight. As I slam the door behind me, a door on the other side of the bedroom opens and Nate's there. He's head-to-toe smug white privilege, from his collared polo to his designer Italian leather shoes. He'll never be my type, but this is my life. I'll probably end up marrying someone like him. Might as well get used to it.

For right now, though, I just need release. I need to get out of my head, because the tequila's only done half the work.

I walk toward him, and he meets me halfway. His mouth is on me before I can say anything. He's all tongue and teeth. Bourbon on his breath. Awkward grasps that have my body tensing despite the fact that I asked for this. He nudges me to the edge of the bed and has his hand on the prize, groping me roughly over my panties. My arousal doesn't belong to him, but

I try to ignore that and kiss him back.

I just need to disappear and forget this warped existence of mine for a while. Can he give me that? Maybe he's a better lover than his foreplay skills suggest. He takes his hands off me long enough to unzip his slacks. Uncertainty falls like a stone in the pit of my stomach when he whips out his dick. It's long and thin and pale, just like its owner.

"You good?" He's got his hands on my hips again, pushing me firmly into the mattress.

I swallow and find my courage. "Turn me around."

He smirks. "You like it like that?"

I nod, because I'm not sure I want to see him when he's fucking me. I can think of something or someone else this way.

Zane. With his strong hands and eyes like a cold December morning. I gasp when Nate takes me out of my fantasy, spins me around, and yanks my dress up over my hips. He's rough in his motions, but I take two fistfuls of the blanket and brace myself for whatever he wants to do.

I wait for him to pull my thong out of the way when instead he takes a handful of my hair and tugs it painfully. I bite my lip to stifle my objection to his roughness.

Smack.

I yelp the second his hand makes contact with my ass. I struggle to get out of his grasp, but he's stronger than I am. Tears well up in my eyes.

He slaps me again, harder this time, and his fist tightens in my hair.

"Nate...no."

He's yanking my thong to the side. *No, not like this...*

I put my hands behind me, trying to push him away so we can end this before it begins. I'm stone sober now, my heart racing with panic.

"Sorry, baby. I should have told you...I like it rough. All the girls want it this way now. You'll see..."

Before I can beg him to stop, a thunderous banging on the door freezes us both.

"Charlotte. Open this door."

"Jesus Christ. Tell him you'll be out in a minute. I won't take too long."

I shake my head even though it hurts to. I don't want this anymore. "We should stop."

"Nah. This guy's cockblocked me for the last time."

I feel Nate's fingers against my pussy, and I can't help it. I scream.

Bang! Bang! Crack!

The sounds of the party carry into the room when the door busts open. Zane kicks it closed behind him, but it won't latch because the wood from the jamb is lying in a dozen splinters on the floor.

"Get your fucking hands off her."

Nate releases me and starts backing away from Zane's approach. He puts his dick away fast, and then his hands are in the air in surrender. "Hey, she asked for it."

Zane looks at me for a second. I yearn for his compassion, but his expression is hard and unfeeling as it always is. It's enough to push my tears over. He slides his intense focus back to Nate.

"Doesn't look like she asked for it." He takes Nate's shirt

and shoves him against the wall with a thud.

"You can't touch me!" Nate's eyes are wide. He's scared to death, and for good reason.

A twisted sneer curves Zane's lips. "You sure about that?" His tone is low and lethal.

"Let's go, Zane. I'm sorry. This is my fault." I barely recognize my own voice. It's watery and weak. I'm an idiot. So stupid.

My words are enough to end the increasing tension between the two men in the room. Nate's still shaking as Zane releases him and comes toward me. I've pushed my dress back down, but I don't feel like the same person who came into this room moments ago.

"Come on," he says quietly. "Time to go home."

I nod and let him wrap his arm around me and coax me toward the door.

"You're going to pay for that," Nate calls after us.

Zane stops us and turns his head back. "I'm sure the senator can take care of it. Because if her father hears about this, that door will be the least of your problems."

More tears fall. I should care that every reckless act is a threat to my father's image, but I barely know the man now. Everyone's too wrapped up in power mongering to notice me or care what I'm doing.

Zane guides me swiftly through the hallway, past the party, and through the front door.

I close my eyes and turn my face into Zane's chest. I feel like everyone can see Nate's hands on me. Have I ever felt so violated? A second later, we're taking the elevator down and

Zane ushers me into a limo waiting outside. I'm still in his arms once we're inside. I usually ride alone, but I'm so grateful he's here now.

The vehicle moves and tense silence stretches between us. My eyelids flutter open and for a few seconds, I take it all in. Zane's possessive hold on me. His cool masculine scent drifting over my senses. It's irrational after what Nate just did to me, but the arousal that burned from Zane's earlier touch is back.

The tears have passed, and somehow being cocooned in his embrace is the most intoxicating thing I've ever experienced. Maybe because I've been so deprived of touch, of attention. And I crave more of it...

I shift so that more of our bodies are touching. My thigh presses against his. My chest aligns tightly with his torso. When I look down, my breath catches.

Zane's erection is unmistakable.

The ache between my thighs can't be ignored either. I lift my gaze and try to rationalize Zane's hard expression with his body's reaction to me. Had I misread him all this time? Does he feel what I feel?

Only one way to find out...

I drag my hand from his chest down to the strained fabric by his thigh. My lips part with wonder when I feel his heat and girth under my palm. That quickly, he snatches my wrist and lifts it away.

"What are you doing?" His voice is a cold snap against the comfort he's given me.

I feel like I have whiplash. Who is he?

"You want me."

The muscles in his jaw bulge, but he says nothing. I struggle to free myself from his grasp, but he doesn't let me go. He tightens his hold, and somehow it's the perfect amount of pressure to make me dizzy with need. The heat between my thighs is almost unbearable.

"Take me," I beg.

His expression relaxes a fraction, and he shakes his head slightly. "You're drunk, Charlotte. The reasons don't end there."

I frown, frustrated as ever. "Nate didn't care and neither do I."

"Not sure if you noticed, Charlotte," he says each word clearly, as if I'm a child, "but Nate and I don't have a lot in common."

"I noticed."

I stare into his dark eyes, trying to communicate that this attraction didn't just crop up in the past twenty minutes. Zane's been protecting my family for months. How long has he wanted me?

I focus on his lips. I lick mine as I imagine how they might feel against me. Is he soft and gentle, or intense and passionate? What does he taste like?

"Kiss me. Just once," I whisper. I have to know how he feels.

"Charlotte..." His suit jacket tightens as he pulls in a slow breath. "This is dangerous."

"Please." The word is a whimper. I know he won't give me everything I want tonight, but maybe he'll give me this one thing. God help me, I need something to channel all this sexual energy toward.

He releases my wrist and cradles my face in his palms. My heart is pounding at his unexpected tenderness. My body is pulsing with anticipation and pleading for more contact. I can't wait anymore. I push up in the seat and press my lips against his with a desperate moan.

I expect him to push me away, but instead he opens his mouth against mine and suddenly we're fully engulfed in the most intense kiss of my life.

He's nothing like Nate. He gives as much as he takes. He seeks and savors. He tastes sweet and smoky. His movements aren't rushed. If anyone's rushing, it's me, because I'm desperate to feel more of him and get him inside me. But his palms never leave my cheeks, and with them he angles me how he wants. Dipping and sucking and exploring every crevice of my mouth with his velvet tongue. Good God, his tongue. If kissing was this good, I couldn't begin to imagine how he'd feel on my pussy.

As if that very thought has a physical tie to my clit, a fresh burst of desire hits me, and I'm drenched with arousal. I deepen the kiss and shift to straddle him in the backseat of the limo. I lower myself so I can grind on his stiff cock. Maybe he'll take me right here...

I moan desperately against his lips. "Fuck me, Zane. I'm begging you."

In an instant, our contact is broken. He rips our mouths apart and plants me back onto the seat beside him. We're both breathless, and I'm momentarily stunned by the lack of contact. I'm feeling cold and deprived, and I don't like it at all.

He drags his hand over his face and stares out the window. He speaks into the hidden microphone in his cuff, which communicates with the driver of this vehicle and the one that follows behind us. "I'm switching vehicles at the next light."

"What are you doing?" I can't help the pleading in my voice.

"The right thing." He doesn't make eye contact, but his voice has that icy final tone to it again. "Good night, Charlotte."

When the car stops, he's gone in an instant.

ZANE

I suck down a second cup of coffee, brush my teeth, and straighten my tie in the vanity mirror. Just another day at the office.

Yeah, right.

My reflection stares back at me. He knows I was almost balls deep in the President's daughter last night, and nothing in this world is going to erase those memories because they felt too damn good.

It's not unusual to get attached to the person I protect, but Charlotte Daley is different. For over a year, I've watched her transform from the picture-perfect daughter—a good girl—to a woman out of control. I've learned not to underestimate her. She's clever and determined, always trying to find new ways to get into trouble even when I'm on her ass constantly. But she can't hide the sadness in her eyes or the emptiness in her demeanor when she's trying to be someone she's not.

She's not a slut, but she's trying it on. I'm guessing it's

to punish the family that has systematically cut her out of their daily lives. My job is to protect them all. Charlotte from herself, and her family from her damaging behavior. Last night, I almost failed them.

I walk through my apartment and belt on my holster. I haven't had to draw my weapon around Charlotte, but I got damn close last night. The vivid memory of Nate Christiansen getting ready to shove his half-hard dick into her has me seeing red instantly. The fear in her eyes was unmistakable. Whatever I'd heard through the door wasn't a cry of pleasure. She was frightened, and I wanted to scare the life out of the little prick for it.

I had my job to think of, though. I sure as fuck wasn't thinking about it when I had Charlotte squirming all over my lap last night.

Damn. I have to see her in less than an hour and hope to hell we can both pretend like it never happened.

I shrug into my jacket, grab my keys, and head out.

◆ ◆ ◆ ◆

"Coffee?"

Chester hands me my third cup as I enter the room.

"Sure, thanks."

We're dressed the same. Standard-issue Secret Service uniform, so no one misunderstands who's shadowing Charlotte wherever she goes. Doesn't deter some as much as it should.

"Anything I need to catch up on?"

Chester shakes his head. He's got a couple decades on me, and it shows in his grays and deep wrinkles. "Nah, it's been quiet. She was sleeping it off most of the day. Must have been quite a night."

I resist the urge to roll my eyes. "You know it."

He chuckles and sips his coffee. If anyone knows what my daily life protecting Charlotte consists of, Chester does. But he'll never know about my indiscretion with her.

Chester's been assigned to Charlotte since the move into the White House, so he knows her routines and behavior now. But I grimace to think about him having last night's shift. Would he have known Nate was hurting her?

He puts his cup down on the pretty silver server and straightens his tie. "Well, I hope you're ready for round two."

I frown. "Pardon?"

He chuckles again. "She's got another private party tonight. She's getting ready now. Should be out soon."

I school my features and nod as if that's going to happen. "Have a good night, Chester. See you in the morning."

He lifts his eyebrows with a nod. "You too. Good luck. You'll need it."

He knows Charlotte is a handful, but he's older and treats her like a wayward niece. He doesn't want to fuck her. If he did...I'd probably have to kill him.

I wait until he's left the room before I make my way toward Charlotte's door. I knock loudly. After almost a whole minute, she opens it. Her eyes are tired but made up with dark black makeup that makes her bright blue eyes stand out even more. Her lips are stained red and glossy. She's wearing a tight black dress with boots that fold over the knee. My cock notices instantly, and I entertain a short fantasy of her straddling me with only those boots on.

I lift my gaze to her eyes again. "Private party tonight?"

"Yup." She fluffs her wavy blond hair but her focus is on the floor.

I'm glad she remembers her bullshit behavior at the party last night. I'm not as thrilled about her remembering our little rendezvous in the limo.

"I'm not sure that's a good idea, especially after last night."

She shakes her head, but avoids my eyes. "I'm fine. It won't be like last night."

"Let's chat, shall we?"

She rolls her eyes, and I have to take a deep breath to keep myself from berating her for acting like a spoiled-rotten brat. I put my hand on the door, silently communicating that we're not finished.

She turns into the room, and I follow her. Her quarters consist of a full suite, a large and opulent bedroom, an en suite bathroom, and a sizeable living room. She walks ahead of me through the living room and into her bedroom. The bed is covered in clothes, and a tray of food and drinks sits on her end table.

"How were you feeling this morning?"

"Not sure why you'd care," she mutters.

"I care because I'm paid to care."

She doesn't say anything and carries on picking out jewelry for her night out. Then I realize how shitty that must sound. Her parents don't care, and they're the ones who are supposed to.

"I'm sorry, that's not what I meant." I am sorry, but I hide all the emotion in my voice out of pure habit.

"Forget it, okay?" She turns toward me suddenly. "I don't need your sympathy, Zane. I don't need your fucking opinions."

"Just my cock."

She narrows her eyes. "Excuse me?"

I walk toward her, my hands casually tucked into my pockets. "You just need my cock. Or was that the booze talking last night?"

Her chest moves unevenly. "I can get laid whenever I want to. Maybe next time I will if you don't break down the goddamn door."

I'm at arm's length, close enough that I can smell her expensive perfume. Her words send a white rage through me, but I don't show it.

"Maybe I won't," I say quietly. "And maybe you'll have someone like Nate taking what he wants from you, and all you'll have left is regret that you let it happen. That *I* let it happen because you said you wanted me to."

Her lips are tight, and I can almost see the sordid memory flash in her beautiful eyes.

"I didn't need you to save me."

"No?"

"No," she snaps.

Little fucking devil. She's an adult, but I've never met one more in need of punishment. There's no one in her world to give it to her. No one's going to take the time to set her straight. No one's going to halt her crash course. By the time someone notices what she's doing to herself, her reputation will be compromised and God knows what she'll have been through.

Were my threats valid? Could I really sit back and watch it happen? Could I stop caring so goddamn much?

No. Fuck no.

This is likely about to be the worst decision of my life, but I'm stopping this shit, here and now. And I could lose everything if it goes wrong.

"You're not going to the party tonight."

Her nostrils flare. "You don't get to tell me what to do."

"That's changing now. Today and tomorrow and every day I'm hired to protect your life, you're going to listen to me."

"Or what? You're going to tell on me? News flash, Zane. No one cares."

"I care. And if you disobey me, I'll redden your ass. I promise you, I can do so much worse than that if you push me."

She swallows hard and searches my gaze. I give her nothing but the face of a determined Dominant. My sexual proclivities have never crossed into work, but all that's about to change.

"You're out of your mind." She shakes her head and moves past me.

I beat her to the door, haul her against me, and take her mouth in a kiss that has me instantly remembering all of last night's temptations. Her anger melts, and I push her against the door as I close it. She groans at the slight shove of her hips against the hard surface. I swallow the sound with another ravaging kiss. Her limbs tangle around me. I know I can take her right here, right now. But that's not what this is about.

I pull back and spin her so her chest is against the door.

"Spread your legs for me, Charlotte."

She hesitates a second before shifting them a couple feet apart. Perfect.

"Hands on the door."

Slowly she slides her palms up over the wood. Then, one by one, I take her arms and fold them behind her back so I can secure them by the wrists with one hand.

I lean in a fraction so I can feel her heat, but our bodies are only touching where I hold her. Her fragrance settles over me, reminding me that she's a weakness. The way I feel about her... The way I've silently lusted after her for too long.

I hover my lips over her neck. I want her so fucking bad.

"Do you trust me, Charlotte?"

"Completely." She answers without a shred of hesitation or doubt.

I'd do anything to protect her, and she knows it. But am I really protecting her?

I lick and kiss my way up and down her neck. She sighs and shifts restlessly against me, but she's got nowhere to go. I suck one particular spot. Not enough to make a mark, but enough to make her shudder against me. Then I bite the overworked area.

She sucks in a tiny breath and then exhales a soft groan. The sound travels right down to my dick, which is instantly hard for her. I want to pull her tight against me and torture the ache in my pants with more of her touch. But I have to stay in control. I tighten my grasp around her wrists and she whimpers and leans back, trying to bring our bodies together.

"Are you wet for me, Charlotte?"

"Yes."

"Show me."

She stops breathing, and I release her. She turns and leans back against the door. Her chest is flushed pink, and her neck is red from my mouth's assault.

"You have a tendency to lie. Show me you're wet, or I won't believe you."

She blinks once and reaches for the hem of her dress. She doesn't move any farther.

"I've seen you in more compromising positions, Charlotte. Now lift up your dress and show me."

Her breathing becomes ragged. She lifts the black fabric up to her hips and pushes the tiny scrap of panties down. I'm so aroused I can barely keep focus on her movements. Her hands frame the patch of light hair between her thighs, making a V.

Open up for me...open up...

I chant the plea inside my head. Suddenly, seeing the pink petals of her wet pussy is the only thing I truly care about. Still, she hesitates.

I shrug out of my jacket, undo my tie, and unbutton the top of my shirt. I glance at her and note the lust in her heavy-lidded eyes.

"Would you like me to fuck you?"

She exhales sharply. "Yes."

"Are you going to that party tonight?"

"No."

A satisfied smile tugs at my lips. "Those are both good answers. Now, pretty girl, I need you to spread your pussy for me so I can see exactly where to fuck you and how hard. I need to see how wet you are."

Her eyes close and her head falls back. "Oh, God…"

Slowly, I come to her. I put a hand on the door beside her head and lean in to whisper against her skin. "I'm bigger than any of these college pricks you've had before. If you're not wet enough for me, I'm going to have to tease some more out of you. Then I'll fuck you slow until I know you can handle more." I trail my touch from the beautiful column of her neck down to her chest where her breasts heave under the bust of her dress. I yank it down swiftly, revealing her gorgeous tits. "And if you're drenched, Charlotte, then I'm going to fuck you very hard and very fast. You're going to come. I'm going to come. And then we're going to do it again, until you're so blissed out from my cock that you can't think about making any manner of bad decisions tonight. Understand?"

She nods. Her entire body is trembling now. I hush her softly before taking one rosy nipple between my fingertips and add pressure until she whimpers.

"Show me."

Doing exactly as I asked, she spreads her legs a little wider and pulls her lips apart so I can clearly see the inner folds of her pussy.

She's fucking perfect. She gives me a little more, trailing her fingers to her opening and dragging its moisture up over her clit. There's no doubt about it. She's soaking wet for me.

"Good girl," I rasp out, because I can barely breathe.

CHAPTER TWO

His eyes own me.

His gray irises darken to a color I've never seen before. Panting with anticipation, I drop my hands beside my body and fall back against the wooden door. I'm captivated. I can't look away. Without breaking our connection, he leans in until his mouth is hovering above mine. Then he inches his hand ever so slowly downward, stopping once he is cupping my sex.

"Do you know what I do to good girls, Charlotte?"

The heat of his breath against my mouth sends a delicious shiver through me. I shake my head, my eyes fluttering. My voice barely registers above a whisper. "No."

He presses his fingertips against my swollen, throbbing clit. "I make them come...hard."

Without warning, he sinks his long fingers into me, stealing my breath as he deepens his reach. My lips fall open with a gasp.

"Can you be a good girl for me?" He breathes the words against my mouth between thrusts. I nod quickly as he finger fucks me with masterful determination.

Harder.

Faster.

Deeper.

My body surrenders to every skilled movement. As he quickens his pace, the heavy ache in my core intensifies. I crave more than his fingers, but the chance to beg him for it slips away. My inner walls are already tightening around his penetration. I need this orgasm more... I fist my hands into his shirt, wrinkling its starched white perfection as my climb nears the crest.

"That's it. Give it to me," he rasps.

The heavy authority in his voice pushes me over. With a trembling bottom lip, I lose myself in the darkness of his irises, allowing the fierce climax to overtake me.

"Oh, God!" I shudder against him as I come on his hand.

He lifts his fingers to my lips, slowly coating them with my arousal. Then, in one delicate sweep, he drags his searing tongue across my mouth.

He sucks in his bottom lip, and then licks his fingers clean. "You're too delicious not to share." He leans in again, crashing his soft mouth against mine. With one swipe of his tongue, he allows me to taste my own flavor. The act is raw and erotic, unlike anything I've ever experienced before with a lover.

I begin unfastening his pants, suddenly desperate to have him inside me, but Zane seizes my wrists, surprising me. The ache in my core throbs. I let out a whimper and bow toward him.

A dangerous look flashes across his face—something calculated, something dark and unreadable. Before I can draw my next breath, he spins me around so I'm shoved flush against the wood grain of the door. He pins me with his weight, grinding his massive erection against my bare ass.

"I should make you earn it this time."

A shiver radiates down my spine at the feel of his hot breath against my ear.

"Beg me, Charlotte."

My heart races wildly. The anticipation is killing me. "P-Please."

He lifts his weight off me. Yes, he is finally going to fuck me—

Whop! His palm meets my ass with a painful sting.

"Beg me like you mean it."

His voice is hard and sharp like the slap. I'm damn near programmed to rile when he tries to tell me what to do. But this is so very different... *He* is different.

"Please, Zane. I'm begging you."

Whop! Whop! "Please what, Charlotte? Tell me what that greedy little cunt wants."

The bite of pain is surprisingly exquisite, heightening my need to epic proportions. My palms are slick against the door. My pussy pulses with the memory of his fingers. My head buzzes with fantasies of him taking me completely, shoving into me with the fierceness his tone promises. Have I ever been more desperate for this kind of possession?

"Please, Zane, take me. I need you. I've wanted this for so long." The words tumble from my lips—admissions I never realized until this moment. *Who am I?*

A good girl. Zane's good girl.

He trails his palms over my ass, never making a sound. Knowing his touch without his intention is absolute torture.

"Take me... Please," I whimper, praying he'll have pity on me.

A low growl erupts from his lips. He's going to give me what I want—

A loud knock shakes the door in front of me, startling both of us. I almost scream, but Zane clamps his hand over my mouth to silence me just in time. In one swift move, his free arm snakes around my waist and hoists me backward against his solid, muscular body. Our sudden closeness stirs the unsatisfied ache that lingers, heavy and deep in my core. I'm pulled so close against him that I can hear his name when it comes through his earpiece.

"Parker? Do you read me?"

Zane releases me slowly and steps back. When I turn, he places a finger over his lips. He brings his arm up to his mouth, presses something on the cuff of his shirtsleeve, and speaks into a concealed microphone.

"This is Parker. Can you repeat?"

Fuck my life.

Feeling defeated and too exposed, I tug my dress back into place. When I glance back up, Zane's slate gray eyes are locked on me. Just like that, he's back to the Zane I know. Cold. Emotionless. Pissed off.

"Roger that," he says. "The First Daughter and I are en route now."

He drops his arm back to his side and begins to button his shirt. "Hurry up and change out of that outfit. Your parents want to see you."

ZANE

She's the President's daughter, for fuck's sake.

What the hell are you thinking? Get your dick under control and focus on the job. I silently scold myself as I follow Charlotte down the long corridor that leads to the sitting room in the central residence. But I can't seem to stop thinking vividly inappropriate thoughts. I can still taste her pussy on my tongue. I can envision exactly where I planned to shove my cock into her willing body. She walks ahead of me in snug jeans and a loose top that falls off one shoulder. Every simple movement tempts me. I've only just begun to discover the treasures of her incredible body.

Guarding the First Daughter on the evening shift has put my extracurricular activities on quite a long hiatus. I can't remember the last time I stepped foot in Crave, the underground sex club where Dominants like myself can keep their needs satisfied and in check. Tomorrow will be the first night I've had off in almost three months, and I've never needed it more.

Things with Charlotte have gone way too far. Once I'm at the club, I'll dedicate every possible second to unleashing this pent-up frustration on a willing submissive. Someone who won't cost me my job and my sanity.

I take in a deep breath. I can practically feel the braided crop in my hand already. But the thought doesn't settle me as much as it should, because the vision my mind conjures includes Charlotte, bent and breathless, welted pink and begging for my cock like she was moments ago.

I'm so royally fucked. I exhale shakily.

Another agent greets us as we approach the sitting room door. He nods in my direction before turning his attention to Charlotte.

"Good evening, Ms. Daley. Your parents are waiting for you inside."

Charlotte gives him a practiced smile. "Thank you."

I step around her and open the door to the sitting room, noticing her body tense as she steps over the threshold. Once she is inside, I reach for the door handle, meeting the President's eyes as I start to shut the door.

"I'll be just outside if you need me, sir."

He lifts his hand to stop me. "Actually, I'd like for you to stay, Parker. This conversation pertains to you as well."

I freeze. Me? What can I possibly have to do with any of this?

I give him a hesitant nod and take my normal stance behind the chair Charlotte claims. Even from this vantage, I can sense her discomfort. Her fists are tight, and she taps her foot nervously on the floor.

From a nearby chair, Charlotte's mother is directing a hard stare at her. Her startling blue eyes are the only thing she and her daughter have in common. The First Lady strums her fingers along the side of her crystal tumbler, arrowing those icy blues on Charlotte.

"Oh, for goodness sake, Charlotte, sit up straight."

Charlotte immediately stiffens in her chair. "Sorry, Mother."

I cringe at her apology. I swear, I don't understand her parents. Granted, they're currently mired in non-stop political ambition, but I've never gotten the sense that they've ever cared about their daughter more than politics. As much as they criticize Charlotte, it isn't any wonder the poor girl acts out like she does.

"What kind of outfit is this? Honestly, Charlotte, do you thrive on being an embarrassment to me?"

I bite down on the inside of my mouth, fighting the urge to say something in her defense. Victoria Daley is much more than the First Lady. Bold and demanding, she uses her power and title to intimidate everyone around her. Those tactics don't work on me. I'll protect her daughter, at all costs, but thankfully I'm not one of the puppets she gets to order around. She has plenty of those running around at her beck and call already.

"Give it a rest, Victoria." The President turns his attention back to his daughter. I wait for his eyes to soften, the way a father's should when he looks at his daughter, but it doesn't happen. Instead, they remain as cold and vacant as the day he hired me to work for his family. "Your mother and I have some important news to discuss with you."

Charlotte scoots to the edge of the chair. "What news?"

"I just got off the phone with the President of Georgetown University. It took calling in some favors, but I've gotten them to speed through your admission into their pre-law program."

She flies to her feet. "What? You can't do that! There's no way I'm leaving NYU!"

"Sit. Down. Now," the President utters through gritted

teeth.

Charlotte pauses a second, then eases back down in her chair. "Please, you can't do this to me. I'm supposed to intern at the Metropolitan Museum this spring. I can't give up that opportunity. I am the youngest art history major to ever earn that internship."

He lets out a chuckle. "You didn't earn that internship. They only gave it to you because your family is sitting in the White House. Besides, you've fooled around in New York long enough. You're twenty, Charlotte. Now is a good time to transfer and get serious. I think we can all agree that a reputable degree in law is preferred over a degree in finger painting."

She tightens her fists until her knuckles are a bloodless white. "Art *is* a reputable degree. It's the career I've been working toward for almost two years."

The President narrows his eyes. Charlotte visibly sinks down into her chair.

"This isn't up for discussion. The arrangements have already been made. Your mother and I have secured you a very nice apartment downtown at View 17."

I nearly choke at his words. View 17 is my apartment building. The President must know this. I school my features, meeting his eyes as he resumes speaking.

"Agent Parker currently resides in that building. I'll feel much better knowing he is close by to keep an eye on you."

"I'm not a five-year-old. I don't need anyone keeping an eye on me."

"Like it or not, Charlotte, you're part of the First Family now, and with that comes certain expectations. I will not tolerate your disobedience or your ungrateful behavior. You are *my* daughter. And you will act accordingly." The President's tone leaves no doubt.

Only when Charlotte stands and bolts from the room do I notice the tears streaming down her face. I was uncomfortable before. Now anger bubbles under my cool exterior at seeing her so upset. I start to follow behind her when the President speaks.

"I'd like to have a word with you, Parker." He turns to his wife. "Victoria, will you excuse us?"

She stands and straightens her dress, lifting her chin up in an aristocratic manner. "Fine, but remember, we're supposed to have dinner with the Petersons in an hour."

"Yes, I remember. This won't take long."

She nods and then glides out of the room as if she owns it.

The President walks to the antique bar across the room and pours himself a drink.

"How are things going with Charlotte?"

"Things are fine, sir." I keep my voice even and calm.

The side of his mouth lifts. "You don't have to sugarcoat things, son. I know my daughter's a handful. I'm quite sure she keeps you and Chester on your toes."

"We manage fine, sir."

Nodding, he nestles the decorative crystal top back into the decanter. "Yes, you've both been doing a remarkable job of keeping her out of trouble. Especially you, having to deal with her evening engagements. Don't get me wrong, Chester is a fantastic agent, but he has a soft spot for Charlotte. I'm guessing that's the father in him." He takes a sip of his expensive brand of bourbon, studying me hard before continuing. "You, however, bring a different element to the job. You're young. Twenty-five, correct?"

"Yes, sir."

"Whether you know it or not, that's one of the reasons I insisted you be assigned to my daughter. Your youth gives you an advantage over most of the other agents. You know what kids her age are thinking, which gives you the ability to stay one step ahead of her without her knowing it. That, of course, is why we secured her an apartment in your building."

He pauses to take another drink.

"As you know, this is a crucial time for me in office. All eyes are on me. I simply can't risk anything hurting my approval rating." He raises his eyebrow. "I trust that you understand what I'm getting at?"

Sure, I do. You want me to become your daughter's twenty-four-hour babysitter.

"Yes, Mr. President."

"Very good." Turning up the glass, he finishes off his drink and motions with his hand. "That's all. Tell Martin outside that Mrs. Daley and I will be leaving soon."

"Yes, sir." I leave, and, after relaying the President's message, I start in the direction of Charlotte's room. Agitation drives my quick steps. I can't believe they are moving her into my building. When I'm off the clock, I'm off the clock. Am I not entitled to have a life away from this job?

Just when I round the final corner, I am met with an agonizing sound. Charlotte is crying. Even from outside her room, there's no denying her misery.

Fuck.

I can't deal with this right now. Crying never solves anything. Why doesn't she get that by now? Why can't she be angry instead? I can relate to anger. I can teach her how to harness it...to control it in ways that will bring her immense pleasure. Suddenly, the thought of her naked body bound and gagged flashes before my eyes. I can visualize the thin leather strips of my flogger slapping against her full, perky tits. I can see the delectable pink lines forming across her flawless skin.

I ignore the stirring in my groin and resume my normal post beside her door. I focus hard on the revolting floral wallpaper pattern across from me—anything for a distraction when all I want to do is barge through her door and pick up where we left off.

I'm hired to protect her, not comfort her. It's not my job nor my nature to feel compassion for her right now, yet I do. Punishing her and turning her into my personal plaything and hopefully a better-behaved First Daughter isn't my job either, yet that's precisely what every cell of my body yearns for.

The longer I stand here listening to her cry, the harder it becomes to ignore those desires.

Turning to face the door, I raise my hand to knock.

I hesitate.

What is it about Charlotte Daley that makes me care so damn much? Before I make the mistake of finding out, I drop my hand back to my side. She's sucking in jagged breaths between her sobs, and my gut clenches.

I return to my designated position next to the door, feeling like the worst human being on the planet.

CHARLOTTE

Chester frowns at me through the rearview mirror of the SUV.

"I don't know about this, Charley. Your father wouldn't approve of me not going in to check things out."

I scoot forward and put my hand on the back of his shoulder. "Oh, come on, Chester. Kat and I are just going to hang out and watch scary movies all night. How much trouble can we possibly get into doing that?"

"Don't bat your eyes at me, Charley Girl." He tries to sound stern, but the smile tugging at his lips gives him away.

Is it strange that I am closer to a Secret Service officer than my own father? Maybe because Chester cares about me beyond his job. At least I believe he does. Since coming to work for our family, he has found a special place in my heart. He always knows what to say or do to make me feel better on my worst days. Of course, being the father of two grown daughters certainly helps with that. He knows what classes I've taken. He knows who my favorite artist is. Hell, he even knows my favorite Starbucks drink. My father is too engrossed running the country to ever care to know any of those things about me. He's a stranger to me in so many ways. I can't remember a day that Chester felt like a stranger to me.

"Please," I beg in my sweetest voice. "I need girl time, and it's embarrassing always having someone following me around. Can't I just hang out with a friend in her own house for once?"

His face visibly softens. "Okay, fine. But I'm not leaving. I'll just keep Lewis company in the guard shack. If you need anything, don't hesitate to call me."

Throwing my hands around his neck, I place a kiss on his cheek. "You're the best, Chester."

"Yeah, yeah." He waves me off. "Go, before I change my mind."

Grabbing my bag, I throw open the back door and head up the paved walkway of Katherine Harrison's house. Kat's dad is a wealthy DC lawyer who my father appointed as the new Attorney General. During this last year on the campaign trail, we have grown close. Unlike the rest of the DC Brat Club, she's more interested in having fun than being seen with important people and being written about in gossip columns. Kat is bold and unapologetic. And, in my very boring, controlled world, she is a dangerous fresh breath of air.

I give a reassuring smile back at Chester in the idling black SUV and press the doorbell. Cathedral chimes echo through the house. Kat answers the front door with a large grin, but frowns when she looks over my shoulder.

"Where's Captain Control Freak?"

I smile at her use of the nickname we'd given Zane and step inside. "He's off for the night. Chester is taking his post at the gate with your security guy."

"Oh." She shuts the door behind me, her shoulders slumping.

I chuckle. "Well, I'm so sorry to disappoint you."

"Oh, shut it. You know I love you. I won't lie, though. I was kinda hoping to see Zane." She puts her back against the door and makes a swoony wistful sound. "I swear that man looks like perfect sin in a suit."

I let out a fake yawn and shrug. "Whatever floats your

boat, I guess."

I never liked the way Kat talked about Zane. Now I can barely contain my irritation. I shouldn't care, but after last night's dizzying almost-fuck and Zane's swift mood shift, I have no idea where things stand between us. Does he really want me, or am I just some stupid mistake that he regrets making? The fact he's off duty tonight makes me think the latter.

"Well, we can't stay here tonight. We have to celebrate your freedom. There's this great club downtown that you have got to see to believe."

I cross my arms and cock my head. "And exactly how are we supposed to get past the two guards at the gate?"

Kat steps forward and places her hands on my shoulders. "Oh, my poor sheltered friend. You really have so much to learn. They make back doors to houses for a reason, you know?" She tips her chin up. "Come on upstairs, and I'll get you all fixed up. I've got a killer red dress for you to wear. Men will be falling at your feet tonight. I guarantee it."

Forcing a smile, I place my hand on the banister and follow her up the stairs. Kat doesn't know it, but there is only one man I really want to bring to his knees. Still, the ripped Secret Service agent I've been fantasizing about for months isn't the only man in the world. Maybe tonight, I'll try to make myself believe that.

◆ ◆ ◆ ◆

Stepping out of the cab, I glance up at the abandoned-looking building. "Wait a minute. I thought you said we were going to a club."

The sides of Kat's mouth lift. "We are. Come on."

She motions for me to follow her, but I hesitate when I see her take the steps that lead down below the ground.

"Hurry up, before someone sees you."

Reluctantly, I follow. "Where are you taking me? This is seriously like a scene out of some slasher movie. Someone's going to end up finding our rotting, dismembered bodies in a dumpster somewhere."

Kat bursts out laughing at the bottom of the stairs. "All right, Ms. Overdramatic. Get your ass down here." She stops on a landing in front of a metal door. It's so rusty, I'm certain we'll need a tetanus shot just from looking at it.

Then I notice the high-tech scanner that is attached to the wall beside the door. Before I can ask Kat how we're going to get in without access cards, she is sliding a shiny black card through the slot. The red indicator light flashes to green and I hear the loud click of the lock as it releases.

She places her hand on the handle and turns to look at me over her shoulder. "Keep an open mind, okay?"

An open mind? Great. This ought to be good.

I follow behind Kat, preparing to be horrified. The instant I step through the doorway, I am rendered speechless. Layers of gathered black satin cover the massive walls of the club from floor to ceiling. Luxurious white leather furniture fills the downstairs lounge, located just to the right of the bar area. Sleek, modern stainless steel stools line the front of a long mahogany bar with intricate designs carved across its front. A flicker of light catches my attention. Above us hangs a massive chandelier, its dangling crystals reflecting flecks of dark red and purple on the walls. No doubt about it, this posh club is unlike anything I've ever seen. But why is a place like this hidden underground behind a seedy entrance? It just doesn't make sense.

"What is this place?" My gaze lands on a group of girls standing in front of us. "And why is everyone wearing red?"

Giving me a wicked smile, Kat grabs me by the wrist and pulls me through the crowd. "You'll see."

ZANE

The alluring smell of leather and sex permeates the air. I take a deep breath, savoring the erotic aromas as they invade my nostrils, bringing with them desire and plenty of satisfying memories.

Goddamn, I've missed this place.

Eager to appease my sexual appetite, I settle back against the leather booth and scan the dimly lit room. Tonight I'll find a submissive that can handle me. I can usually gauge the right fit by a woman's body language alone. One by one, I eliminate the girls in my line of sight, some of which I've already had in the past.

Too fragile.

Too inexperienced.

Too clingy.

As picky as I'm being, I know it's going to be virtually impossible for me to find what I want. Nothing short of a mind-blowing fuck will make me forget about Charlotte.

I'm about to lose myself in one of a dozen fantasies I've created around her when the pulsating bass of a new song reverberates loudly throughout the club. The sexual energy in the crowd is palpable and thrums steadily in my veins. I'm already half-hard, and all I've done is think about the one girl I need to get the hell out of my head.

On the other side of the room, a bright spotlight flashes from behind a translucent curtain, revealing a sensual silhouette of a woman's figure as it arches off a table. Up and down. Side to side. She bucks her body like a wild animal, stretching her limbs to their limit as she pulls at the restraints.

The tall curtain suddenly drops to the floor, and the crowd quiets to a murmur. A naked brunette lay spread eagle on the table, her expression as rapt as her earlier gestures behind the curtain indicated. Her Dominant takes the stage, wearing only a pair of tight black leather pants. In his right hand, he grips the braided handle of a leather riding crop.

My palm itches and visions flash behind my eyes. Visions I need to banish from my mind.

The Dominant paces back and forth, ruthlessly teasing the woman's body with the hard tip of the whip until she is trembling. He raises his hand into the air and brings it down hard on the inside of her raised thigh. I bite my lip. Blood rushes to my cock.

The delicate lines of the woman's body tense as she accepts the painful blow. Her Dominant doesn't give her time to recover before he's slapping a series of blows against her other thigh, and then her swollen pussy. The longer I watch the exhibition on stage, the heavier the ache in my balls becomes. If I don't get a release soon, I'm going to lose my fucking mind.

I finish off my drink, wipe my mouth with the back of my

hand, and glance up in time to see two girls enter the club—a brunette and a blonde—both dressed in red.

The color red is very important at Crave. It indicates an available submissive. Needless to say, it's become my all-time favorite color.

Without explanation, my attention fixates on the hot blonde. I drink her in, groaning at how the short dress clings to her tight body. I strain to see her face, but between the distance and the bright stage light, I can't make anything out. It doesn't matter. With a body like that, she won't be available long, and my patience has expired.

I slide out of the VIP booth and set out in full pursuit of her before someone else stakes a claim. Maneuvering through the crowd of people, I quickly work my way toward her. By the time I reach her, her brunette friend has disappeared. She's all mine.

I step behind her and place my hand gently on her hip. "Want to play?"

Blonde hair flies against my face as she spins around. My heart stops.

Charlotte?

Her blue eyes widen. I'm not sure if it's her shock or the flash of fear in her eyes, or maybe the way the tops of her breasts peek out over the bust of her dress. Whatever it is has my cock fully hard.

Our identical response comes out in perfect unison. "What are you doing here?"

I narrow my eyes. "Never mind why I'm here. How in the hell did you get into this place?"

Charlotte purses her lips. "Wouldn't you like to know?"

I'd give anything to take her over my knee right now. "Don't get smart with me, Charlotte."

"You're off duty, Zane. What exactly are you going to do about it?"

I tug her against me and settle my hand at the small of her back. My thoughts scatter with the full body contact before they gather again around a new plan.

"I'm about to show you."

CHAPTER THREE

It's too much. The pulsing energy of the club. The need for release that threatens my better judgment at every turn. But she's here. In red. Unprotected. And I can't help but take that as a sign that I need to finish what I started.

The perfect pressure of her body molding to mine isn't helping. The familiarity of it should be alarming, but it only fuels my irrational possessiveness. No one else gets to command her body, use her, please her. No one but me.

My head is nearly buzzing with that last thought. I exhale a rough sigh and contemplate the private room I've reserved for the night when she's ripped from my arms.

She stumbles backward, and I now recognize her brunette friend.

Katherine Harrison's middle name is trouble, and I bite down on the urge to call Chester and ream his ass for letting Charlotte find her way here with this little devil.

Katherine's eyes are steady, her lips tight. "Charlotte, let's go," she says, worry lacing every word.

She's wise to worry. Katherine may be trouble, but her

father's a mean son of a bitch. My thoughts flash back to the last time we escorted her to attend a private event with Charlotte at the White House. He released her into our custody, but not without a litany of foul-mouthed threats making it clear he felt rather above the law his position was meant to uphold.

I can't imagine the man's ire if he knew his daughter was advertising herself as a submissive in an underground sex club. I mask a grimace before noticing another familiar face.

A man at the bar turns my way, as if hearing a silent call. Demitri has been running Crave for as long as I've been a patron. He's also the most perceptive Dominant I've ever met.

I lift my chin, signaling for him to help me unfuck the current situation. Hauling the girls back home isn't that straightforward, and I need a minute to regroup.

"Stay here. I'll be right back." I shoot Charlotte a hard look and hope the girls heed my warning.

Crossing the room, I meet Demitri as he approaches, keeping the girls in my periphery.

"Zane, it's been a long time," he says with a heavy Czech accent that I've learned to decipher over the years.

He holds out his hand and shakes mine firmly. He's at least a foot taller and several pounds of muscle heavier. He rarely needs to rely on brute force to enforce club rules, though. Nothing misses his appraisal. He recognizes a dangerous Dominant before a sub can suffer under his wrath. And when it comes to the women who kneel for him, the only weapons he wields are his mind and his cock. His head games are unmatched and the women he commands worship him with a godlike reverence.

"I've missed this place," I say with a smirk, because despite the current debacle, I'm at home here.

"This place," he sweeps his arm in a broad gesture to the room, "misses you, my friend. What keeps you from us?"

"Work," I answer with a sigh, all too aware of being suddenly back on the clock. "I need a favor, if you don't mind."

"I am at your service."

I glance back at the girls, whose faces are filled with a defiant kind of worry. They're trying to be brave, but they are minnows thrown into a sea of piranhas at the moment. Fresh rage burns through me. Charlotte's disobedience enrages my mind—and fuck if it isn't making my cock want things too.

She needs punishment.

I can't deny it. And I can't deny the way she complied with the slightest hint of pressure. From my hand around her wrist to my hips pressing her to the door. She submits when she tastes my control. *She needs this...*

"Those girls..." I search for the right way to say it.

Demitri follows my gaze and an easy smile settles on his lips. "Are kittens. I've seen the dark-haired one here before."

I frown. "Does she play?"

He shakes his head. "She watches. Fascinated. Disturbed by what she sees, but can't stop looking. She hides in the shadows." His icy blue eyes are fixed on her. "Like I said...a kitten." He says the last word softly.

"Their fathers have claws."

He lifts an eyebrow.

"She's the daughter of the Attorney General. The other..." I swallow hard, because I should be ashamed of what I'm about to say. "That's the President's daughter."

Demitri blanches—something I've never seen. Even here, surrounded by sexcapades in progress throughout this underground haven for freaks, I can see this news has rattled him.

"I protect her," I say. "I'll get them both out of here soon enough. But I need a minute with the blonde. Can you watch the other one while I'm gone?"

He nods wordlessly, fresh tension lining his suit-clad shoulders. "Introduce us."

CHARLOTTE

I hold Katherine's hand, which is hot and slick against mine. Shit. What kind of mess has she gotten us into now? I'm not happy to see Zane here, but that doesn't keep my curiosity from running wild. Did he follow me here? Or did we both happen to find ourselves in this peculiar place?

As he approaches with an enormous blond-haired man flanking him, I have the strong sense I'm about to find out the truth. I'm not entirely sure I'll like it.

"I can handle this," Katherine says in a whisper.

Before I can talk her out of whatever crazy shit she's thinking, the men are ahead of us. Two impenetrable columns of dominance and...*sex*. Yes, I know the look in Zane's eyes as he rakes me in, and hell if I don't recognize it in his comrade's as he fixes his stare on Kat.

Her lips part like she's going to speak but shut a second later.

"Katherine, Charlotte. This is Demitri Nicoloff. He's

a friend of mine, and he runs the club. Katherine, you'll stay here with him while Charlotte and I..." Zane swallows before uttering, "talk."

Katherine's eyes go wide, her panic evident now. "You can't just leave me with—"

Demitri extends his hand, palm up in invitation. "Come," he says, his voice low and firm. "You're safe with me."

A few seconds tick by as Katherine regards him, her mouth slack, her body frozen as if she's fallen wordlessly under some sort of spell. But instead of taking his hand, she straightens, releases her tight grip on my hand, and marches past Demitri. His lips curve into a sly smile as he pivots and follows her into the crowd, leaving Zane and me alone again.

Then, before I can argue, Zane is tugging me in the opposite direction, down a short hallway and through a doorway that leads us into a small empty bedroom of sorts. This must be where these people come to... My imagination rushes to fill in the blanks. Anything could happen in here. Suddenly my heart is racing with panic, and maybe a touch of excitement, because the hungry look in Zane's eyes is threatening to knock me down. That and I've never seen him like this before. Casual. Jeans that strain against his muscular thighs and a black collared shirt that sets off his olive skin and dark hair.

Fuck me, he's a gorgeous creature. An unrecognizable song plays outside, but the rhythm seems timed to my heartbeat, pulsing through my veins and throbbing between my legs. Will he always have this effect on me? Am I doomed to ache for him this way?

He rolls up his sleeves, one at a time, revealing tattoos on his forearms that I've never seen before. I swallow hard, because suddenly I feel powerless.

"What are you going to do to me?" My voice shakes, and I ball my fists to still my anxious trembling.

Zane slants his head, his expression unmoving. "That's an interesting question. I have a lot of options right now, and endless inspiration."

He's standing beside what appears to be a window covered with a thick red curtain. Yanking it to the side, he reveals a scene that puts the ones I'd briefly witnessed on the main floor to shame.

In a room that mirrors ours, a woman is gagged and bound, on her knees before a man I assume is her Master. I've read enough smut between coursework to know how it works. But I'd never imagined I'd find myself in a front-row seat watching it play out in a sex club.

The man deftly unclasps the gag, unzips his pants, and presents her with his cock. As he does, her mouth drops open wide.

"She's offering herself," Zane says, pinning me with his stare before walking slowly toward me. "That's what a submissive does. She offers herself. She obeys."

I clench my teeth, because I have a feeling he's not just talking about the people fucking around in the other room. He's demanded my obedience before. In the heat of the moment, I'd been willing to give it to him.

Zane circles around me, like a lion eyeing his prey. Meanwhile, on the other side of the window, the Master's cock disappears into the woman's mouth in one violent thrust. The pane of one-way glass that separates us offers us a soundless view. I can't look away. A dozen solid, short pumps into her willing mouth, and then a short reprieve as he yanks her head back by a tight fistful of her hair. I imagine she's gasping, struggling to breathe through the performance. I suck a deep breath of air into my lungs.

Then I feel the heat of Zane's body behind me, his fingertips trailing up the side of my dress.

"She's giving him everything he needs. Her submission. Her tight throat. Her need to breathe. Pure surrender, Charlotte. Absolute trust, even with the most vital element... The air she needs to survive."

I tense as Zane skims his hands down my arms and then circles my wrists firmly. I bite my lip, because whenever he does it, I want to come apart. I want to fall to my knees and give him my air... Everything I have.

"And do you know what comes next?"

His voice is a whisper over my skin. His lips graze the place where my neck and shoulder meet. Then his tongue, warm and velvet, travels slowly upward.

I shake my head slightly, my breaths coming fast. *Show me*, I silently beg as I feel his lips again, a tender kiss at my pulse.

"What comes next?"

"Reward," he mutters and sinks his teeth into my flesh.

I gasp, but his hold on my wrists tightens, keeping me in place. My eyes roll back and a pained moan escapes my lips. I'm so wet, so needy for him. I shift my ass backward, seeking the evidence of his arousal. It's there, trapped inside his clothes. God, how I wished we hadn't been cut short yesterday. He was right there... So close to being inside me.

"Watch," he orders gently.

My eyes flutter open slowly, just in time to see the man through the window pulling out of the woman's willing mouth and pumping his release across her lips.

Heaven help me. I can't help but imagine Zane's taste on my lips. Another rush of arousal soaks my panties with the mere thought.

"Did you enjoy that?"

I nod, because what's the point in denying it? I'm painfully aroused.

"I want this, Charlotte. And I think you need it."

I ball my fists tighter, because he can't possibly know how much I need it right now. "I need *you*," I whimper, comfortable in his bonds, but struggling for more contact.

He tisks softly. "I don't think you're hearing me."

"I hear you fine, Zane. Goddamnit, stop torturing me. Do you get off on this? Making me crazy for you and never satisfying me?"

He stills. I can't even feel him breathing. And when he finally speaks, it's firm and clear.

"Yes, I get off on this. And I think you do too. Watching that woman being used by her Master turned you on, didn't it?"

"I don't know." The lie feels sour on my tongue, but the truth frightens me more.

"I think you know. I think you're soaking wet with the

thought of it being you."

He's right but I can't say it.

"What if I bound you and pushed you to your knees, Charlotte? Would you offer yourself to me?"

My skin is on fire as desire and embarrassment fight for control over my body's responses. "Zane," I utter breathlessly.

"Let's find out, shall we?"

In a flash, Zane releases his hold on my wrists and binds my arms behind me with something I can't identify. Firm pressure on my shoulders brings me to my knees. The floor is cold and hard, but somehow the slight discomfort only brings this act of submission into stark relief. Inherently, I understand this isn't supposed to be comfortable.

I peer up at him as he rounds to stand before me.

His lips part slightly. "You really are beautiful. Just like this."

He shakes his head, like he can't believe what he's seeing. The wonder in his eyes, the warmth where I only ever saw cold detachment, does me in. I lick my lips, let my eyes fall closed, and open my mouth.

The next touch isn't one I expect. His palm slides across my cheek, tenderly.

"Charlotte," he whispers.

I open my eyes to see more heart-wrenching reverence in his eyes.

"Are you ready?"

I nod.

"Say it."

My heartbeat stutters and the truth breaks free. "Use me.

I want you to use me, Zane."

His eyes darken as he unfastens his belt with his free hand, threading his fingers through my hair with his other. When his cock is free I almost whimper. He's long and thick, and my pussy clenches painfully. I open for him again, because my body wants him in any and every way. And when he invades my mouth, it's firm but careful.

He stays there and closes his eyes as his head falls back. "My God," he breathes.

I weave my tongue along the underside of his cock, drawing his attention back down to me.

"Flatten your tongue, beautiful. Your throat's going to feel me next."

I relax my jaw and tongue, readying myself to accommodate his next thrust. When it comes, all I can feel is his loud groan as it vibrates through me, spurring my own. Then the painful grip of his fist in my hair as he pumps into me, one fierce thrust punctuating the next. With my arms bound, I can't steady myself. I'm anchored to him, his rhythm and his needs.

When I think I might pass out, he pulls me off so I can suck in a frantic breath of precious air. But when I take him again, it's almost sweeter than air. The desperate sounds breaking free from his lips feed my own desire. More, faster, harder, deeper... I'm buzzing and pulsing, so high on giving him pleasure that it's sweeping through me like a wildfire.

"Good girl. So close," he rasps, pulling me off once more before shoving me back down onto his beautifully engorged cock.

My knees hurt. My throat stings. I've never wanted someone's orgasm more than my own. But I want his more than I want air…

A second later he gives me both—desperately needed space to breathe and then his release, warm on my tongue. I moan again and tears fill my eyes. They trail down my cheeks as I suck and lick him clean. I don't know why I'm crying. Pent-up frustration, relief, confusion…

I don't have a chance to think it through before he tucks himself away, unties my bonds, and lifts me into his arms. He lowers us onto the bed, hushing me as he wipes my cheeks.

"You were perfect. Utterly perfect," he whispers.

Then his lips touch mine, and we're lost in a hungry kiss. I savor every sweep of his tongue. The mix of his smoky taste and his come mingling on our tongues is so unexpectedly intimate.

Desperate for my own relief, I shift my hips up to meet his. I'm so wet, I know my panties must be destroyed. When he slips his hand under my dress and into them, we share a groan.

"Remember what I said? What do good girls get?"

I buck my hips into his touch. "Good girls get to come hard."

"That's right. They get rewarded, Charlotte. I can't wait to see you come for me."

I nearly scream when he slips two fingers deep into me. Instead, I curl my fingers around his biceps, digging my nails into his shirt and the flesh beneath.

The corner of his mouth lifts a fraction. "The rooms are soundproof. You don't have to be quiet here."

When he deepens his penetration, his invitation is all I

need to cry out. Like before, he sets the rhythm and I quickly fall into it. I feel like I'm being ripped apart with desire, and Zane is the only one who can keep me whole. I'm begging, pleading, and screaming his name like he's the only god worth my prayers.

"I need to... Zane... Oh, my God, I need to come. Please!"

My erratic breathing and the wet sounds of his movements inside my hypersensitive tissues fill the air.

He sucks at my neck, his voice warm at my ear. "I know you do, baby. And you're going to. You're right there, aren't you?"

He adds another finger to the effort and fucks me faster and harder until I'm coming apart at the seams.

"Yes!" My throat is raw from being fucked savagely and screaming in ecstasy.

"Look at me."

The demand in his tone sobers me enough to meet his stony gaze. I'm right there, but apparently still one more command away from coming. If sharing his taste on my tongue was intimate, this is more...

"Please," I beg.

He nods.

"Come for me like a good girl, Charlotte."

Permission.

I start to slip when he shifts his angle to one that nudges my clit with every stroke. I open my mouth to scream but the sensation steals my voice, my breath, and all rational thought. I'm breaking apart into a thousand pieces under his touch. My vision goes black. I'm shaking as I go under. A thousand moments of frustration and anger and resentment go up in the flames of my orgasm.

I need this...and I'll only ever need more.

As I come down, my eyelids flutter open, and it's his intense stare that makes me whole again. In that moment, everything returns, like a phoenix made from all the flinty relics of time passed, black like the pupils of my gray-eyed lover.

He slips from me but pushes up my dress until we can both see the mess we've made.

"I think we've wrecked your panties," he says solemnly.

I laugh and am rewarded with a rare smile from Zane. It's another wave of relief in the wake of my orgasm.

Seemingly undeterred, he slides his fingertips through my soaked folds and teases my clit, sending sharp jolts of pleasure through me.

He bites his lower lip. "How the hell am I supposed to let you leave this way?"

Only then do I realize he's hard again, and the only thing keeping him from me are his jeans.

And Katherine.

And the fact that he's been hired to keep me safe, not fuck me raw.

The warm haze of my orgasm has officially dissipated, because none of those things occurred to me when I was on my knees taking his cock like my mouth had no other purpose. Or when he was three knuckles deep inside me, sending me to the stars, to a beautiful place where reality didn't matter.

"I should get back to Katherine," I say softly.

He nods and makes a small sound of agreement. "You're

right."

He rolls off the bed without a word, pauses to adjust himself before he goes to the window, and closes the curtain to the now empty room. His heavy sigh echoes off the walls, and as I straighten my dress, I worry that he regrets all of this. I worry that maybe I should too.

When he comes back to me his face is an unreadable mask. He helps me to my feet, tucks my hair behind my ear, and fixes the fallen straps of my dress.

"I'm going to call Chester, and he'll take you both home."

My chest tightens.

"Don't worry. He's not going to rat you out," he says, like he can read my mind.

"How do you know?"

"Because he never does, except to me. And he's certainly not going to rat us both out. Even if he wanted to he wouldn't. He owes me a couple favors."

I frown. "Like what?"

"None of your business."

I huff and open my mouth to speak. Before any words come out, his hands are on my cheeks, his mouth covers mine, and our tongues are tangling again.

Reality can fuck off because I'm addicted to this man's taste, his touch... Hell, everything about him turns me inside out.

But he pulls away before I can think about getting to his cock again.

"Charlotte, listen to me. We're going to talk about all this. About us. But not tonight. For right now, I need you to do what

I say."

The side of me that is hardwired to defy Zane wants to argue, but I decide to hold it back. "Okay."

His shoulders relax and some tension releases from the gorgeous planes of his face. "Thank you."

I nod, and he makes a quick call to Chester, letting him know our location. Then he takes my hand and leads us back into the club's main area.

After a few minutes, we spot Katherine and Demitri at one of the private seating areas. When we approach, she's flush-faced but seated a safe distance from the man who only takes his eyes off her to acknowledge Zane.

"Leaving so soon?" His accent is familiar, but I can't quite place it. Eastern European, I think.

Zane nods. "It's time. Miss Harrison, let's go."

Katherine doesn't argue, but her hands are shaking as she grabs her purse.

"Are you okay?"

She doesn't answer me, but Demitri rises beside us.

"Let me show you out."

He rests his hand on the small of her back, and I swear the color rises full force in her cheeks as we make our way toward the exit. Katherine splits as soon as she sees the black car and Chester waiting beside it.

But something keeps me planted on the other side of the threshold. I turn and Zane is there, his presence giving me the same safety and comfort it always has. But everything's different now. I tangle my fingers into his shirt, and he holds me against him. We seek out each other's mouths, but the kiss can't last long.

"Go, Charlotte."

"I don't want to."

He kisses me harder, biting my lower lip before ripping away. "Go," he says more firmly. "I can't go out there and have anyone see me with you off duty."

I sigh, but somehow I'm missing him, craving him all over again. What is he doing to me?

He kisses me one last time and then presses his finger to my lips.

I nod. I can't tell a soul.

CHAPTER FOUR

I make my shameful walk toward the car and Chester. His stance is typical, but for the first time in over a year, the kind smile I'm normally greeted with is absent. The rigid lines of his clenched jaw and tightly pursed lips are enough to send my stomach plummeting.

I can handle my parent's disappointment, but not Chester's. He's never once let me down, but tonight I've undoubtedly let him down. I don't know if I'll ever be able to gain back his trust.

Avoiding his gaze, I slide into the back of the car. My ass barely hits the leather seat before the door slams shut. Yep, he's definitely pissed.

Katherine is slumped forward in the seat beside me, her face buried in her perfectly manicured hands. "Oh, my God. We are so fucked!"

Outside my window, Chester is talking on his cellphone. I assume he's busy orchestrating a plan with Zane to get us out of this.

"It's going to be okay. Zane's handling everything."

"What?" She drops her hands away from her face, revealing the thick black streaks of mascara that now stain her cheeks. "Are you kidding me right now? Do you seriously think this isn't going to get back to our parents? I bet he's dying to bust us on this."

I've never seen her this out of sorts before. I suppose I am being abnormally calm, especially considering the amount of trouble we are both facing. But for some reason, I trust that Zane will come through on his promise.

"No, he's not. He promised me that he'd cover for us."

She squints her eyes. "How can you be sure?"

"Just trust me, okay? Chester will get us back to your house, and no one will ever be the wiser. Tomorrow we can forget any of this ever happened."

Except it's highly unlikely I will ever forget about this night. Not after the mind-blowing orgasm Zane just gave me.

Katherine turns her body until she is completely facing me. Only then can I fully see the fear in her eyes.

"Charlotte, if my dad finds out..."

I reach over and take her trembling hand into mine. Katherine's father is legendary for his aggressive temperament. He's ruthless in the courtroom. It's one of the main reasons my father appointed him as Attorney General. As hard as my parents are on me, I can't imagine what her home life must be like.

"He's not going to find out." I force a smile and give her hand a reassuring squeeze. "I promise."

Our talk abruptly ends when Chester opens the driver's side door and situates himself behind the wheel. As we pull away from the curb, I settle back against the seat. Outside, the buildings of the city fade into a blur. When I close my eyes, my mind drifts back to the private room in the club. I touch my fingers against my lips and smile. I can still taste Zane's release on my tongue.

The warm satisfaction I feel blooms, fed by so much more than the orgasms we gave each other. Something about submitting to him on the cold hard floor of that club has forever changed me. The experience woke something inside of me—a hidden desire that I hadn't known existed. Already I crave more, need more. Our time tonight had been cut short. Now I'm aching for him to fill me with his cock. I can't think of a single thing I want more than to have him inside me.

Stretching me.

Claiming me.

But will we ever have a chance to be alone that way again?

After dropping Katherine off at her house, I find myself dreading the drive home. I keep thinking Chester's going to lay into me at any second, but a heavy silence fills the car instead. The longer the silent treatment goes on, the more torturous it becomes. Unable to handle a second more of it, I lift my head to catch his stare in the rearview mirror. He frowns and shifts his eyes back to the road.

"Go ahead. I know you're dying to give me a lecture about all of this."

He lets out a heavy sigh. "It's not my place nor my job to lecture you. But it is my job to protect you. What you did..." He pauses and then shakes his head. "I can't keep you safe if you go and sneak off like that. You may not realize it, but you put a lot of things at risk tonight. My job included."

There's a heavy pull in my chest as the guilt of what I'd done settles over me.

"I'm sorry, Chester. I wasn't thinking. The last thing I want is you losing your job over something stupid I did."

Chester eases the car over onto the shoulder of the road, places his arm across the seat, and turns around to face me. "Charley..."

I'm so relieved to hear him call me by my nickname.

"I'm much more upset at the idea of something happening to you than I ever would be about losing my job. Got it?"

My heart warms at his words. I tilt my head and give him a shy smile. "So...does this mean you're not going to say anything about tonight to my parents?"

He furrows his brow. "What good could possibly come from me doing that?"

"I don't know. Maybe you'll luck out and get reassigned so you wouldn't have to deal with me anymore."

He lets out a soft chuckle. "Like it or not, you're stuck with me, kid."

"Thank you, Chester...for everything."

My words hold much more meaning than he will ever realize. But the tender look he returns makes me wonder if maybe he already knows that.

Chester gives me a wink. "Let's get you home, Charley girl."

◆ ◆ ◆ ◆

Come for me like a good girl, Charlotte.

"Charlotte! Are you paying attention to me?"

My mother's voice snaps me out of my fantasy. Fucking hell. Even smoldering daydreams about Zane aren't safe from her bitchy reach.

"Yes, Mother. Of course, I'm listening." I straighten in my seat and smile tightly. I've become a pro at placating her, especially over the past year.

She glares a moment at me, then at her assistant, a young intern. Rebecca isn't much older than me. I'm sure her dream internship position at the White House turned into a nightmare when she was assigned to my mother. I wouldn't wish that job on anyone.

"Do you have Charlotte's weekend agenda prepared?"

I resist the urge to roll my eyes. Why is she so insistent on having these schedule briefings with me? I never have any say in the high society luncheons, boring fundraiser speeches, and flamboyant charity events that fill my daily calendar. I'm expected to go to all of them without complaint.

"Yes, Ms. Daley. I have it right here." Rebecca fumbles through the leather binder in her hand.

When she doesn't produce the schedule quickly enough, my mother lets out a loud huff.

"Today, Rebecca."

The poor girl is so nervous she nearly trips as she steps toward me. I give her a smile as I take the schedule from her shaking hand. I hate seeing her catch my mother's wrath. Anyone who deals with her incessant demands on a daily basis deserves some sort of sainthood.

At first glance, I'm shocked to see that my morning and afternoon are completely clear. A whole day off? That hasn't happened in months. But as I turn the page to check my evening schedule, my stomach drops.

"Wait a minute. We're having dinner at the Christiansens' tonight?"

"They're hosting your father's law school alumni dinner, remember? We discussed this in detail last week."

Now I remember, but that had been before the incident at Nate's penthouse. I don't want to be anywhere near him now.

"Do I really have to be there?"

My mother grimaces as much as the collagen fillers in her face allow. "Of course you have to be there. This is an important dinner for your father. It would be extremely rude for you not to attend."

"But—"

"Will you give us a moment, Rebecca?"

She keeps her eyes on me as Rebecca leaves us alone in the sitting room. I take a steeling breath and try to prepare myself for the verbal lashing I know is imminent. But my mother only smiles tightly and folds her hands over her crossed knee.

"I'm not blind, Charlotte. I know you've had your eyes set on a certain young man for a while now." The sweetness in her voice is a marked diversion from her usual snippiness toward me, and, well, everyone.

My jaw drops a fraction. How can she possibly know how I feel about Zane? Have I been that obvious this past week?

"I encourage you to pursue him. Your father and I think very highly of him."

I shake my head in disbelief. "What? Who are you talking about?"

"Nate, of course. That's why you're nervous about going

tonight. Am I right?"

The sound of his name causes a wave of nausea to hit me. God, no.

Just as I open my mouth to argue, a knock on the door interrupts us. Rebecca steps one foot inside the room, shielding the rest of her body behind the door.

"I'm very sorry to interrupt, Ms. Daley, but the guests for your ladies brunch are beginning to arrive downstairs."

"Very well, I'll be right down."

My mother waves Rebecca out of the room, stands, and smooths down the front of her crisp navy dress. Like a wrinkle would ever try to defy Victoria Daley. Every day she's donning a new designer suit, always dressed to perfection.

On her way past me, she stops and lifts a strand of my long blond hair. She drops it after a second. "For heaven's sake, Charlotte, do something with your hair before dinner tonight. You'll never hold Nate's interest looking like this."

And with that, she leaves me alone.

ZANE

Dinner with the Christiansens?

I scan tonight's schedule with disgust. The last thing I want is Charlotte hanging around the piece of shit who tried to force himself on her, formal dinner or not. After what he pulled at the party the other night, he's lucky I hadn't broken more than his damn door.

Reeling, I toss the paper onto the desk and make my way to relieve Chester from duty. After his double shift, I'm sure he's more than ready to get out of here. True to form, I find him posted outside the indoor White House pool. His shoulders are slumped forward slightly. A closer look at his face reveals dark circles beneath his eyes.

"Jesus, man. You look like shit."

He stretches his arms above his head and gives me a tired smile. "Then I must look like I feel. These long shifts are making an old man out of me fast."

I nod toward the door. "Everything all right with her?"

His brows knit together. "She's been in there swimming laps for over an hour. Ever since her meeting with her mother this morning, she hasn't been herself. I don't know what's going on, but she seems to be upset about something."

I know exactly what she's upset about. But I won't be filling Chester in on those details. The less he knows about the incident with Nate, the better.

"I'll see if I can get it out of her."

He lets out a chuckle. "Yeah, good luck with that. I imagine she's still pretty pissed at you for spoiling her fun last night."

I smirk in his direction. "She'll get over it."

Chester shakes his head. "You really might consider taking some lessons on women, son. They don't forgive or forget too easily."

Not wanting to broach that topic, I quickly change the subject.

"Listen, I appreciate you keeping last night under wraps. I know I was asking you to risk a lot by doing that."

He loosens his tie, his face warming with a smile. "She's worth the risk, son. Not much I wouldn't do for that girl."

Me neither.

Chester lets out a long yawn.

I slap him on the shoulder. "Go get some beauty sleep, old man. You're starting to show your age."

"Watch it there, kid. I may be older than you, but I'm still young enough to kick your ass."

"Bring it. I'm ready anytime," I tease.

He waves me off and turns to leave.

Once he's completely out of sight, I ease the door open to the pool and slip inside. Thankfully the indoor pool is not under video surveillance. It gives me the perfect opportunity to talk to Charlotte alone without the prying eyes of the other agents.

I stand next to the edge, admiring how the lean lines of her legs and arms glide through the water. Not many women have been able to hold up to my stamina in the bedroom, but endurance won't be an issue for her. She may be a party girl lately, but she stays in shape.

When Charlotte finally spots me, she makes her final strokes toward the ladder next to where I'm standing. After smoothing back her hair, she grips the sides of the metal rail and slowly climbs out of the water. My cock instantly comes to life at the sight of her dripping wet in her tiny black string bikini.

God, the things I want to do to that body.

Without saying a word, Charlotte turns her back to me and bends over to retrieve a towel from the chair. Her barely there bikini inches up her perfect round bottom, exposing the cheeks of her ass. The little minx knows exactly what she's doing. But she's playing a dangerous game with me. She just doesn't realize it yet.

"We need to talk," I say.

Charlotte turns back and rolls her eyes with a sigh. "Always so direct."

"Did you say anything to Katherine about last night?"

"What do you think?" She squeezes the towel around her wet hair, seemingly oblivious to my concern.

"This is serious." I motion between us. "I don't have to tell you how dangerous this is. Neither one of us can handle something like this being exposed to the public. My career would be over, and you, Charlotte, would become a national scandal overnight. That means Katherine can't know anything. No one can."

"I know that. And that's why I would never do anything that might jeopardize us being together."

She wraps the towel around her waist, walks toward me, and reaches out to touch my face. I catch her wrist before she makes contact. Once she hears what I have to say, she may not feel the same way.

"Let's get something straight. I'm not offering you romance. I'm not going to be sending you flowers or vying for your affection. If you agree to this, it will be a discreet relationship based on trust. It's sex. Nothing more. No matter how intense the attraction is between us, you must never misread lust for love. I'm only interested in you surrendering your body to me, not your heart. That's never going to change."

She blinks a few times. "So we'd be like that couple at the club. You tell me what to do and I do it."

"In a way, yes. Your obedience will be rewarded. Your

defiance will be punished. You may learn to enjoy both. It's that simple."

"What if I do something wrong that isn't my fault? Will you still punish me?"

I see a flash of fear in her eyes at every mention of punishment. She has no idea that one day she might enjoy the punishment as much as the reward. For now, I'll use her fear to my advantage if it can steer her away from bad behavior.

"Defiance is a choice, Charlotte. You don't understand it now, because you're spoiled and willful. But when you intentionally defy me from here forward, you'll know the action warrants a consequence. You'll know what your decision will cost you. It could be a night of pleasure. It could be the simple act of sitting comfortably had I not reddened your ass as punishment for acting out. So before you try to defy me, just make sure you're willing to pay the price."

When she doesn't speak, I continue.

"I'm offering you an outlet. I know what you go through every day, better than most. I believe you may need this every bit as much as I do."

"But that's just it. Why would I want someone else to control me? I have enough of that in my life already as it is."

I release her wrist and slide my thumbs rhythmically over her pulse point. "Submission is more powerful than you realize. It's my job to find your limits. It's your job to decide how far those limits get pushed. You will always have a safe word to protect you." I step closer, our bodies nearly touching. "This is about pleasure as much as it is about pain. I will never do anything to you that you don't want me to do. You're the one with the control, Charlotte. Not me."

She doesn't speak, only searches my gaze. I can't help but wonder what's going on in her head.

"Talk to me. Tell me what you're thinking."

She looks to the ground between us. "It's just... Those girls at the club... Will you be doing this with them too?"

I'm not sure what's more disturbing in this moment—the prospect of being unfaithful to Charlotte or her believing that I could be. I cup her face gently with my hands, forcing her to look me directly in the eye.

"I only want you, Charlotte. I'm willing to risk everything to have you. But if I'm going to do that, I have to know you're going to follow my rules. Are you willing to do that? Are you willing to surrender yourself to me?"

Her beautiful blue eyes flutter. Something pulls in my chest, something I haven't felt in a long time.

Fear.

What will I do if she says no? What if she wants the affection that I can't offer her? After tasting her sweet lips, her luscious cunt, how will I ever be able to walk away from her? How will I ever be able to handle another man having what should be mine?

Just as the questions in my head begin to send me into a silent panic, I hear the most beautiful word fall from her lips.

"Yes."

I exhale a breath I didn't realize I was holding. *Thank God.*

I walk her backward until her back hits the concrete wall and I crash my mouth against hers. Stroke for stroke, our tongues hungrily move against each other, tasting, savoring.

Charlotte drops her hand between us, teasing her touch along my erection. Groaning, I break our kiss. If I don't put the brakes on now, I'll end up fucking her over a lounge chair.

"Not here." Cradling her face in my hands, I drag my lips tenderly across hers. "But tonight you're all mine."

CHARLOTTE

"Well, well, well. If it isn't America's Little Princess."

Freezing mid-step, I turn. Nate is standing at the top landing of the staircase that overlooks the Christiansens' foyer. With his brown curls slicked back against his head, he's almost unrecognizable. Up until this moment, I'd managed to avoid any interaction with him during tonight's guest introductions. My luck has just run out.

Dressed in a tuxedo, Nate straightens his bowtie and descends the staircase with a leisurely swagger. Once he's reached where I'm standing, he gives me a wink.

"You know, if I didn't know better, I'd say you were purposefully trying to avoid me tonight."

I square my shoulders, unwilling to let him intimidate me. "But that's just it, Nate. You *do* know better."

"Ouch. Someone's got their panties in a twist." He holds his finger to his lips, his expression mocking. "No wait. You prefer thongs, right?"

I flinch at his words. Without the tequila-fueled courage coursing in my veins that night, I never would have initiated things with him in the first place. The fact he knows what kind of underwear I wear is mortifying enough, let alone that we almost had sex.

Thank God Zane got me out of there when he did. Becoming another notch on Nate's bedpost is something I'll never want.

I cross my arms. If I am to ever get through tonight's dinner, I've got to stand up to him. "What do you want, Nate? If this is about the other night, you need to get over it."

He takes the final step that closes the distance between us. "Get over it? You left me fucking hanging the other night. You owe me."

"I don't owe you a goddamn thing."

I turn to leave when he grabs me by the arm and jerks me back. I flinch at the pain. I try to pull out of his hold, but that only makes him tighten his grip. His roughness instantly reminds me of the way he handled me on the bed the night of the party.

"Girls don't tell me 'no' and get away with it."

I stare into his dark, soulless eyes, sickened by the thought of how many girls he's made victims.

"Let me go before I scream. Zane will have you on your ass in front of everyone in seconds."

Nate releases my arm at my warning, but not without issuing one of his own.

"He won't always be around to save you, Charlotte. And, when that day comes, I'll be waiting. One way or another, you're going to give me what I want."

Heart pounding, I hurry to the adjacent room where guests are beginning to gather for dinner. When I spot Zane across the room, the relief is instant. Somehow I feel safe enough to breathe again. When our eyes lock, he leaves his post and comes toward me, his stride confident and measured. A moment later, he's close enough to touch. All I want is to fall into his arms and forget everything, but I know better.

"What's wrong?" His voice is low so only I can hear his hushed concern.

I shake my head, rubbing the sides of my arms with my hands. I should stay and suffer through this dinner. I can already hear my mother's insufferable nagging if I skip out, but Nate's words have me nauseous.

"Zane... I just need you to get me out of here."

I shoot him a pleading look. His expression hardens. I know he wants more details, but I can't talk about things here. Especially not with Nate a room away. Right now, I just want to go home.

Zane lifts his arm to speak into the small communication device. "This is Parker, requesting return transport for Miss Daley." He returns his attention to me. "Wait right here. I'm going to tell your parents that I'm taking you back home." The muscle in his jaw flexes. "And when we get there, you're going to tell me everything."

ZANE

The twelve-minute drive back to the White House is agonizingly long. The haunted look in Charlotte's eyes has ebbed away, but I have to know who put it there in the first place.

Once we arrive, I keep a safe distance, following behind her as we make our way inside and up to the second floor. The instant she's in her bedroom, I'm right there, closing the door behind us.

"Start talking."

She shakes her head. "It's okay, Zane. Nate just caught me off guard, that's all. I should have known better than to let him get under my skin like that. I'm sorry to worry you. I probably overreacted."

She's lying. As visibly shaken as she'd been earlier, I fear this is far more than that fucker Nate running off at the mouth.

"You're lying. I saw your face. Did he threaten you?"

She wraps her arms around her body. "Nate won't let what happened go. He says I owe him. He…"

When she hesitates, I cradle her face, forcing her gaze to mine. "He what? Tell me."

"He said he's going to make me pay for leaving him hanging. I guess he doesn't think you can protect me forever and eventually he'll get his chance."

A murderous rage surges through me. I should have broken his neck when I had the chance. Through other agents, I'd heard numerous stories about him taking advantage of girls. With his father's help, all of those allegations have been silenced. He thinks he's above the law, untouchable.

"Listen to me. There's no way in hell Chester or I would ever let something happen to you. Nate can't touch you. He just wants you to think he can. These kinds of guys thrive on fear."

She lifts her gaze up at me. "I just want to forget that night happened. I want to forget how far I let him go. I was so stupid."

I hush her and bring her against me. Once she's there, she squeezes her arms around my middle and exhales a quiet sigh.

I curse myself for all the times I stood by, watching her hurt from afar when I could have held her this way, given her an ounce of comfort when her family gave her none.

"Please... Make me forget," she whispers against my chest.

Please.

That quickly, I'm unraveling, as if that one little word is tugging on a string wound around my self-control.

What is she doing to me? How can one woman make me this weak?

"Charlotte..."

"Please, Zane. I need this."

Still, I hesitate, trying to make sense of the power she's gaining over me, one forbidden moment to the next. Sex isn't the issue. I gave up pretending like I didn't want to bury myself between her thighs the second she showed up at Crave in red. But my infatuation for her runs deeper than I care to admit. I want to do far more than fuck her. I want to crawl inside of her soul, possess her, save her, ruin her from ever wanting another man. I only know one way to do that...

I step back and the dejected look in her eyes nearly brings me to my knees. She has no idea she's already won.

I slide my jacket off and toss it onto a nearby chair. Relief softens her features. I can't wait to see rapture claim them.

"When we are alone like this, you will refer to me as 'sir,' understood?"

Her lashes lower, shadowing her eyes. "Yes, sir."

I begin working the knot loose on my tie, relishing the flush in her cheeks as she says the words. "Take off your dress."

I follow her hand as she slides down the metal zipper on

her side. Then she gives a final tug at the jeweled shoulder clasp, sending her midnight blue dress to pool at her feet. Without asking, she unclasps her strapless bra and slides her panties to the floor. My breath hitches at the glorious sight before me. From head to toe, I devour every delectable curve of her naked body.

There is no comparison. She's the most beautiful thing I've ever seen.

I come closer, stopping once I'm directly in front of her. "Give me your hands."

Without hesitation, she obeys, extending her arms out to me.

"Good girl," I murmur.

She smiles softly and follows every movement as I weave my black silk tie over the delicate skin of her wrists. I secure the binding with a single knot, leaving the remaining fabric to hang loosely. Then I take her bound hands into mine. Back and forth, I tenderly rub the pad of my thumbs over her wrists, relishing the fact that her flawless skin will soon bear the markings of her restraints.

"Do you trust me, Charlotte?"

She looks up at me. "Yes, sir."

"Good. Give me your safe word."

She swallows hard. "Silk."

Her choice has my dick throbbing. One thing is certain. After this, I definitely won't be able to look at my neckties the same way.

My patience wearing thin, I tear the blankets off the four-poster bed and nudge her back onto it. Its enormous size makes her look small and vulnerable, a circumstance that inspires both the hunter and the protector in me. The mattress dips as I sink my knee into the bed beside her.

"Lie back with your feet facing me, and put your hands above your head."

Crawling over her body, I use the remainder of my silk tie to secure her arms to the braided wood post behind her. After giving her restraint a quick test, I rise up and take a moment to appreciate the sight below me. Bound and naked, Charlotte is a Dominant's wet dream.

"Remember, no matter what you do or how much you beg me, I won't stop what I'm doing unless you say that word. Understand?"

"Yes, sir."

I don't miss the quiver in her voice. Still new to the experience, Charlotte has every right to be afraid. Tonight's only the beginning of what I have in store for her.

I free my belt from around my waist. It whooshes through the loops. Starting just below her neck, I trail the smooth leather down the front of her torso. The silk knot above Charlotte's head strains as her back arches up off the bed.

"Oh, the things I want to do to you, pretty girl."

I drag my gaze down her body, lingering over her full luscious tits. My cock aches to slide between them, to fuck them unmercifully. But not tonight. Tonight, when I come, it will be deep inside Charlotte's tight pussy.

"Spread your legs apart for me. Let me see how wet you are."

At my command, her legs fall open, giving me a perfect

view of her beautiful pink opening. My focus drops to the small rim of her anus. I bite my lip so hard it could bleed, because I know one of these nights, I'll have that too.

I glide my fingers up through the slick heat of her sex, groaning at how drenched she is. "You're already soaked for me."

Craving a taste, I bring my fingertips up to my mouth and savor her flavor.

"So fucking delicious."

Desperate for more, I position myself between her thighs, slide my hands beneath her ass, and yank her to me. She lets out a loud gasp when my mouth reaches her sex. The ruthless flicking of my tongue across her swollen clit sends her bucking against the restraints. Holding her writhing body in place, I plunge my tongue inside her and feast on her pussy like a starving animal.

"Oh, God!" She screams, arching up off the bed.

I don't want to stop, but I can't hold back much longer. I reach for the condom in my pocket. I'm ready to rip it open and plunge into her, but something holds me back. Protection is vital in my relationships. I've never questioned it before. Not until now.

I know Charlotte's on the pill. I'd seen the prescription on her bathroom counter plenty of times. After my recent healthy physical results, I know I'm no risk to her.

Dizzy with the prospect of having her bare, I lean in, flick her clit with my tongue, and breathe her in. "How many men have had you, Charlotte?"

Her answer comes out on a ragged breath. "One. Just

one."

Relief hits me, then an unexpected tension. The good news is she's had one other partner. That bad news is that means someone else has been inside her, and now all I can think about is wiping the memory of him clean.

"Did you always use protection?"

"Yes, sir."

She's mine. I have to make her mine.

My possessive thoughts drown out all the rational ones. Need claws at me from the inside out. "I want to fuck you raw, Charlotte. Tell me there's enough trust between us for that. I need to feel when you're coming on my cock."

Need to come inside you... Need to mark you.

"Yes. I trust you. God, yes."

That's all I need for my desire to win. I unfasten my pants, shove them past my hips, and slide up her naked body. She's stripped, and I'm still fully clothed. The inequity only adds to my arousal. Her added vulnerability is like a shot of something strong on top of the already intoxicating experience of being nearly inside her. Gripping the base of my shaft with my free hand, I align the tip to her glistening opening. I push my hips forward, gasping at the overwhelming sensation of taking her bare.

The muscles of her tight channel resist my girth at first. I lock my eyes with hers, savoring the hazy mix of desire and apprehension I see there. Her bottom lip trembles. I catch it with my thumb and hush her little whimpers as I press my lips to hers.

"I've got you," I whisper, rocking gently, joining us a little bit more with each thrust.

She's so tight. I'm ready to lose my mind, but somehow I find the patience to take her slowly as her body adjusts. When she's taken all of me, I let out a groan.

"Holy fuck. Your pussy is gripping my cock so tight."

One glance between us to where my cock is buried inside her perfect body has me ready to explode. I still my movements and grasp her hip to hold her firmly in place. One more thrust and I'll be coming inside her long before I'm ready to. I take a few deep breaths and ease out of her, then slowly push back in. Each time I sink into her is better than the time before. Thrust for thrust, our bodies move in perfect sync.

"How does that feel, baby?"

"Amazing." Her voice is breathy, and her eyes flutter closed. "Fuck me. Please fuck me, sir."

With a growl, I give her exactly what she asks for. Less restraint, more of everything else. The loud sounds of our bodies coming together echoes through the room.

Crashing my lips to hers, I swallow her tiny moans. I push her knees out and spread her legs wider, giving me deeper access to her core. When I feel the tip of my dick hit her cervix, it's everything I can do to keep from coming.

"You're so deep," she moans, rolling her eyes back.

I quicken the pace of my forceful thrusts, feeling her inner walls as they tighten around me. She's close, so fucking close. And, I'm right there with her.

"Zane!" She lets out a trembling cry.

"That's it. Come for me, Charlotte. Fucking come on my cock."

She arches away from the bed, shuddering as the climax rips through her.

"Your pussy is mine, Charlotte." A feral sound rips from me with one final drive of my hips. "Mine," I rasp against her damp skin.

Mine.

CHAPTER FIVE

CHARLOTTE

Slivers of sunlight slip into my bedroom through the tall curtains. I roll over, bury my face in my pillow, and notice some new aches in my muscles. I wince and then remember...

With a lazy grin, I stretch, embracing the discomfort. Lately I'm used to waking up with a pounding headache and a fuzzy account of the night before. But my memories of last night with Zane are crystal clear. And vivid enough that I spend the next twenty minutes replaying them in my mind until I'm squirming against my sheets and wishing he were here to relieve the throbbing between my thighs.

I could get myself there, but I'd rather he did. I turn and reach for my phone on the bedside table. Then I type out a text for Zane and hit send.

I can't stop thinking about last night. Thank you...for everything.

A few seconds go by before a reply comes back to me.

Are you sore?

I draw my lower lip between my teeth as I respond.

In all the best ways. I can't wait for you to make me sore again. I'm so wet already just thinking about it.

I roll to my back and slide my hand into my panties, hopeful that he'll take the bait. I see three little dots indicating that he's typing. Then they disappear and the phone rings.

"Zane—"

"Under no circumstances are you to touch yourself without me."

I can't help it. A rush of defiance fires through me. "That's not fair."

"It's not your job to decide what's fair. I decide and you obey. And I'm telling you that you'd better get your pretty little fingers off that perfect little cunt right fucking now. Unless you want me to paddle you later, which I'm happy to do. But I'm not sure if you're ready for that yet."

I whisper a little "fuck" under my breath and grip the phone tightly. How does he do that? Turn my defiance into a desire I have no control over in a matter of seconds? Slowly I slide my fingers back up to my belly, but not before giving my clit a little extra pressure. I don't know why I'm intent on teasing myself, when every minute between now and seeing Zane again will be heavier because of it.

"I need you," I mumble. "Relieve Chester early. I'm begging you."

He releases a quiet sigh and his silence encourages me. Maybe there's a chance I can allay this ache yet...

"I need you inside me, Zane. I've never felt anything like that, and I'm going crazy without it. You can sneak in. I'll play sick and we can spend the day in bed. Just me and you—"

"Charlotte, listen to me."

I hold my breath at his sharp command.

"After I hang up, you're going to get up, shower, and get dressed for your day. You're not going to wear any underwear. I want you to feel every breeze, every scratch of fabric, and every brush of skin against skin."

"What if I get wet?" God, I'm so fucking wet already, what he's demanding is going to be pure torture.

"Then I suggest you dress accordingly," he answers abruptly.

"When can I see you?" I'm whining...begging. Jesus, what the hell is wrong with me? I have no idea how Zane has me under this spell, but I'm praying to the ceiling that he has a surprise visit in mind. Something...*anything* that I can look forward to while I battle this unexpected withdrawal.

"You will see me at precisely five o'clock, like you do every day. And when I get there, I expect easy access to your pussy. Because I'd very much like to fuck it."

"Oh, God," I breathe, tightening my free hand around the sheet to keep from touching myself.

"I will know if you've come without me, Charlotte. I'll know the second I look into those baby blue eyes, because I've been watching you lie to me for months."

That small layer of truth on top of his dirty talk sobers me a bit. I feel the guilt first, then the urge to defend myself. I've been living in political hell—not for months, for *years*. He'll never understand that.

But he is right. I've lied. I've made his life more difficult, and I've threatened his livelihood with my carelessness. There's just as much at risk now, though. Maybe more. Deciding to pursue this relationship with Zane is undoubtedly dangerous, but it's also safer because no one has ever made me feel this way. Even as I burn for another intimate moment with him, knowing he has a plan for us gives me a calm like I've never known.

"I'll wait for you."

I utter the promise, and I intend to keep it. But the rebel in me has other plans.

ZANE

I step out of the fitness center on the ground floor of View 17 and take the elevator to my apartment, cooling down and catching my breath from a five-mile run on the treadmill. I can't remember the last time I woke up with this much goddamn energy. Between wrestling with my guilt over pursuing Charlotte to longing for her as though she's my next breath, I haven't had much solid rest lately.

But last night something changed. The sex was out of this world, without a doubt. Charlotte wasn't the only one waking up flooded with memories of the way our bodies came together. But her submission... Once she gave in to me, it was like a missing puzzle piece just fell into place. I spent the past half hour trying to make sense of this new peace that's got me buzzing from the inside out.

Whatever it was, or is, I'm not giving it up anytime soon. If I'm not completely addicted to her body—which I am—then I'm on my way to being a true junkie when it comes to this level of satisfaction. How will I ever want it to end?

Doesn't matter. It will. Eventually.

I rip my earbuds out and open the door to my apartment, unwilling to consider an end when I'm this fucking high on the woman. Her phone call this morning has me hard every time I think of it, and I can't keep my eyes off the clock. Delayed gratification has its benefits, and tonight I plan to thoroughly enjoy them.

I'm about to jump into the shower and get ready for work when Chester calls my phone. In my line of work, almost nothing gets my heart beating fast. But it's racing now. Nate couldn't have gotten to her... There's no way.

"Chester, what's up? Is everything okay with Charlotte?"

His gravelly laugh hits my ear and the relief is instant. "Yes, our Charley girl is just fine. Up to her usual antics, I suppose."

My relief quickly morphs into anger. "What's going on?"

I swear to God if she's gallivanting around with her friend Katherine or anywhere within a mile of Nate Christiansen, she's going to get the paddling of a lifetime. She'll need to get used to it at some point anyway.

"We're heading your way shortly. She had breakfast with her mother this morning and asked to move into the apartment early. She thought it was only fair since she's being forced to stay in DC for the foreseeable future."

"And what did Mommy Dearest say?"

That earns another chuckle from my colleague, but it fades into prolonged silence, which tells me the exchange was likely tense.

"We'll talk about it when we get there. The place has already been furnished and her people arranged it so she could stay there starting tonight. Our team scoped out the building and we'll have people posted before she arrives. Just wanted to give you a heads up to report to the penthouse tonight."

"See you then."

I hang up and start pacing the floor of my living room, because I'm anything but relieved right now. My cock, of course, thinks this is an excellent development. But having her a few floors away from me every night is no less dangerous than fucking her in the residence. In fact, it's even riskier because Chester will be in my backyard while I'm off duty now. Charlotte has promised obedience, but I still don't trust her to make smart moves when she's grown used to chasing every impulse lately. Now *I'm* her impulse.

I take my pacing into the bathroom, strip down, and shower quickly. She'll be on my doorstep in two hours, and when she arrives, I'll need a whole new game plan.

CHARLOTTE

My apartment is teeming with black suits when I arrive. Per the usual, every window, door, vent, and access point will have to be thoroughly checked to ensure my safety. Chester is especially tense, probably because I dropped this on him unexpectedly. Despite this, he seems to share a bit of my enthusiasm about the move. No doubt witnessing the negotiation with my mother this morning earned me an ounce of empathy.

Agents come and go, reporting details to the people posted outside through their devices as I attempt to unpack. I should be thinking about the usual things. How I plan to decorate and move things around so this new place feels like home. It's significantly bigger than my apartment in New York. But all I can think about is where Zane will make me his again. I'm sure it won't go down the way he planned it this morning, because we're in new territory now. But I'm determined to have him tonight, even if he's annoyed about this unexpected move.

I feel him before I see him enter my room, a prickling heat on the back of my neck. And the second our gazes lock, I know he's less than pleased. His eyes are like cold granite, a perfect match to the rock-hard body he hides under his suits.

I clear my throat and push past him into the main living area. "Okay, everyone out!" They've been casing this place for hours. I need alone time. Now.

Slowly the other agents file out, and Chester mutters a few words to Zane that cause his expression to soften ever so slightly. When we're finally alone, I approach him cautiously. Something about his dominant posture keeps me from reaching out to touch him.

"I've been waiting all day for this." Nothing in my voice hides my relief or my wanting.

"What the hell do you think you're doing?" He hasn't raised his voice, but the words are clipped enough that I know I'm in trouble.

I shrug, trying to seem casual. "The move was inevitable.

I figured I'd speed things up is all."

"You didn't feel the need to discuss it with me this morning?" The tendons in his neck tighten, and I resist the urge to run my palms along them, coaxing out his more forgiving side. Or maybe his sexier side...

"I didn't think of it until after we talked," I say softly. "I remember you saying you wanted easy access to me. So here I am. I obeyed." I shoot him a coy smile, because I'm certain Zane doesn't consider this obedience in any way, shape, or form.

"And what do your parents think of this new plan?"

My smile fades, but I try to ignore the stab of pain I feel. "It's an inconvenience, obviously. Just like everything else that has to do with me. But ultimately it was a means of getting me out of my mother's daily life a little sooner. In her words, she won't have to worry about me looking the part of a respectable First Daughter so much anymore. So," I shrug again, "here I am. Maybe they can forget I exist, for real this time."

My longing for Zane is momentarily suspended by my pain. With the pain has always come loneliness, even in the most crowded rooms. I close my eyes, because I don't feel that way when I'm with Zane. Maybe that's what brought me here tonight. Not the unquenchable desire to feel him pounding possessively into me—though I desperately want that too—but the deep desire to feel wanted again...by someone who might truly care. The way he swept me away from the situation with Nate last night tells me he might.

I open my eyes when I feel his fingertips feather gently across my cheek. There's new warmth in his eyes.

"She's a cruel woman. Standing idly by while she hurts you has been one of the most difficult parts of this job. She makes it impossible for me to truly protect you because of who she is."

I cover his hand with mine. "You protect me as much as you can. But you do more than that." I can't ignore the electricity that's vibrating between our bodies. I've never felt this way with someone. No one...ever. "You save me, Zane."

When he pulls in a shaky breath, his suit strains at his chest. When he releases it, his touch falls away. I look down. Have I shown him too much? I've moved into his apartment building, and now I'm saying things I shouldn't. Things that make me sound vulnerable and pathetic. I'm pretty sure that's not what he meant when he asked for my submission.

I shake my head and swallow over the unexpected emotions burning my throat. I thought tonight would be all about fucking. I wasn't expecting to show him so much of myself.

"Did you do as I asked?"

"Huh?"

I lift my gaze again, only to drop it to where he's drawing his hand up my bare thigh.

"Were you thinking of me today?" His rising touch moves past the hem of my dark denim dress.

"All day," I confess breathlessly, trying not to move as he makes his ascent to the apex between my thighs.

"And were you wet, thinking of me?"

"Constantly. I—" I stumble over the confession that wants to burst free.

"You what? Tell me everything, Charlotte." He stares at

me intently, demanding the truth.

"I want you so much... My body aches for you in a way that almost frightens me. I spent half the day out of my mind imagining how you'd fuck me tonight, and the other half terrified that you'd punish me and I'd never be satisfied."

His slow-traveling hand finally reaches my bare pussy. I jolt from the slight contact of his fingers on the outside of my lips. I'm wound so tight, I think I could come with a few well-placed flicks at this point.

"I think we both know you should have talked to me before you had Chester drop you on my doorstep."

I nod. I should have, but I was desperate.

"Did you want me to punish you?" His voice is low. Not threatening. In fact, it's almost hopeful.

I shake my head, but then I stop. Am I being honest?

"I don't know. You have a way of turning pain into pleasure. You make me want to try things, even if they scare me sometimes."

He tilts his head slightly, but I can't read him.

"Then I think now is a good time to try some of those things. Go to your bedroom. Put your hands on the bed. I want to see your ass in the air, dress up around your hips. Do you understand?"

I nod but my feet are frozen in place.

He lifts an eyebrow. "Now."

Without another word, I do as he says, my heart swelling and racing. I clear my new king-size bed of my suitcases, my hands shaking as I do. Then I position myself in front of it and hike my dress up as I bend over.

My pussy throbs unbearably. Somehow it's worse than ever. Maybe because I can feel the air like a kiss on my wet, sensitive tissues. Maybe because I don't know what he's capable of...

My palms are moist and prickle against the bedspread, but I keep my fingers spread wide, my ass perched high.

Everything I do now is to please him.

I've stepped into another world, a place where my daily reality bleeds away and Zane is my king, me his willing subject. I close my eyes and take a slow, deep breath. Then I hear his quiet footfalls as he enters the room.

He stops by the doorway. The absolute silence has me trembling again. Then he moves behind me, and I hear his shoes creak as he bends to sit on his haunches. A breath hits the back of my thigh. I fist the bedspread and stifle a whimper.

He hushes me softly, even though I haven't made a sound. "If I touch you, you'll go off, won't you?"

Hell yes, I will. "I've been waiting for you for hours."

He makes a quiet sound in his throat, which sounds like acknowledgment. His palms graze the backs of my thighs up to my cheeks, spreading them apart, causing the flesh to sting. I jolt and he hushes me again.

"Just looking, sweetheart. I almost forgot how perfect you are here. Almost. I can't wait to slide into this little heaven." He barely traces the outer lips of my pussy with his tongue. "Going to come right here, fill you up until you're dripping."

I whimper and push my hips up, hoping it gets me closer to the sweet torture of his mouth. Just a few licks...

He tisks and straightens behind me.

Smack!

His hand comes down hard on my ass cheek and I cry out, not so much because it hurts but because the abruptness startles me.

"Use your safe word if you need to. Otherwise, scream into a pillow. I can't have people thinking I'm murdering you in here."

"Okay," I reply shakily.

His palm comes down again, just as hard as the first time. Maybe harder. I bite my lip as he creates a rhythm. Quick slaps, rotating between the two sides, peppering my ass and thighs with stinging heat. I reach for a pillow and muffle a cry into it when he starts his rotation again, hitting flesh that's already felt his punishment.

Sirens go off in my head. My thoughts whirl and scream at me. *What the fuck are you doing? You're the President's daughter. How can you let him degrade you like this? Is this who you are now?*

"Yes!" I cry into the air as his palm makes contact once more.

I whimper and brace myself for more strikes, but they don't come. Then his lips are everywhere, whispers of warmth and reassurance against my burning ass and thighs. *So beautiful. Perfect. Such a good girl. Going to fuck you now.*

The sound of his zipper almost brings tears to my eyes. I'm so wet. So ready. Then his cock drives into me with one fierce shove, and our moans mingle in the air. He's still dressed, the same as he was last night. His suit pants are rough against my sore ass, adding awareness to the pain as he pounds his way toward our pleasure.

The tangle of sensations has my mind whirling again. Because I like it, but I know I shouldn't. Still, I relish the discomfort because nothing—absolutely nothing—has felt as good as his cock claiming me in this moment, in the wake of his punishment.

My whole body jars with each thrust. His strength and the way he fills me up like no one ever has feeds the climb toward my climax. I'm wrapped around him like a vise, and so on edge. The only thing keeping me from coming is the certainty that doing so would bring this all to an end. And it feels too fucking good to end yet.

But behind me, Zane's rhythm falters and his grip on my hips grows firmer. He shudders, and I know he's close.

"Zane," I cry out his name, because my control is slipping too.

"Fuck, you feel so good." Thrust. "Ah, Charlotte... Come for me, baby." Thrust. "Let me fill you up now."

I fly apart as he fucks me wildly, my name and mindless promises on his lips. I scream into the pillow, lost in the orgasm, lost in every incredible sensation of our bodies coming together. In a split second, I remember one word from last night. *Mine.* I came even harder when he said it. Now I'm crying *yours* in my head as the sharp pulses of pleasure level out. *I want to be yours.*

I whimper when he slips out of me. When he groans and spreads my cheeks apart again, I know he's watching his release drip out of me. I feel it, warm and slick, trailing down my inner thigh. Now that I know how much pleasure it gives him to mark me, I resolve to give him plenty more opportunities in the future.

"Up on the bed now. I'm going to get a cloth to clean you up," he says quietly, giving my ass a little pat.

I inch farther up the bed and wait until he returns with a cloth, which he uses to clean away the evidence of our incredible sex. When I think he's done, he sits down, dipping the bed, and begins to rub lotion on my sore backside.

I turn my head to watch him. He's still fully dressed, as put together as he was when he walked in an hour ago.

"Why are you still dressed?" I mumble against the bed, closing my eyes against the sensation of his fingers kneading and massaging me.

"Because, despite the fact that I just screwed your brains out, I'm still working."

I make a sound of displeasure. "I don't like sharing you with your job."

"This job is the only reason I'm allowed within a hundred feet of you. We should both be thankful for it. If anyone ever found out..."

I open my eyes and recognize the flash of worry in his. "I promised you I wouldn't tell anyone."

"I believe you. But now that you're here, in the building, we need to discuss some ground rules."

I frown. Because I don't like rules, and because he's no longer massaging me. He's shifted off the bed and is straightening his tie.

"Get dressed. We need to talk," he says before leaving the room.

CHAPTER SIX

Charlotte emerges from her bedroom wearing a pair of tiny black lace panties and a matching tank top, which is not at all what I meant when I told her to get dressed. She's wearing less now than when I fucked her ten minutes ago.

She plops herself down onto the tan leather couch and tucks her legs beneath her bottom. "All right, let's get this over with. Lay the rules on me."

"Well, for starters. Try not to wear shit like that around the apartment while I'm around."

Charlotte looks down and scrunches her forehead. "What's wrong with what I have on? I sometimes sleep in less than this."

I suppress a groan at the visual.

"As much as I love seeing that tight little body of yours, you can't prance around the house half-naked. Unless I instruct you differently, you have to be decent when I'm with you. I don't have to tell you how bad it would be if your mother dropped by here unexpectedly and found you dressed like that."

She huffs, grabs a throw pillow off the couch, and hugs it tightly to her body. "Fine, what else?"

"No parties and no surprise visitors. It's too risky to invite people here without the proper clearance."

"What about Kat?"

I hesitate at her request. I don't consider Katherine a positive influence, but I know she's a close friend, which Charlotte doesn't have in abundance.

"Katherine's visits are fine for now, as long as you two can behave. Everyone else will have to be approved by either Chester or me before they step through that door. Got it?"

"Yeah, I got it."

Her tone is clipped, but at least she's agreeing to my demands. For now.

"Third, my apartment is completely off limits. My privacy is very important to me."

Charlotte narrows her eyes. "How is it fair that you get to know everything about me, yet I know nothing about you?"

"It's my job to know everything about you. That's how I can effectively keep you safe. What goes on in my personal life, behind closed doors, is my business, not yours."

"So ridiculous," she mumbles under her breath.

I harden my jaw before I speak again. "Fourth rule: No—"

"Jesus! You mean there's more?" Charlotte slaps her hand on the arm of the couch. "I thought when I moved in here that you'd ease up with all the rules, not pile more on."

"What did you expect? Did you think you and I were going to cook dinner in the kitchen and watch movies all night? My job is to protect you. Not play house."

She pushes herself up off the couch, glaring at me with her icy blue eyes. If they were daggers, I'd be dead.

"Believe me, I'm completely aware of why you are here, Zane. But that doesn't give you the right to be such a dick about it." She moves past me toward the kitchen.

I can hear the disappointment in her voice and immediately hate myself for hurting her. But I need to keep things in check between us. If deeper feelings take root, no good can come of it.

I follow her into the kitchen, but she's faced away from me, arms crossed, leaning her hip against the counter. I indulge a look at her perfect ass, but draw my attention to the taut line of her shoulders. I brush a finger down her spine. She shivers and softens a bit.

"Listen," I say quietly. "I know I may sound harsh, but we need to keep our heads straight about all of this. We have to keep our feelings out of the arrangement."

She spins quickly. "Can you honestly look me in the eye and tell me that when we're having sex you feel *nothing* for me?"

Of course, I feel something for her... More than I'd care to admit. The connection between us, especially when we're intimate, is unlike anything I've ever felt before. But those feelings are dangerous for both of us. So, instead of telling her the truth, I look her dead in the eye and lie.

"I don't have those kinds of feelings for you, Charlotte."

Her face falls. Her defiance melts away. In its wake, the hurt there is enough to rip my fucking heart straight out of my chest.

She tries to push past me, but I seize her by the arm and spin her around to face me.

"Go to hell!"

I bring my face close to hers. "You don't have the right to be angry with me. I haven't misled you in any way. The terms of this relationship were made clear from the beginning. This isn't romance. It's fucking."

She flinches at my words. "Get out." Her voice is low and pained.

"Charlotte…"

I loosen my grip and she slips away, her eyes blazing with emotion. "Go do your job and leave me the fuck alone."

CHARLOTTE

"You lucky bitch." Kat shoves the bag of bagels into my chest and pushes past me.

After last night's argument with Zane, I needed a distraction. If anyone can get my mind off things, Katherine can.

She stops in front of the long wall of windows that offers a panoramic view of downtown. "God, I'm so jealous of you right now. I can't believe they actually let you have your own place."

"Your parents are traveling constantly, Kat. You have the place to yourself all the time."

Returning to the kitchen, Kat slips off her cherry-red peacoat and places it across the back of the stool. "It's not the same, trust me. I've been trying to convince my parents to let me move into an apartment for over a year now. My father finally said he'd consider it this summer. Until then, I'll have to live vicariously through you." She situates herself in the seat and braces her elbows on the counter, resting her face in her hands. "So, tell me. How does freedom feel?"

"Freedom? It's a little hard to feel free when you have a bodyguard posted at your door twenty-four hours a day. Not to mention one that has an apartment two levels below you."

Kat's jaw drops. "Wait a minute. Zane lives in this building?"

I place a couple of plates on the counter. "That's the reason my father picked this building. He liked the idea of having Zane close by to keep an extra eye on things. So, basically, I traded one jail cell for another."

She reaches in the bag for a bagel. "Think of it like this. You're like Rapunzel. Stuck up here on top of the tower just waiting for some handsome prince to climb up and rescue you."

I let out a short laugh. "Yeah, well, I hate to break it to you, but fairytales aren't real. No one's coming to rescue me."

She drops her hands down away from her face and scrunches her nose at me. "God, you're depressing as hell, you know that? We really have to work on finding you a guy."

I concentrate on cutting the bagel in half. "I've got enough on my plate with school starting. Getting a guy is the last thing on my mind right now."

"When do your classes start at Georgetown?"

"My parents and I are supposed to tour the campus tomorrow morning. I'm sure they'll want me to start as soon as possible, especially since I'm already heading into the pre-law program three weeks late."

Katherine's expression suddenly hardens. "I hate them for forcing you into this. I wish we could convince them to let you go to Howard with me. They have such an excellent art program there. You're way too talented to give it up."

I shake my head, trying to keep myself from gaining hope from her words. "There's no way that's ever going to happen. My father looks at an art degree like it's a kindergarten diploma. He already thinks I've wasted the past year and a half in school as it is."

"That's ridiculous. No one should ever have their entire future dictated to them."

As much as I appreciate my best friend coming to my defense, I can't waste any more energy on it.

"My father's the President of the United States, Kat. That means, for at least the next four years, he has complete control over me and my life. It doesn't do me any good to try and fight it."

Katherine opens her mouth to argue, but I hold my hand up to stop her.

"Enough talk about me and my pathetic life. What are you doing tonight? Want to grab some dinner and maybe see a movie?"

"I'm sorry, but I can't. I've already made plans."

I cross my arms and lean across the counter. "Plans? As in date plans?"

She tucks a strand of her dark hair behind her ear. "Not really. Well...actually, I'm not really sure what to call it."

"Anyone I know?"

Instead of answering, Katherine shoves the rest of the

bagel into her mouth and diverts her eyes to the bottle of water in front of her.

A smile spreads across my face. "So it *is* someone I know."

Kat swallows and finally makes eye contact. "Do you remember the guy at the club the other night? The one Zane left me with?"

My eyes widen. "You mean the guy with the accent? Demitri? That's who your date is with?"

She gives me a hesitant nod.

I drop the knife onto the counter. "Have you lost your fucking mind? Zane will go apeshit if he finds out you're sneaking back into that club."

"I'm not going to be sneaking in. Demitri invited me back as his guest."

"What? How did he even know how to get in touch with you?"

"I was so upset when we left the club that night with Zane that I accidentally left my phone on the couch. Demitri had it couriered to my house the next day—but not before he added his contact information. When I called to thank him, he invited me to come to the club tonight."

"And you're actually going? You saw what kind of things go on at that place. Besides, you don't even know this guy."

Katherine pulls her bottom lip in between her teeth, blushing. "I can't explain it. There's just something about the club that I'm drawn to."

She casts her eyes low. I sense there is more she's not telling me.

"Is it Demitri or the club you're really drawn to?"

She releases a small sigh, giving me the answer without words.

"One look in his eyes the other night... It was like I was under some kind of spell. I've never felt anything like it. It was unnerving, but thrilling in a way I can't explain. I can't walk away from that again without exploring it."

I understand that feeling far more than she can ever realize. Maybe that makes both of us crazy. I already know what I'm doing is dangerous, but Katherine is the risk-taker and I always worry one day she'll take things too far.

"Just promise me you'll be careful. Don't let him push you into doing something you're not comfortable with. And if you see yourself getting into a bad situation, call me. I'll get you out of there—even if I have to have Zane come in there after you."

Katherine waves her hand dismissively. "I'll be fine, I promise. Speaking of Zane, have you ever wondered why he was there at the club that night?"

"I try not to think about it too much," I lie. The truth is, I've thought a lot about why he was there that night. It sickens me to think about what would have happened if we hadn't bumped into one another. Just the thought of him fucking another woman enrages me.

"I'm sure he was there trolling for a submissive. Who knew Zane was a Dom? Fuck, I get hot just thinking about it." Kat fans herself with her hand. "Whoever gets tied up and spanked by him is one lucky bitch."

I choke on my drink, spewing water across the counter.

Katherine's eyes widen. "You okay?"

I wave her off and clear my throat, trying to recover from

the coughing spell. "Yeah, I'm fine. I just swallowed wrong."

She relaxes back onto the stool. "I'm glad I can talk to you about all this. I was so afraid you would judge me over it."

"I would never judge you, Kat. You're my best friend. You can always tell me anything."

"That goes both ways, you know. I wish you'd talk to me more instead of holding things inside like you do. It really worries me."

I swallow hard, because she has no idea what I'm holding inside lately. I would give anything to be able to confide in her right now. But my relationship with Zane is a secret no one else can bear.

Katherine reaches for another bagel, glancing at her watch. "Shit. I've got to go. I'm going to be late for a meeting with my advisor." Easing off the stool, she grabs her coat and slides her arms through the sleeves.

I walk her to the door and give her a quick hug. "Thanks for bringing the bagels."

"You're welcome. I'll call you tomorrow with details, okay?"

"You'd better," I tease, closing the door behind her.

ZANE

The doorbell rings incessantly. I'm ready to kill whoever is on the other side of the door. I rub the sleep out of my eyes and squint at the time on my watch.

It's ten thirty in the morning.

Shit. I haven't even slept an hour. I'd been so upset from last night's argument with Charlotte that I'd had a hard time falling asleep when I got home this morning. Now that someone is practically sitting on my doorbell, it seems I won't be going back to sleep anytime soon.

Peering through the tiny glass peephole, I spot my younger sister, Lauren, on the other side. She's dressed in her navy blue airline uniform, which tells me she's looking for a place to crash for a few hours between flights. I gave her a key to my apartment last year to avoid these instances, but she always forgets it.

Blowing out a long breath, I open the door to let her in. Before I can say a word, Lauren holds her hand up to stop me. "Save your breath. I already know what you're going to say."

I smirk and step back so she can come in. With our parents both gone, Lauren is the only family I have left. I rarely get to see her unless it's on occasions like this. Sometimes I think I prefer it that way. I'm not the same brother she grew up with.

She props her bag by the door and rolls her shoulders with a tired sigh. "You know I hate bothering you like this, but the airline is too cheap to put us up in a hotel for this short a layover. I've been flying for sixteen hours straight. I just want a hot shower and a nap before I have to head back out again. I'll be out of your hair in no time."

"Help yourself. I'm going back to bed. I've got to be up in a few hours for work."

Lauren places a quick kiss on my cheek. "I'll be quiet as a mouse. You won't even know I'm here."

I let out a chuckle. "You and quiet have never belonged in the same sentence, sis." I wave my hand and turn to leave the room. "Good night."

After shutting the bedroom door behind me, I climb back into bed and pull the duvet over my body. I end up tossing and turning for another hour. Rolling onto my back, I throw my arm over my face, begging my body to find a way to give in to the exhaustion.

It's pointless.

I can't stop thinking of Charlotte. Everything about her haunts me. The hurt in her voice when I lied about harboring deeper feelings for her. Then the anger drawing color into her cheeks as she kicked me out to spend the rest of my shift posted outside her door. As if wondering what she was thinking that whole time wasn't torturous enough, now I'm dedicating all entire fucking down time to it too.

I groan and rake my hands through my hair, tugging at the roots out of pure frustration.

My thoughts are as vivid as they are loud. Every time I close my eyes, all I see is Charlotte's perfect round ass perched up high in the air, her pussy dripping wet from her arousal and my release.

Goddamn. I'm so fucking hard.

I try to fight it, but the heaviness in my balls grows more and more unbearable by the second. I'm desperate for a release, anything for this tension to leave my body. I throw back the covers and slide my boxer briefs down past my hips. My erection springs back against my stomach. I suck in a hard breath when my hand slides over the sensitive head of my dick. Slowly, I inch down until I reach the base of my cock.

Images of Charlotte's luscious tits are getting me there faster. I drop my head back against the pillow and lift my pelvis, fisting my dick faster, harder. I grip the sheet beside me with my free hand as my back arches up off the bed. One last pump and I feel the hot release shooting up my stomach. Breathless, I collapse back down onto the mattress, still shaky from my climax.

As I lay there staring at the ceiling, all I can think about is the girl two floors above me who's turned my whole world upside down.

CHARLOTTE

View 17's fully equipped fitness room is beyond impressive, and exactly what I need to clear my head about Zane. I toss my towel over the treadmill bar, step onto the track, and glance around the room. Other than the guy on the workout bench behind me and Chester lingering near the door, the place is empty.

I quickly power on the machine and work my pace up until I'm running. My ponytail bounces against my shoulders as I continue upping my speed. I stare through the bay of windows in front of me, visualizing myself running far away from everyone and everything in my life. It may be wishful thinking, but it still helps drive me during my workouts.

Sweat beads on my face. I welcome the heavy burn in my chest and the painful strain in my calves. Mile after mile clicks by on the screen. My body begs for me to give up. But instead, I push harder, dig deeper.

My mind drifts to my argument with Zane. Foolishly, I'd expected him to care more about our relationship. His words had hurt, but kicking him out because he didn't feel the connection that I did wasn't exactly fair.

I've thought of little else today, and the more I dwell on it, the more I realize just how horrible I'd treated him. He'd made me no promises.

I just hadn't expected to feel so connected to him. But no matter how much I ache for him to return those feelings, I have to accept it isn't going to happen. I could walk away from our arrangement, but right now having any part of him is better than not having him at all.

Of course, that's only if he still wants this. After our fight, I wouldn't be surprised if he decided the relationship was more trouble than it was worth. The thought of never having him inside of me again is too unbearable for me to even imagine.

I hit the power-down button and slow my strides, working my way down to a steady walk to cool off. Once my heart rate begins to return to normal, I step off the treadmill and reach for my towel to dry off my face.

I have to do something to fix this before it's too late.

◆ ◆ ◆ ◆

I hold my breath as the elevator comes to a rest at the fifteenth floor. When the metal doors open, I turn to face Chester.

"Do you think you could wait here? I'm just going to slide this beneath his door. I promise I won't be long."

Nodding, he motions with his hand. All he knows is that Zane and I had an argument and I'm trying to make peace, which is technically true. What Chester doesn't know could land us all in deep trouble.

"Go ahead," he says. "His apartment is just around the

corner. Apartment fifteen E. I'll wait here."

"Thank you, Chester."

My heart pounding in my chest, I proceed down the long hallway toward his apartment. I glance down at the envelope in my shaking hand. Maybe I am taking the cowardly way out by writing out my thoughts. But apologizing to Zane face-to-face is too intimidating to bear. I refuse to let our fight fester until his next shift.

The sight of the bronze apartment sign 15E sends a mixture of terror and exhilaration coursing through my body. I know I'm pushing his new boundaries by coming to his apartment. My intention is to make peace. I worry Zane will only see this as defiance. Either way, I'm willing to take the risk. And the punishment, if necessary.

Just as I'm kneeling to slide the envelope beneath the door, I hear movement coming from inside the apartment.

Shit.

I hadn't expected Zane to be awake this early. Before I can stand, the door suddenly opens in front of me. My attention lands on a woman's bright pink toenails, and then rises slowly to follow her long, toned legs. She's wearing a gray, oversized men's shirt that hits just above mid-thigh. Her dark hair is long and tousled like she's just gotten out of bed. When I finally make eye contact with the gorgeous raven-haired beauty, I'm certain my heart has shattered into a million little pieces.

Is she why he doesn't want me coming to his apartment?

She leans into the doorjamb, causing the shirt to inch up higher on her thigh. "Can I help you with something?"

I rotate the envelope in my hands. "Oh, um... I was just

going to leave this for Zane."

She gives me a lazy smile. "He's still sleeping. But you can leave it with me if you want. Who should I say stopped by?"

Fuck. What do I say? I can't give her my name. I've got to get out of here.

I take a step back. "On second thought, I think I'll just wait and catch him another time."

She tilts her head, drawing her perfectly arched brows together. "Are you sure?"

"Yes, I-I'm sorry to have bothered you." Mortified, I turn and leave.

As I round the corner back to the elevator, I toss the envelope into the garbage bin. How could I have been so stupid?

The elevator door is chiming and Chester smiles as I approach. I do my best to mask my rioting emotions and keep it together.

"All set to head back upstairs?"

I manage a nod and step inside, trying like hell to hold back the tears until I can be alone in my apartment.

Chester swipes the access card through the reader to access the penthouse level. There is a sudden jerk as the elevator starts its journey to the top floor. I close my eyes, but all I see is the beautiful woman from Zane's apartment. My chest constricts as I fight to hold the sobs in. By the time the door opens on my floor, I'm already losing control of my tears.

"Don't worry, Charley. I'm sure Zane has already forgotten all about what happened between the two of you." Chester's ill-timed words slice right through me.

Zane may forget, but I never will.

I curse to myself a dozen times on the way into my apartment. How could I be so naïve? How could he take advantage this way?

I resolve then and there, I never want to lay eyes on Zane Parker again.

"Chester, do you think you can have another agent cover Zane's shift tonight? I just don't feel comfortable with him being around so soon after our argument."

His eyes narrow when he sees my tears. "What's really going on here, Charley?"

I'm so desperate to have someone to talk to, but I fight back the urge to tell Chester everything.

"It's...personal." I swallow down another wave of tears. "Can you arrange for another agent, or do I need to call my mother?"

His expression hardens. "No, that won't be necessary. I'll take care of it."

Without another word, Chester closes the door behind him, leaving me to deal with my anger and tears alone.

CHAPTER SEVEN

I stagger into my apartment, my legs weak from the crushing workout I'd just endured. The place is empty again. Lauren left as if she'd never been here, as promised. Briefly, I regret that we hadn't had time to catch up a little. Even coffee would have been nice. With my head so caught up with thoughts of Charlotte, though, maybe it would have been a waste of time. Then again, maybe a little womanly advice could help me figure out what the hell to do with this girl. No, she's a woman. A spoiled brat, maybe. But Charlotte Daley has the heart and body of a woman, and I've never been more mesmerized by any other in my life.

I guzzle down a glass of water, refill it, and reach for my phone. The home screen shows a handful of missed calls from Chester. He never calls before my shift unless something is wrong. I call his number and start pacing the kitchen.

"Where the hell have you been, Parker?" Chester's sharp tone throws me off. Something has to be really wrong for the old man to lash out at me.

"In the gym. I forgot my phone in my apartment. What's

going on? Is something wrong with Charlotte?"

"I'd say so."

"Tell me." I curl my free hand over the edge of the counter and hold my breath, bracing myself for bad news.

"Get yourself cleaned up. And don't bother dressing for your shift tonight. You've got the night off. I'll be down at your place in a few minutes."

"Wha—"

Before I can press him, he ends the call.

"What the fucking fuck," I mutter to myself.

If Charlotte was hurt, he'd tell me right away. I take solace in that and head to the bedroom to clean up. I take a quick shower, dress in street clothes, and pace some more until Chester shows up at the door.

"Are you going to tell me what the hell is going on?" I say the second I open the door.

When I step to the side, he slips past me. He takes a casual stroll across the living room, slowing in front of the windows that look out onto downtown DC. My God, this is maddening. I'm ready to head up to the penthouse and get the details from Charlotte personally. I have a few things I want to tell her anyway.

"She's got a better view," Chester finally says, his back still to me.

"She's the First Daughter."

He turns slowly, leveling a stony stare my way. "You're goddamn right, she is."

I swallow hard, because I don't like that look in his eye. If I didn't know better, I'd think he knew I was taking Charlotte to bed every chance I got. Instead of playing dumb, I stay silent. If he knows something, I'll let him spill it first.

"You know Charley is like family to me, right?" His hands are tucked in his pockets, and his stare never wavers.

I nod. "I do. I get the sense that it means the world to her too, considering the treatment she gets from her parents."

He looks down at his shiny black shoes and back up to me again. "Are you sleeping with her?"

Fuck.

Chester and I never mince words, but his blatant accusation throws me completely off guard.

Lie. I should lie and save my own ass, but I just stand there like an idiot. I'm certain my silence speaks volumes when Chester's taut expression folds into a grimace.

"Goddamnit," he mutters, turning his back to me again.

I shove a hand through my hair and then draw it down my face. How do I excuse my behavior? Chester will never understand my reasons for luring her into bed with me to begin with. I'd be willing to bet he's never spanked a woman for pure pleasure in his life.

I should explain that I fucked up. I made a huge mistake.

But as I practice the excuses in my head, they sound flimsy and weak. Because I regret nothing. The truth is, Charlotte means everything to me.

"I care about her too, you know."

He turns back, his expression softer. "I know. I'm not blind. She may have been oblivious to the way you looked at her these past few months, but I wasn't. Remember, it's my job to read people's intent before they have a chance to act on it."

I wince, because I had no idea Chester suspected how I'd felt this whole time.

"If you knew, why didn't you intervene earlier?"

"Because I didn't believe you'd be stupid enough to act on it. You're paid to protect her, Parker. What the hell were you thinking to take things this far?"

I lower my head, shame weakening my justifications.

"There's nothing I can say to make you really understand. I thought I was protecting her. She's been out of control. You know that."

He points a finger in my direction, his grimace deepening. "So you take her to bed? You think you can tame her with a forbidden relationship that risks the reputation of the entire administration? You're going to lose your goddamn job, and she's going to catch hell from that sadistic mother of hers. And I'll be lucky if I get to stick around after it all goes down. Then who's going to protect her? What happens then?"

"No one knows about us. No one but you."

"Well thank you, Jesus. I'd like to hope neither of you were stupid enough to start shouting it off the rooftops."

He paces in a circle, and I wait for him to keep shouting, giving voice to all the doubts I've been harboring for days.

"What now?" I finally say.

"I'm not going to waste my time telling you to stop sleeping with her, because I know you won't. And after I saw that look in her eye today..." He shakes his head.

I frown. "What look?"

"I don't know what you did, but you'd better fix it before she starts getting therapy from her girlfriends about all the heartbreak her bodyguard is giving her."

My heart starts beating faster. "Katherine..."

"She's out shopping with her right now. They're going out for a girls' night, and I smell trouble."

"I have this shift. I'll take care of it."

"I told you, you're relieved tonight. Her request. She threatened to get her mother involved if I didn't find a replacement."

I curse inwardly and roll through my options. I'm not letting her slip away that easily.

"Find her for me. I'm about to crash her party."

Chester takes a few strides toward me. "I'll get you her location. But you better watch your ass. Don't do anything stupid."

"I can handle this."

He doesn't look convinced. "Fix this or I will. And you may not like the way that goes down."

I nod tightly, because I can read between the lines. Chester's a comrade, but his loyalty is to Charlotte first.

And if I lose my job or get reassigned, I'll never see Charlotte again.

CHARLOTTE

"This one or this one?"

Kat peers at my reflection in the tall mirror. We've been in her closet for at least an hour, contemplating every red dress she currently owns.

She's already dolled up in a red lace bra and underwear that has me terrified about how far she'll go with Demitri tonight. There's only room for one terrible decision maker in this friendship, but of course I can't tell her that. If there's any silver lining to today's heartbreak, it's that I could tag along with her to Crave and make sure she doesn't do anything crazy.

She's holding up a pleather minidress that screams "woman of the night" and a thin-strapped V-neck dress with a flowy bottom and a slit up the side. I point to the latter.

"That one, I think."

She rolls her eyes with a sigh. "You *think*? This is important. I need you to focus."

"I am focused. That one." I glance down at my watch. "Speaking of staying focused, when does Demitri expect you?"

Kat slips the dress on and spins in front of the mirror as she assesses my choice. "We didn't set a time, which works out perfectly. You and I have time to take a detour on the way. I got a last-minute invite to a party. I need a drink or two before I see him again."

"What party?"

She shrugs. "I don't know. Some rooftop thing. Someone in my study group is getting us in. Should be fairly anonymous, I'm hoping."

"Okay." I stand up and check my appearance in the mirror again. A basic black cocktail dress for me tonight. Nothing too flashy or revealing.

I strongly consider opting for one of the losers in Kat's red dress pile, but tonight is about moving on, not advertising myself for another fucked up sexual relationship. I think back to the woman on her knees at the club, taking her Master's violent thrusts. The thought of submitting to anyone but Zane makes me nauseous.

I plan to disappear in the shadows tonight. If nothing else, the club will be a much-needed distraction with its many characters and torrid sexual displays. Plus, the way Kat has been buzzing around her place preparing for her next encounter with Demitri has me on high alert. I need to be there for her tonight, first and foremost.

After another half hour, I force her out the door. The back door, of course. We'd called a cab to help us make our escape as we'd done before.

Twenty minutes later we're in the crush of a raging rooftop party. House music thumps at a level loud enough to muffle every conversation we pass on our way to the bar. Outdoor heaters buzz and the walls that line the enormous balcony are lit up with vibrant blue and purple beams. So far, we haven't run into anyone we know.

Kat orders four shots, flattening her hand over my mouth when I try to protest.

"Don't argue. Just drink."

I brush her hand away. "I don't know this guy very well, but I'm guessing he wants you conscious when you show up at Crave."

She waves me off. "I'll be fine. I just need to take the edge off. And *you*." She lifts her shot and clinks it with mine. "You need to get laid. Tonight."

I down the first shot with her, but my brain won't accept the prospect of hooking up with anyone new tonight. Zane is still heavy in my system. But maybe when the alcohol hits, he'll start to fade away. As I take the second shot, I'm not even sure

I really want that.

I gasp after the sugary concoction funnels down my throat. Gross.

"What the hell is in this?"

Kat starts answering, but her voice and the music blur into the background when I see Nate over her shoulder. He's several feet away. I don't recognize the people around him. All I know is that I don't want him to see me. Not tonight. Not without Zane or Chester.

For the first time, I regret that I've made every effort to thwart their protection. There was a time when I was confident I could handle someone like Nate. But now that he's threatened me, I know without a doubt his resentment and strength are enough to overpower me no matter how much I fight back. A vision of him exposed and ready to fuck when I'd offered myself to him flashes to the front of my mind, causing the shots to curdle in my stomach.

"We should go," I say, interrupting whatever Kat was saying.

She frowns. "No way. I need at least one more."

I roll my eyes. She's my best friend, but I swear to God she'll put me in my grave one of these days.

"Whatever. Order your drink. I'm getting out of here."

"What? You're ditching me?" Her red lips are agape, like I've just devastated her whole night.

"Let's just say this party isn't anonymous anymore. Text me when you're ready. I'll meet you at the front door."

As she scans the crowd, I slip away without looking back. I'm afraid one last glance at Nate will draw his attention toward me. Hopefully I can hide out somewhere inconspicuous while Kat drowns her anxiety. The party inside the expensive condo is no less jammed with people. I'm relieved to find the room filled with strange faces, vaguely aware of how comfortable I've become with loneliness.

It's better than getting hurt by the people who pretend to care…

I close my eyes and Zane is behind them. Those gray eyes and dark lashes, his full lips claiming me. *Mine.*

I open my eyes when a strong arm bands around my waist. The strike of fear that hits me softens instantly when I recognize Zane in front of me.

"Zane, what are you doing here?"

"I'm getting you out of here," he says in his usual business-like tone.

I rile instantly and shake out of his embrace. "I'm here with Kat. And this isn't your shift. How did you find me?"

"You think a night off means you can disappear and make shitty decisions? It's my job to know where you are twenty-four hours a day, and if you haven't noticed, I take it pretty seriously."

I resist the urge to slap him for barking at me. But something else dawns on me as I try to piece together him being here.

"Chester helped you find me, didn't he?"

"Obviously. He figured you and Katherine would be up to no good tonight, as usual, and tracked your phone."

"Then why isn't he here instead of you?"

The tight set of his jaw has me worried.

"Zane..."

"We need to talk," he says, eyeing the front door again.

"I can't leave without Kat."

He rolls his eyes, takes my hand, and tugs me down the nearest hallway. Together we duck into a bathroom that's more lavish than mine and boasts more square footage than most undergrads' apartments.

He slams the door, locks it, and turns toward me. "Have you told Katherine about us yet?"

My jaw falls. "Is that why you came here? You're worried about me exposing you? Well the answer is no, I haven't. I don't plan to. And for the record, there is no 'us.'"

I expect him to go all he-man on me and convince me that I belong to him, but he doesn't. He's eerily still.

"If this is about last night...you caught me off guard. I'm not used to talking about relationships. Or feelings, for that matter. I know I came off as cold, but I didn't mean to hurt you."

My heart picks up its pace, but any hope I try to cling to is shot down when I remember the woman in his apartment.

"You did hurt me. I obviously care more about this than you do. But I agreed to your terms, and I was ready to accept them all over again. Maybe it was stupid of me to assume exclusivity, but I did."

"That's not stupid at all. If anyone else touches you, I swear to God..."

"I'm not talking about me, Zane." I take a step toward him, raising my voice as I do. "I've been with one other person before you. You think I'm going to let you come inside me while you're fucking other people? How naïve do you think I am?"

His eyes widen. "I'm not fucking anyone else."

I almost want to believe him.

"Then who's the beauty in your apartment? Another submissive from the club? You expect me to believe that someone like you wouldn't have a girl on the line ready every time I kick you out of my apartment?"

He shakes his head and then stills. "Jesus. Charlotte, that was my sister."

I laugh and turn away, wrapping my arms around myself. "That's rich."

He spins me toward him, and for a second, I want to climb into his arms and let him kiss me until I can't breathe anymore. Why do I want him so badly?

Because you're gullible and weak. The perfect submissive. Why else would he choose you for this sick game?

"You don't need to make excuses, Zane. Really." I look away, suddenly exhausted. All I want is to go home, crawl into bed, and forget Zane ever happened. "I wrote you a letter. I was going to tell you that I wanted to try again, try harder. But when she answered the door, I knew I couldn't be who you needed me to be. I can deal with the pain and the punishments, but seeing her there did something to my heart that hurt so much worse."

He touches my cheek, sifts his fingers into my loose curls, and guides my gaze back to his. "I've only ever lied to you once. I'm telling you the God's honest truth now. Lauren is stunning, but she's my sister. She's a flight attendant, and she crashes at my apartment between flights sometimes. And when we get home, I'd be happy to supply the family photos to prove it to you."

I part my lips, my mouth suddenly dry. I want to believe him, but I still feel like such a fool. If he's lied to me once...

"You asked me if I felt nothing when I was inside you, and I lied. The truth is, I feel everything when I'm with you. I feel your heartbeat against me. I feel your anger and your pain and your loneliness. I feel when you need to come, just before you give me everything. I feel you open yourself up to me, and I want to crawl inside and live there, be with you, protect you, fill you up with everything that's missing."

Zane is gutting me with his words. Tears pool in the corners of my eyes. I couldn't speak if I tried.

"You're everything I need. All I've ever wanted," he utters softly. "I lied to you because I don't trust myself. It's so dangerous to feel this way. I could lose everything. But I can't lose you."

"Zane..."

His name leaves my lips in a breathless sob, disappearing as his mouth covers mine. With his lips comes relief. With his tongue, a wave of deep satisfaction. Somehow, despite everything that still stands between us, the huge chasm that will keep us from ever having a normal relationship, I believe that everything will be okay. Someway, somehow.

Our kiss deepens, and Zane lifts me onto the cool countertop. He slips my panties down deftly, never breaking our connection, like we already know this dance by heart. Sliding me to the edge and parting my legs around him, he frees his cock from his jeans and presses into me slowly.

My head falls back as he pushes deeper. Somehow this physical connection becomes the embodiment of all the feelings I've been fighting. And when he roots, twining his arms around my torso so we're flush, so close, completely connected, I could cry. I've never known intimacy like this.

I whimper his name when he thrusts again. He whispers mine into my ear, kissing down the column of my neck as he fucks me gently. When I open my eyes, I see a dozen versions of us making love on the counter of this opulent room. The different angles of our reflection reveal everything—my rapture, something like awe and anguish tightening Zane's features, my fingers clawing into his shirt, the muscles of his ass tightening with every thrust.

I have a strong sense that in this moment Zane is giving me something he's not used to giving anyone.

I hold him closer against my chest and tighten the grip of my thighs around his hips. Silent praise, silent pleas for more.

I love him. I've loved him since before I agreed to be his...

But I can't say the words that bloom around my heart and make my chest hurt.

Before I can convince myself otherwise, he groans, driving deeper. The friction is divine, but the way he hits the deepest part of me... That's pure heaven. My eyes roll back, and I stifle a cry. Never in my wildest dreams did I imagine sex could be this way. With Zane, everything is intense. Everything is incredible. The places he takes me, no one ever has.

"Charlotte," he rasps against my skin, "You're mine. I can't let you go. Tell me you're mine, baby."

"I'm yours," I say, sliding my fingers against his scalp,

tugging the damp roots of his hair. "I've always been yours."

With that, his tempo increases. I feel him everywhere. I tighten and tense.

"Come for me, beautiful. Give me everything. Everything you have. Give it all to me."

I lean back, propping my hands up on the vanity so he can fuck me harder and deeper. I give up his heat and his heartbeat against me, but I gain the visual of his gorgeous features as he gazes down, riveted to where our bodies meet. He holds my thighs apart. Smoothing caresses become tight desperate grasps that will leave bruises tomorrow. Both give me equal measures of satisfaction.

Energy collects in my belly and builds with every deep drive until I'm trembling. The erotic visual of our bodies joining, his thick cock shoving into me, and me accepting him with ease—all of it takes me down.

"Zane!" I scream as I come, a tearful proclamation on the edge of my lips... *I am undeniably...yours.*

ZANE

I find a cloth and clean her, as I always do. The truth is, I want to collapse into a dreamy slumber with her nestled by my side, my seed warm inside her all damn night. But that's a fantasy all its own.

I have no idea where all this is going. I can't overthink it right now. Not when I just poured my goddamn soul out. Not after I just fucked her in someone's bathroom, with a party raging beyond every wall. Far in the background I hear Chester telling me not to fuck this up.

I probably am, but what can I do? I can't think straight around this woman. I'm falling hard and fast. This isn't who I am, but it's quickly who I'm becoming.

A loud bang hits the door, and we both jolt. Playtime is over. She slides off the counter and straightens, slipping her hand into mine, which feels so goddamn right.

I open the door, and Katherine is there. She's pale, nearly green, and holding herself up by her hands pressed on each side of the doorframe.

"Kat, are you okay?" Charlotte goes to her, but Kat steps back as if a mere touch will set her off.

"I... I'm going to throw up."

We both move to the side and into the hallway, giving her privacy as she locks herself in the bathroom.

"Well, well. Look who it is." A high-toned male voice echoes from behind us.

Charlotte's hand is in mine again in a death grip, but I tuck it behind my back as I turn.

Nate Christiansen stands a few feet away, drink in hand, a smirk plastered all over his smug face.

"We meet again," he says, his bleary-eyed gaze floating from Charlotte to me. "You're the one getting that prized Charlotte Daley pussy then? So that's why she's not giving it up anywhere else." He purses his lips. "Too bad."

In an instant, I'm made of stone. My blood is ice. I'm ready to pound this man-child into sand. I drop Charlotte's hand behind me and take a step forward.

"You're not going to talk about the President's daughter like that in front of me. Do you understand?"

He laughs weakly. "Right. Maybe I'll just let her parents know that she's fucking the help. What are you going to do about it then?"

My breath catches and my thoughts tumble. What has he seen?

Nothing. It's all conjecture. He may have noticed we were holding hands. Or that we were in the bathroom together. Who cares? He's drunk. We could have been helping Katherine, who I can faintly hear heaving on the other side of the door. Still, I'm not on shift. I really shouldn't be here, but I can even explain that, with Chester's help.

I take an intimidating step forward, and Nate steps back, raising his hands.

"Maybe we can work something out, big guy. Tit for tat." He laughs again. "You can't be that attached already. I'll keep my mouth shut, and you can look the other way. I just want to hit it once. Just a little taste. Who can it hurt?"

I ball my fists tightly and exhale.

"If you even so much as breathe in her direction, I will end you. Do you understand?" I'm seething. My chest rises and falls rapidly.

He has the nerve to smile back at me. Maybe the alcohol is giving him the courage to challenge me. But the evil glint in his eyes tells me differently. He knows exactly what he's doing. He's pushing my buttons, taunting me for a reaction.

He takes a step closer, narrowing his eyes at me. "I wasn't asking for your permission. I don't need it." He looks to Charlotte, raking his eyes down her body. "Enjoy her while you can. Because, one way or another, I'll have my way with

America's Little Princess."

Nate's expression darkens and he winks at Charlotte, as if she could be anything but repulsed by his words. She's completely still, her expression tight. But I recognize the fear in her eyes.

A murderous rage unlike anything I've ever felt before overtakes me. I could kill him. I could wrap my hands around his pale throat and choke the life out of this sick little bastard. But I can't. Even thinking that way could get me in a world of trouble.

Instead, I pivot back and knock on the door. Katherine stumbles out a few seconds later, her eyes red and her face as pale as it had been.

"You okay?" Charlotte wraps an arm around her.

Kat nods, and I nudge Nate against the hallway wall as we pass.

A few minutes later, I have the three of us downstairs and situated in my Audi. I shoot a look to Kat, who's in the backseat. "If you're going to puke in my car, give me a heads up. I'll pull over."

She sighs. "I'm fine. I just..." Her head falls into her hands. "What am I going to tell Demitri?"

I frown and look to Charlotte, whose bottom lip is trapped between her teeth.

"Demitri?" I ask in a low tone.

She offers a quick nod. "He reached out to her. They were supposed to meet up tonight at Crave."

"I blew it," Kat sobs. "I'm such an idiot. I was so nervous... I screwed it all up."

She collapses sideways in the back seat of the car, and I resist the urge to roll my eyes.

"I'll take care of it, okay? Demitri is a friend," I say.

She doesn't answer. I maneuver through traffic while Charlotte is mostly silent, staring out at the city as it passes by.

I grab my phone and pull up Demitri's number. He answers in his thick accent.

"Zane."

"I have your date," I say quietly.

He's silent.

"She drank too much. I think you make her nervous. In any case, what the hell were you thinking inviting her back?"

He laughs. "Ah, sweet temptation. You know how it is. What about your little pet? Have you given her up yet?"

I tense my jaw and glance over to Charlotte.

He laughs again, interrupting my mental cataloguing of all the ways I'm crazy about her.

"I guess not," he answers for me. "You are right, though. The kitten is trouble, but the kind I like." He sighs. "She's drunk, yeah?"

I glance back to where Kat snores quietly in my back seat. Her house is only a mile away.

"She's done for the night."

He is silent a moment. "I'll reach out to her tomorrow. You won't see her at Crave again. This is perhaps the way it should have been."

"I'll let you break the news. Talk soon."

Katherine won't be happy, but that's for her and Demitri to work out. Charlotte's detail is still idling outside of Katherine's apartment. I end the call and dial Chester. When he picks up, I speak.

"Chester, I'm bringing Katherine home. Then I'll be on my way to View 17 with Charlotte."

He makes a gruff sound in his throat. "How did it go?"

Charlotte's gaze is fixed on me now.

"Everything's fine. Katherine's had too much to drink, but she'll be fine. What do you want to do about Charlotte?"

"I assume you're tucking her in?"

I stifle a laugh. But, truth be told, I have every intention of spending the night with her. A fuck in the bathroom isn't enough for me. I need to be inside her all night. I need to hear her scream again.

"Unless it's an issue, I'd prefer to stay with her tonight. Can you take over early to avoid any awkwardness?"

I hear him sigh. "Sure. I'm only fifty-five. Who needs sleep at this age?"

I smile, because I believe that past his scolding and reservations about all this, he does care about us both. He might even be hoping like I am that somehow we can find a way to make this work.

"Thanks, Chester."

I hang up, trusting that he will take care of the rest. When I drop Katherine off, Charlotte goes up to get her settled. She returns a few minutes later. Her bare thighs are almost more than I can bear as I pull away. I want to pull the car over and do unspeakable things to her.

I resist the urge and drive toward our building. I park in the underground garage, and we take the elevator up to her apartment. Somewhere on the journey, I'm lost between two sides of myself. The one that swore to protect her and the other that's committed to loving her all night.

She threads our hands together and leans her head on my shoulder as we ascend. The gestures are intimate, which should alarm me. Then I remember how coldly I'd treated her the last time we were here together. If I want to keep her close physically, something has to change.

Once we pass the threshold of her apartment, I make a choice. I shut the door behind us, take her into my arms, and consume her mouth. We kiss slowly, deeply. I'm ready to drag her to the bedroom and show her exactly what she means to me when a sound stops me. Her stomach, growling loudly.

She smiles under my lips. "Sorry."

I pull back. "When's the last time you ate?"

She shrugs. "Katherine brought bagels over earlier. I was too upset to eat before we went out though."

I frown, take her hand, and lead her into the kitchen. "Sit," I say, gesturing to one of the stools.

She sits and tucks her hands under her chin as I move to the refrigerator.

"What are you in the mood for?"

"Anything that can soak up those awful shots Kat made me drink at the party."

I shake my head and shove down all the things I want to say about her wayward friend. I'm sure she has some redeeming qualities, but they're hard to rationalize when she puts Charlotte in compromising situations time and again.

I open and close a few drawers, piecing together a plan to

feed us. Suddenly I'm feeling famished too, and if I want to be with Charlotte all night the way I'd like to, I'll need the fuel for it. "How about eggs, bacon, and toast?"

"Sounds perfect. You don't have to cook for me, though, Zane. I can do it."

"I've got this," I say firmly.

Before I can stop her, she shimmies off the stool. She comes around the island as I set out a carton of eggs and a package of bacon. She slides between me and the counter, using her ass to nudge me back so she can open a drawer with some mixing bowls nested inside. I graze my palm over her perfect curves, but she straightens and starts cracking eggs before I can take advantage of her position.

I sidle up behind her so her back is flush with my front. I lower my lips to whisper in her ear. "Are you trying to get me to feed you or fuck you, Charlotte?"

"Feed me first," she says softly. "Then..."

I pull her earlobe between my teeth and bite gently. She stops cracking the eggs for a second and sighs.

"Then what, baby?"

"Then... Then you can fuck me."

I growl, tighten my hold on her, and force myself to take a calming breath. Something about the word "fuck" passing between her pretty lips has the power to completely derail any willpower I'd mustered. But it's my job to take care of her first.

Against every instinct, I step away, grab the bacon, and find a skillet in her cupboards. For the next few minutes, we work together quietly. The air is thick with sexual tension and the smell of breakfast on the stove.

"Go sit. I'll make you a plate," I say, turning off the burners.

She smirks but doesn't argue. I serve this woman nearly every waking moment, and somehow I can't bring myself to stop. I make our plates and sit adjacent to her at the kitchen island. Charlotte doesn't waste any time getting started. I'm equal parts satisfied that she's eating and angry at myself for upsetting her enough to kill her appetite earlier.

"I know you said this isn't something to expect, but"—she pauses to take a bite—"I have to admit, this is kind of nice."

I nod slowly and chomp on a piece of perfectly crispy greasy bacon. "I don't usually share meals with other people, so I can't argue with you there."

She tilts her head, like something has taken over her thoughts. "Why don't you?"

I hesitate a moment and think about her question. I've spent more time with Charlotte recently than anyone in a long time. But why?

"I guess I've gotten used to it." I set my fork down onto my now empty plate and contemplate whether to tell her more. She's given so much of herself to me, though. Suddenly, the thought of holding back seems unfair, not to mention dangerous if it drives her away. "Acclimating from the military wasn't as easy as I'd thought it'd be. I lost touch with the guys on my team and never really connected with new friends when I moved to DC. It was always about work."

"What about your family? You must get together for holidays sometimes."

I shrug, not making eye contact. "Lauren's always jet-setting for her work, so we rarely see each other for any decent stretch of time. My parents died a few years ago. They used to give us a reason to take time off and be together as a family. I guess that sort of fell apart."

"I'm so sorry, Zane."

I shake my head. "You don't have to be. It's not like you have it much better."

She winces and I regret my words.

"Sorry, I—"

She reaches for my hand and squeezes it. "I know my parents can seem cruel. And, let's face it, they are sometimes. But it wasn't always like that. Things just got really intense when my father's career got put on this presidential path. Nothing lasts forever, though. One day, I hope we'll be a family again. A real family."

She smiles weakly, and the sadness I see there nearly guts me.

"And if I'm wrong, and that day never comes, well then one day I'll make my own family. I won't always be theirs to control. That's what I loved about New York. It's nothing like DC. I felt like myself there. I could envision a life and a future outside of state dinners and campaign appearances. A life that would actually make me happy."

"Charlotte, baby..." I don't know what else to say. I want to hold her and give her a reason to be happy. But maybe all I can do is give her an escape, a temporary reprieve from this life consumed by circumstance and an uncompromising family.

She rises before I can say more. "Are you staying with me tonight?"

I turn on my stool, and she settles between my thighs,

running her hands up the taut denim.

I capture her face in my palms and stare into her eyes. In an instant, I'm caught up in her perfection, her beauty, her innocence. All of it has me whipped up and strung tight, ready to worship her every minute I can. "All night," I murmur.

She bites her lip. Something like happiness sparkles in her eyes. "In that case, I want something from you."

I lift an eyebrow. "You think you can call the shots now, Miss Daley?" My tone is low and unwavering, the inevitable sex we're about to enjoy heavy in my thoughts.

Her gaze darkens a little bit. Enough to show me that she feels my dominance and takes pleasure in the promise of it. She lowers her eyes and toys with the hem of my cotton shirt.

I lift her chin and kiss her softly. "What is it, Charlotte?"

She blinks. Her pink lips part slightly. "I've never seen you naked. I don't know if it's because you need to hold something back with me, or—"

I don't think twice. I tug my shirt off and toss it to the floor. "There," I say. "Better?"

Without a word, she skims her palms over my shoulders, across my chest, and finally, trails them down my abs, stopping at the button on my jeans. "Wow."

I try unsuccessfully not to grin, but her unfiltered appreciation for my physique satisfies something deep inside me.

She shakes her head slightly. "Sometimes I can't believe this is real. That I get to touch you like this."

Seconds go by, her hands roaming, my breath catching and releasing under her touch. Being with her at the party earlier tonight seems like ancient history. I need to possess her again, need to bind us tighter. I halt her motions, stand, and brush my lips across hers. She lifts into my arms and threads her fingers roughly into my hair.

With a groan, I tug her dress off and drag her into the bedroom where we fall onto the soft mattress, hands roaming, mouths claiming, hips reaching for contact. I can't wait a minute more to have her.

Tonight is ours, I decide. Tonight, this incredible, beautiful woman needs something she's never been given. Something I've never been able to offer. Something forbidden, however brief.

As I strip her naked and pull our bodies together, I resolve to spend every waking moment making love to her. Cherishing her. Making her believe, without a doubt, that this is real.

CHAPTER EIGHT

Lost in my thoughts, I stare out at the night skyline from Charlotte's living room. Snowfall begins to blanket the city below. With the taste of Charlotte's sweet essence still fresh on my lips, it takes every ounce of restraint I have to keep myself from going into her bedroom and sinking my cock back into her. My hunger for her body is insatiable. Even after a nearly sleepless night making passionate love to her, I still crave more.

With every thrust into Charlotte's body, I felt like I was embedding myself deeper and deeper into her soul. But the more we're together, the more the balance shifts. She claims as much of me as I do of her. I want to hold on and never let go. I want to scream to the world that she's mine. But our world together only exists behind the walls of this apartment. After last night, I'm not sure how much longer I can be okay with that.

A sudden sound of shuffling feet behind me brings me out of my thoughts. My gaze heats as I watch Charlotte's reflection in the glass. A long sheet draped around her body, she comes up behind me and places a tender kiss on my shoulder. She snakes her way between me and the window, pressing her body against mine. My cock strains inside my jeans. With nothing but the thin material of the sheet separating her naked body from me, it's everything I can do to not take her against this window, right here and now.

Jesus, will I ever get enough of her?

I cradle her face in my hands. "You should be asleep, baby."

She trails her fingertips down my chest, inching downward to the waistband of my jeans.

"Now that I've finally gotten to appreciate you undressed, I don't ever want to see you any other way."

If I'd known how much she'd relish my nakedness, I wouldn't have held it back from her so long. Even I couldn't deny the intoxicating sensation of our bare bodies against each other's last night. Her mouth on me, her hard nipples grazing my chest, her sweat slick against mine.

Just as she reaches for my belt, I stop her. She looks up at me with those breathtaking blue eyes. Without a doubt, she owns every part of me.

"Take me back to bed." She uses a sweet pleading voice that works on Chester but has never worked on me.

Something's changed though. I want to give her the world, make every wish come true, satisfy every desire. She eases from my grasp and laces our fingers together. She kisses my knuckles, letting her tongue slip across my skin as she goes.

Fuck. I exhale shakily. There isn't time. My shift—the one I'm not even supposed to be working—is almost up.

I run the pad of my thumb tenderly across her plump

bottom lip. "You know I can't. Chester will be here in less than fifteen minutes."

A flash of mischief lights up her eyes. She releases her hold on the sheet, allowing the fabric to pool at our feet. "Then you should hurry."

That quickly, I accept her challenge.

I spin her around. With a little pressure, she leans forward.

"Put your hands on the glass and keep them there."

"Yes, sir." Charlotte places her hands against the windowpane.

I unfasten my jeans and shove them past my hips. I rotate my pelvis, grinding against her ass. "What's wrong, baby? Tell me what you want."

Her eyelids flutter closed. "Mmm. I want you."

Stepping back, I deliver two hard slaps against her bottom. I admire the pink outline of my hand that forms across her flawless skin. Urging her feet apart with my foot, I grab her by the waist and pull her ass out to me.

"You already have me. I'm right here. If you want something else, you'll need to be specific."

Teasing her unmercifully never fails to satisfy. But the clock is ticking down on my willpower and the time we have together. I grip the base of my cock and line up to take her, ready to join us no matter what she says.

"Fuck me, sir. Make me sore. Every minute you're not inside me, I want to feel the memory of when you were."

My eyes roll back and I hold nothing back when I shove into her. I bite hard into my bottom lip at the overwhelming sensation.

Her low moan matches the need clawing at me from the inside out. I slide my palms up her naked torso until I'm cupping her full breasts in my hands. When I give her nipples a firm tug, her pussy retaliates by clamping down around my shaft like a vise.

"Jesus Christ. Your pussy is too goddamn good. I'm not going to last."

I adjust my stance and tilt her hips, changing the angle to gain deeper access to her core, causing her to cry out again, louder this time. I thrust again, inspired by the desire to take her harder than I had last night.

"That's it, baby. Take every inch of me."

She lets her head hang between her outstretched arms and lets out a long moan. "God, Zane, you're so deep. Please, don't stop."

I tighten my hold on her waist and quicken my thrusts, feeling the heavy ache in my balls intensify. The sensation of her climaxing around me takes me down with her. With one last fierce shove, I drive my cock deep inside of her. I try to still my body, but the orgasm ricochets through me. Every time with Charlotte seems more intense than the last.

I don't want our time to end, but I know it has to. The alarm on my watch goes off just as I'm pulling out of her. Chester will be here any second.

I give her a hard smack on the ass, eliciting another little whimper from her. "I need to go, baby, before Chester walks in here and has a heart attack. I'll call you once I get in my apartment."

Charlotte bends to collect the sheet from the floor as I

jerk up my pants. Not bothering to cover her nakedness, she leans in and gives me a slow, seductive kiss.

I muffle a curse under my breath and head toward the door. With time ticking down, I make it outside just as Chester steps off the elevator.

CHARLOTTE

From across the room, I can see the impression of my handprints on the floor-to-ceiling window. Every inch of my body still hums from our endless night of lovemaking. Each time Zane came, he would demand my eyes. I recognized a vulnerability in his stare, a kind of desperation I can't explain. He looked at me like I was some sort of mirage that would disappear if he blinked. All I could do was hold on to him and prove through my body that I wasn't going anywhere, that I was undeniably his.

I wish I could stay home and linger in the memories we made last night, but real life is calling again. I pull on a heavy peacoat and walk toward the long wall of windows, peering down below. The fresh layer of snow makes everything look so crisp and new. A couple walks hand in hand down the street. I can't help but envy them. I wish I could do those things with Zane. I don't know how it will ever be possible. I can't make him choose between me and his career, but I worry that is where this is all heading. As strong as our feelings are, neither of us will be able to hide it from the world for much longer.

Movement in traffic catches my attention. Four dark SUVs and a limousine pull up to the front of the building. The large entourage causes onlookers to gather across the street to watch. Moments like this make me wish I were invisible. Right now, I'd give anything for a normal life out of the spotlight where Zane and I can be together.

I trace my fingertips over one of the handprints on the window.

One day.

♦ ♦ ♦ ♦

As I approach the limousine parked next to the curb, I have the unmistakable feeling of being watched. Hugging my coat to my body, I turn and glance back up at Zane's window. Although I can't see anything from this far down, I have a feeling he's there looking down on me.

"Charlotte! Stop dawdling and get into the car. You're letting the cold air in."

I turn away from an invisible Zane, noting the pang in my heart as I do, and step off the curb into the limo. Not even my mother's condescending tone can ruin my blissful Zane hangover this morning.

Once I settle into the backseat, I realize that my father isn't in the car. "Is Dad meeting us there?"

My mother shakes her head, keeping her focus on the paperwork in her lap. "He won't be joining us. Something important has come up. He's confident you'll agree that Georgetown is the best choice. The tour is mostly a formality."

Of course, something has come up. It always does. I thought my father would at least show up, though, since he's the one forcing me to switch schools in the first place. But over the past twenty years of my life he's missed virtually every important event—recitals, plays, even my high school graduation. In my father's work-driven world, politics and business come before anything else, even his only child.

I rest my head back against the leather seat when my phone chimes with a text. It's from Zane.

I can still taste you on my lips.

My body flushes from the dirty text. I bite down on my lip and send him a reply—one that will definitely gain his full attention.

I can still feel you inside me.

His reply is almost instantaneous.

Good. I want you to think about me every time you move today.

I smile, knowing I will.

Trust me, I'll be thinking about you all day.

There's a brief pause and then another message chimes.

Promise me that you will stay close to Chester today.

I frown at the message. I like the playful Zane, not the serious one.

I'll be fine. Don't worry about me.

I'll always worry about you. You're mine, Charlotte. Say it.

I cross my legs. Even through text, my body reacts to his possessive tone.

I'm yours. Always yours.

"Here we are."

I lift my head at my mother's voice and look out my window.

The gothic stone clock tower of Healy Hall comes into view as we pull through the gates. The large crowd of people gathered on the steps at the front entrance of the building should surprise me, but it doesn't. This is not the inconspicuous college tour I was hoping for this morning, but it's the one I should've expected. My father can never be bothered, and my mother can never do anything low-key. Everything's always a goddamn media opportunity.

Plastering a fake smile on my face, I step out of the car and wave in the direction of the clicking cameras. My mother and I pose for a quick picture together on the top of the steps before we're ushered inside the building.

After a half hour of countless introductions, I am completely overwhelmed. When Chester asks to speak to me, I welcome the opportunity for a break.

"Campus security wants to meet with me to go over a few

things. Agent Larson will be taking over my post until I return, okay?"

Masking my disappointment, I nod back at him. "Thanks for letting me know, Chester."

I resume my place beside my mother, trying not to seem bored out of my mind as more eager faces gather around us for an opportunity to speak with one of us. My stomach plunges when I spot Nate Christiansen's face in line.

Turning away from my mother, I pull out my phone and shoot Zane a quick text.

Nate is here.

I know he probably won't see the text until he wakes up, but with Chester not here, I'm anxious.

Zane's response comes surprisingly quickly.

Stay by Chester.

I fire off a quick response.

He's in a meeting. Agent Larson is assigned to me.

A painful nudge in my side makes me jump. I turn. My mother's eyes narrow into slits, the way they do when she's silently warning me to correct myself. I drop the phone back in my pocket, trying to ignore the constant buzzing against me. Zane has got to be going nuts right now.

Blowing out a long breath, I prepare for Nate's greeting.

Immaculately dressed in a navy sweater and tan pants, he looks completely reformed from last night.

Nate leans in to give my mother a kiss on the cheek. "You're looking lovely this morning, Mrs. Daley. It's so good to see you again." He then turns his attention to me. "Charlotte, always a pleasure. We missed you the other night after the dinner."

I nod tightly. "Something came up."

He grins. "Of course. Well, I hope you're as excited as I am about the tour."

I turn to my mother. "Excuse me?"

She smiles broadly. "As a current student, Nate has graciously offered to be the one to give you the full campus tour today. Isn't that lovely of him to take time out of his schedule to do that for you?"

My eyes widen, but I cling to my composure. "Absolutely lovely."

Nate extends his arm for me to take. "Shall we get started?"

I hesitate, but I'm not sure how I can get out of this without causing a scene or upsetting my mother. Swallowing down the rising bile in my throat, I loop my arm through his, careful to keep our bodies as far apart as possible. The sooner we can get this over with, the better.

My mother looks at our joined arms and beams. Something tells me she's already planning our wedding in her head. Stepping forward, she waves her hands to usher us on. "You two have a wonderful time."

My heart pounds. "You mean, you're not coming along?"

"I have a very busy day today, Charlotte. I simply don't

have the time. Besides, I'm leaving you in good hands." She leans in and places a rare kiss on my cheek—which I know is only for show—and smiles at Nate. "Thank you again for doing this, Nate."

"It's my pleasure, Mrs. Daley. This gives Charlotte and me the perfect chance to catch up on things."

Just as I start to pull my arm away, Nate places his hand firmly over mine, preventing me from slipping free from his hold. My whole body is rioting from being in such close proximity to Nate, but I've been raised to smile under duress and endure discomforts with grace. Today, apparently, is no exception.

I allow him to lead me out of the room and through a long hallway lined with closed office doors. The instant we are far enough from the crowd, I yank my arm free from his and halt in my tracks.

"What the fuck do you think you are doing, Nate?"

A smug smile splits his face, revealing his perfect teeth. "Just like your mother said. I'm giving you a tour."

I shake my head violently. "I don't know what kind of scheme you and my mother have conjured up, but there's no way in hell I'm going anywhere with you."

I glance around, hoping to see Agent Larson, but he's not here. As a matter of fact, no one is around at all.

Nate prowls closer. "What's the matter, sweetheart? Looking for someone?"

I open my mouth to scream, but he quickly silences me by covering it with his hand. In one forceful shove, I'm slammed against the wall behind me.

His hand traps the scream in my throat, and with the rest of his body, he pins me painfully between him and the wall. All I can do is tremble and stare back into his evil eyes.

"I told you, Charlotte," he says, his breath hot on my cheek. "He won't always be around to protect you."

ZANE

I pace the floor of my living room as I listen to the endless ringing. My muscles are jumpy and my stomach is somewhere in my throat.

"Come on, come on, baby. Pick up. Please, pick up."

This is my tenth attempt at calling her. I've texted her at least thirty times and still haven't gotten a single response. Chester isn't answering his phone either, which only makes matters worse. I now wish I'd filled him in on Nate's latest threats. Maybe if I'd spent more time doing my job and less time feeding my obsession with Charlotte's luscious body, I would have.

When the call goes over to her voicemail again, I sling my phone across the room. "Goddamnit!"

Something's wrong. I'd felt it the moment I watched her get in the back of the limo. I'd been so unsettled by it I hadn't been able to sleep, though my body sorely needed rest.

I should have trusted my intuition and tagged along with them to the university. At least then I would have been there to keep Christiansen in check.

My phone starts to ring. Stumbling forward, I practically trip over my feet to get to it. Once I see Chester's name on the screen, I don't know whether to feel relief or panic.

"Chester? Please tell me you're back with Charlotte."

"No, Larson's with her. I'm still going through a walk-through with campus security. What's going on?"

"Radio him now and see if she's okay."

"What are you talking about? Of course she's okay."

"She messaged me earlier that Nate Christiansen was there with her. Since then she hasn't responded to any of my calls or texts. Please, Chester. Just do a check-in with Larson. Believe me, I want to be wrong about all of this."

Chester pauses. "Is there something you're not telling me about her and Christiansen?"

I hesitate, but then I realize nothing can be worse than admitting that I'm sleeping with the First Daughter, which I've already done. So I tell him everything as quickly as I can. From the first few times Nate tried to make moves on her, to the time I nearly shoved him through a wall, to his latest intoxicated threat. The more I tell him, the sicker I feel.

Chester's silent when I finish. He sighs into the phone. "Goddamnit, Parker. You should have told me this sooner."

"Trust me, I know."

"Okay. Hold on."

I listen as Chester speaks in the background. "Larson, can I have an update on the First Daughter's location?"

There is a brief pause as he waits for an answer through his headpiece. "What? Why are you not with her?"

I tighten my grip on the phone as Chester's conversation plays out.

"How long has she been gone? Goddamnit. Lock the campus down now. No one gets in or out until we locate her."

I grab my keys and head for the door.

"Do it now. We have reason to believe she could be in trouble," he continues, his voice muffled by the rustling of his movements.

Everything feeds my panic, and I can only think one thing. I have to get to her. I'm already getting in my car when Chester comes back on to speak to me.

"Parker, she's with Nate. Her mother arranged a private tour with him and bailed on them. She told Larson to stand down and give them privacy. They're locking down the campus now to look for them."

"Goddamnit."

My tires squeal as I pull out of the garage and onto the busy street. I weave in and out of traffic as scenarios start to play out in my head. The tour, the meeting. It was all too coincidental.

"Chester, how long did you know about this security meeting that you were in today?"

"They approached me this morning. Why?"

In that moment, all the pieces click. "Motherfucker!" I slam my hands down on the steering wheel. "Nate planned all of this, Chester. I guarantee you he's already taken her off the premises. He wouldn't have gone through this much trouble if he was going to keep her there. Have them check the surveillance videos of people leaving. I'm on my way there now."

"We'll find her, Parker. Charley's a smart girl. She's going to be all right."

"I hope you're right, Chester."

I hang up and press down harder on the accelerator.

"Hang on, baby. I'm coming for you."

CHARLOTTE

Once Nate pulls into his parent's driveway, I know he's brought me here to settle the score.

"You're never going to get away with this, Nate. Any minute now Chester will realize what's going on. When he does, he will turn this city upside down looking for me. This is kidnapping. Do you realize that? Even your father can't get you out of this one."

"Kidnapping?" He throws his head back and laughs. "Do you honestly believe anyone is going to believe I kidnapped you? Your mother is practically salivating at the idea of you and I being together. Even the ice queen isn't immune to my charm."

"You might have her fooled, but Chester knows you've threatened me," I lie.

He puts the car in park. "I'm afraid Chester is going to be preoccupied for a while. By the time he's finished, you and I will be long done with our little visit."

I grip the edges of the seat so he can't see me trembling. "You think you're just going to rape me and get away with it? If you lay a hand on me, you'll be destroyed."

He shakes his head. "No one's going to believe you, Charlotte. Especially after everyone sees all the dirt I have on you."

He reaches behind the seat and retrieves a large yellow envelope and drops it on my lap. "Have a look at those and tell me what you think."

I stare down in shocked silence. With shaky hands, I unfasten the metal clips on the end of the envelope and tilt it on its side. A large stack of photos slide out into my lap. The photos are numerous...and explicit. The first ones show me bent over Nate's bed. He must have secretly taken them the night of his party.

"I must say that the video is even better than the pictures. Of course, I conveniently edited out the part where your boyfriend interrupted us."

I swallow hard. "Zane will tell them the truth about everything. His word and mine are better than yours."

"Is he also going to tell them how he fucked you in the bathroom at the party last night?"

I clench my jaw and attempt to school my features. "You were drunk last night, Nate. You have no idea what you saw. Katherine had gotten sick in that bathroom. Zane and I were only trying to help her."

He smirks at me and points at the stack of glossy photos in my lap. "You might want to keep looking through those. I saved the best for last."

I slide my shaking hand over the pile and freeze once I see the last group of photographs. Picture after picture is of me and Zane naked in front of my living room window. Judging from the angle, they look as though they'd been taken directly across the street from my apartment. But this was from this morning. How does he have these?

"A little word to the wise. If you want to keep your relationship a secret, you might not want to fuck your boyfriend in front of an open window."

I narrow my eyes at him. "You were spying on us?"

"Technically, no. That would be the guy I hired to follow you. And I must say, Charlotte, you gave him some winning shots. Who knew you were such a naughty girl?" I flinch when he touches the side of my face with his finger.

"I'm tired of playing games, Nate. If you're trying to blackmail me into sleeping with you, it isn't going to work."

"Oh, but you're missing the point. I'm not blackmailing you. Blackmailing means you have a choice in the outcome." He pulls a pistol from under his seat and rests it in his lap. "And right now, I'm afraid you're all out of choices."

ZANE

I answer my phone on the first ring. "Chester, please tell me you've found her."

"I just had Christiansen's phone pinged for a location. He's at his parents' residence here in Georgetown."

Changing lanes, I take the upcoming exit. The Christiansens' house on Cherry Lane is less than a mile away from here.

"I'm just a couple of minutes from there. Are they sending units for backup?"

"Listen to me, Parker. The White House isn't considering this a kidnapping."

"What are you talking about? You and I both know she didn't leave with him of her own free will."

He sighs, and even through the phone I can sense his frustration. "I have pleaded with her mother, but she refuses to believe her daughter is in any sort of danger."

"Fuck her mother. There's no way in hell I'm standing down on this."

"I'm not asking you to. I am on my way now. She shouldn't have ever been left alone."

Nate's house comes into view. I ease my Audi up next to the curb and park. Nate's silver Porsche is parked in the driveway.

"I'm here, but I don't have a visual on Charlotte," I report through the phone.

"Do not engage until I get there. You're too emotionally involved in all of this, Parker. This is not the time to be irrational. You've got to think with your head, not your heart. I won't have Charlotte getting caught in the crossfire of this, do you understand?"

I grab my gun off the seat next to me. "He's got the woman I love, Chester. I'm not waiting."

"Goddamnit, Park—"

I end the call and step out of the car. Holding my gun to my side, I inch my way toward the house. When I reach his parked car, I notice a trail of footprints in the snow. Raising my weapon, I quickly follow the prints across the yard.

As I approach the corner of the house, I hear Charlotte pleading with him.

"Please, Nate. Don't do this."

"Keep begging, princess. You're only making my cock harder," he says, his voice tight with anger.

My blood boils, and it's everything I can do to keep my rage in check. Chester was right. I'm too emotionally involved.

I can't risk Charlotte getting hurt because I'm not thinking clearly.

Swallowing down my anger, I place my side flush against the brick wall and carefully poke my head around the corner to check their location. I spot them just as they reach the edge of the pool house. Nate has a tight hold on Charlotte's right arm, tugging her toward the back entrance of the mansion. And just like I had suspected, my smart, beautiful girl is fighting him every step of the way.

"Let her go, Christiansen," I shout. Heart pounding, I step into view and align the crosshairs of my gun on Nate's head.

They spin together, Nate shielding his body behind Charlotte. Her beautiful blue eyes, so full of terror and pleading for me to help, instantly lock to mine.

Hang on, baby.

I see a flash of silver as Nate reveals the Glock in his hand. When he presses the barrel against her head, panic and adrenaline spike my blood.

I hold my breath and wait for the perfect opportunity to pull the trigger. But with Charlotte writhing in his hold, I can't risk taking the shot.

"Drop the gun, Parker, or I'll put a bullet in her pretty little head."

"Zane." She whimpers, tears glistening in her eyes.

"He can't help you, sweetheart. Not this time," he sneers.

I clench my jaw. My whole body is coiled tight with rage. I breathe in and out slowly.

Stay focused.

Stay calm.

"It's over, Nate. You're surrounded," I lie.

Where the hell is Chester?

As if Nate can read my thoughts, he twists his lips into a devious smile. "Do you seriously expect me to believe that? You're here alone. A stupid move, I might add."

"He's not alone. Drop the weapon, Christiansen." Chester steps out from the other side of the house, his gun aimed directly in Nate's direction.

The sounds of screeching tires and approaching sirens echo from around the other side of the house. Within seconds, Nate's entire head is covered in snipers' red dots.

"Let. Her. Go," I demand, my finger itching to pull the trigger. I need this sick fucker's hands off my girl. Even more, I yearn to be the one who puts the bullet in his head.

Seconds that feel like minutes go by. Nate reluctantly lowers the gun, and the smallest measure of relief soothes my adrenaline spike. Except I don't see regret or defeat in his eyes. They're empty and dark as he releases her.

The instant she's free, she runs in my direction. She stumbles at first and gets back on her feet. Tears stream her cheeks.

I take swift steps toward her, but then I freeze. Nate lifts his arm and points the gun straight ahead.

No.

I lunge forward, haul her to me, and turn to shield her body with mine. Shots hammer through the air and mingle with Charlotte's terrified scream and shouting voices all around us. I grunt when a searing pain slices through my shoulder.

We fall to the icy ground below, my body covering hers. A

few more shots ring out. Then silence.

"Parker!" I hear Chester shouting.

I look up slowly. Nate's limp body lies on the ground several feet away. Blood saturates the snow all around him. The relief is dizzying. She's safe. He'll never get to her again. I push into the icy slush and roll myself off Charlotte, ignoring the pain thrumming in my shoulder.

"They got him, baby. You're safe now."

My breathing is ragged and my heart is pumping wildly. Charlotte doesn't move or speak. She's trembling. And covered in blood. It's not mine.

More blood seeps out from beneath her. Her eyes are glassy, her lids heavy.

"Baby?" I scramble to my knees and rip open her jacket.

Her shirt has turned a deep red. I rip it down the middle to find the source of the bleeding. The wound puckers below her collarbone and gushes. The bullet that went through my shoulder must have hit her.

"No. No, no, no!" I place the heels of my hands on it, bearing down hard. I lift my head as Chester approaches. "She's been shot. Get some help. Now!"

"The First Daughter has been shot. We need EMS immediately," Chester reports into his earpiece.

The warm rush of liquid seems endless as it seeps through my fingers. Fuck, there's so much blood, and I can't get it to stop no matter how much pressure I apply. This isn't happening. Terrified, I glance up at Chester's face and see the fear mirrored in his eyes.

"Zane." Charlotte's voice is so weak that it comes out as a

whisper. She's so pale. Her body shakes from the shock.

"Shhh, baby. Don't talk. Everything is going to be okay. Help is almost here."

"I-I love you. I was too scared to tell you before." A tear slips free just as her beautiful blue eyes begin to slowly shut.

Panic grips my chest painfully. I can't live without her. Desperation unlike anything I've ever known overtakes me. She's slipping away.

"No, no, no. Charlotte, stay with me!"

Then I'm being tugged backward.

"Stand back, sir. We need to get through," the paramedic orders from over my shoulder.

The whirring of a helicopter landing nearby almost distracts me enough to pull back. But I can't. I shake my head, unwilling to leave her side. I push harder against her wound. She can't leave me. I have to tell her how much I love her.

Chester wraps his arms around me and forces me away. "Come on, son. Let them do their job."

The next few minutes are a blur. The paramedics are all over her, obscuring her from my view. Then they're lifting her onto a gurney and make a run toward the waiting helicopter.

Never in my life have I felt so helpless. So without hope. The helicopter lifts into the sky, taking her away from me.

She can't leave me like this. I whisper her name over and over like a prayer that can keep her breathing. Hot tears course down my face. I drop to my knees and sink into the blood-soaked snow.

I was supposed to protect her.

But I've failed her.

CHAPTER NINE

ZANE

I haven't slept in forty-eight hours. Once upon a time, my body had been trained for sleep deprivation. Torture. Emotional duress.

Nothing could have prepared me for this.

Waiting is the worst torture.

No one has let me close to her...

My legs dangle like dead weight off the hospital bed as I wait for my discharge papers. I'd refused pain meds so I could keep my head clear. After everything that's happened today, I'm still on high alert. As soon as the doctors let me out of here, I'm going to find her.

When Chester walks through the door, I jump up and move toward him. I stumble and brace myself on the bed when my vision goes patchy black and then back to normal.

"Slow down there. You okay?"

I nod and remain on my feet. "I'm fine. I'll be fine." I hesitate and fresh worry creeps in. "How is she?"

His lips thin, and I think I might be sick. The throbbing in my shoulder can't even distract me from the very real possibility that Charlotte could be dying right now. Or dead.

"We'll know more soon," he finally says.

I walk toward him, preparing to shake him until he tells me everything. "Chester, don't placate me, goddamnit."

"She's got the top doctors in DC," Chester says in his best soothing voice. The worry lines in his face ease slightly. "She lost a lot of blood, but she's going to be fine, I promise you."

I shake my head, adrenaline still spiking my veins hours after they'd patched me up. "You don't know that. Where is she?"

"She's in surgery. No one's getting to her right now. Not even her family. Go home and get cleaned up. I'll call you as soon as she's out and we know more."

I glance down at my hands. They're still smeared with red. My clothes are a bloody mess. Charlotte's blood mingled with mine. I ball my hands into angry fists. I want to fight my way to her, but I know deep down there's nothing I can do. I had my chance to protect her. I'm powerless now.

Tears sting my eyes as I suck in a shaky breath.

Hell, I can't remember the last time I cried. But I can't remember ever feeling like my heart was being torn out either.

I was supposed to protect her. The shield of my body wasn't enough. I swallow hard and relive the horror in my mind for the hundredth time. I should have seen it coming. I should have known Nate wasn't going to give up.

Chester puts his hand on my arm and squeezes tightly, jolting me to the present. "I know you're upset."

I blink, but emotion clogs my throat. "I let her down, Chester. I failed her so completely. What if she doesn't pull through? How am I supposed to live with that?"

"You can't think like that," he says gently. "Let the doctors do their work, Parker. Go home and get some rest."

"Rest? You expect me to sleep while she's in there fighting for her life?"

I point to the door, but she's far beyond that threshold. She's probably on another floor, protected by a wall of men who were hired to do what I failed to do today. I'll never know where she is because Chester knows better than to tell me in my current state of mind. He's right. But I can't rationalize much of anything right now.

"I'm going to have one of the guys give you a ride home, all right? I'll call you the second I hear anything."

I nod, because my throat hurts so damn bad I'm not sure I could speak if I wanted to. All I can do is wait and pray there's a God that can save her.

I stare at the counter where my phone sits. The creases of my hands are stained dark brown. I'm still a goddamn mess. I can't wash her off. I can't move until I know she's okay.

I don't bother putting on the news. Chester will know more before they do.

I resist the almost painful urge to call him for an update. I fold my hands together and drop my forehead against them.

She's going to make it. She has to. God, please...

My chest tightens painfully. I can't remember the last

time I prayed. Not even when my parents passed. I was too hurt. My anger at having lost them too soon consumed me. Something is different now. I'm beyond angry. I'm devastated... I'm desperate.

Just as my thoughts begin to take me down a dangerous path, my phone rings. Chester's number lights up the screen. My hands are shaking so badly I can barely answer it.

"Chester. Is she okay?"

"She just got out of surgery. She's stable."

I pinch the bridge of my nose and release a breath I feel like I've been holding for hours. "Thank God."

"The bullet punctured her lung, but they've repaired it. She's going to be okay."

The relief hits me so hard I'm dizzy again.

"Parker... There's something else."

"What is it?"

Chester hesitates and my panic starts climbing again.

"They found some photos of you with Charlotte in Nate's car. I don't know all the details yet, but it doesn't sound good."

"Photos of us? What the hell does that mean? I'm her bodyguard. I'm with her all the time."

"I haven't seen them. I just know they're damaging. You're being placed on mandatory leave until things settle down."

"Fuck." I slam my fist onto the counter. "I need to see her, Chester. I need to apologize. Tell her how I feel. She almost died for Christ's sake."

He sighs on the other end of the line. "I hope you get your chance, Parker, but it's out of my hands now. Get some rest tonight. Tomorrow you'll need to come in and give a full report. I'm guessing you may have some hell to pay with her father too."

Sitting across from the President of the United States in the Oval Office should be a thrill, but I'm anything but thrilled.

"Parker." He offers a tight smile. "How's your shoulder?"

"Fine, sir."

"Good. I don't have a lot of time, so we'll make this brief." He tosses an envelope across the desk. "Take a look at these."

I open it and a stack of photos slides out. I riffle through them, preparing for the worst. I bite back a curse when I get to the last ones of Charlotte holding herself against the window. My figure is behind her, less clear but still obviously me. I knew the photos would be damaging, but I wasn't sure what to expect. Between her nudity, our position, and the rapt expression on her face, there's no doubt she's in the throes of passion. I graze my thumb over the corner of the photo. Despite the awful position in which I now find myself, I can't ignore how beautiful she is. I'd give anything to see her right now, but I worry the likelihood of that is dwindling with each passing minute.

These photos are beyond incriminating. And the threat of them being splashed across the tabloids has me in knots. One more fuck-up on the pile of mistakes I've made when it comes to her.

Slowly, I return the photos to the envelope and place them on the desk. I stay silent and wait for the verbal lashing I deserve.

"I'm not going to waste time lecturing you on the consequences of taking advantage of my daughter. I think we both know you compromised your career the second you stuck your dick in her."

I blink hard at his crude remark but make every effort to school my features.

"What's more concerning to me is that Nate Christiansen was in possession of these photos minutes before our people shot him to hell. You understand how that looks, right?"

I try to piece the day together with this new information. Nate would have used the photos to coerce Charlotte into sleeping with him. Deep down I know she wouldn't, so he would have resorted to brute force, or the threat of a weapon.

"He threatened her numerous times. Your wife ignored her concerns and insisted that Charlotte go with him unprotected."

The President slams his fist on the desk and rises. "You keep my wife out of this!" He takes a few ragged breaths and slowly lowers back down in his seat. "You've got one chance to tell me the whole truth. I need to know with absolute certainty that there was no foul play here, or I'm going to have the senator asking questions. Then I'm looking at a potentially career-ending scandal. Not to mention the end of Charlotte's reputation, in case that's anything you care about."

Every muscle in my body is strung tight. I'm ready to go off on him, but I have to keep my cool. Charlotte's reputation is tied to her father's, and I need to keep her safe the only way I can now.

"I understand, Mr. President."

The muscles in his jaw flex. He leans back and gestures for me to speak.

"Nate Christiansen tried to rape her at a house party a couple weeks ago. She was drunk. I intervened...aggressively. Not long after that, Charlotte and I"—I swallow hard, because I'm about to lay out all my transgressions to the most powerful man on earth—"began a sexual relationship. Nate continued threatening her. He assured her I wouldn't always be there to save her. I can only assume he involved himself in the campus tour as the perfect opportunity to get her alone. He was obsessed with..." I close my eyes and exhale slowly, trying like hell to stay composed. "I believe having sex with Charlotte would have been the ultimate trophy for him, and being denied it repeatedly drove him to make some very poor decisions. As long as I've known him, he's always acted above the law. I don't think he realized in that split second when he pointed his gun at her that he would pay the ultimate price." I look down at my hands, tracing the lines in my palms. "To be frank, he was a spoiled brat. Someone took away his toy and he threw a tantrum. I'm not sorry he's dead, but I had no idea about the photos until after all this happened."

I lift my head to meet his hard stare.

"And what about you, Parker? Was Charlotte a trophy for you too?"

I wince. "No, sir."

He shakes his head slightly. "Doesn't matter now anyway. Hopefully she's learned a powerful lesson." He leans in and slides his hand over the envelope containing the photos. "These will disappear. Senator Christiansen will never know about your affair with Charlotte so as not to confuse the issue. Nate will be painted as a jealous lover with mental instability. Something like that." He drums his fingers. "Needless to say, Charlotte's things will be moved out of View 17 as soon as she's well. In the meantime, she'll be recovering at the residence."

A beat of silence passes, but I sense there's more.

"I'm not happy about what you've done, Parker. I should discharge you immediately. But the fact remains that you took a bullet for my daughter. I'm willing to reassign you as long as we're clear on my expectations."

I wait for him to continue, but the dread in my gut tells me I'm not going to like his expectations.

"You are *never* to seek her out again. No phone calls. No texts. Don't try to use your relationships with other agents to get close to her. The second I find out you do, you're finished. Your exit will not be pleasant and it will not be honorable. You are being given a second chance from someone who rarely offers them, so take this as a blessing and disappear from her life gracefully. Don't make this messy."

Take this as a blessing.

You've failed her.

Let her go.

"I understand," I say again, but my voice breaks.

CHARLOTTE

"I want to go back home." I ease back onto my old bed awkwardly.

"This is home. For now." My mother's voice lacks its usual icy punch, but it's hardly warm. She covers me with a blanket without making eye contact. "The staff will take good care of you here."

"I'm fine," I lie. I'm weak and my bandages need to be changed regularly, a task I can't manage with full range of motion of only one arm. But if I was back at my apartment, I wouldn't need to. I'd have Zane.

"You're not going back to your apartment, Charlotte," she says, as if reading my thoughts. "Those photos." She shakes her head almost violently. "I don't need to tell you how much damage you could have done with your recklessness."

No one had mentioned the photos in Nate's car while I was in the hospital. But as soon as the fog of anesthesia cleared, I remembered them. The threat of exposure hangs like a cloud over me now. Someone must have found them. Maybe that's why I haven't seen or heard from Zane since the shooting.

My heart breaks every time I think of him. The wild look in his eyes when he'd discovered I shared the bullet that had ripped through him. The details were a blur. Everything had happened so fast. But Zane's face is imprinted clearly on my memory.

My mother switches on the bedside light. I grimace at the sudden brightness.

"Can I at least have my phone now?"

She rolls her eyes and goes to speak with the staff who hover nearby, ready to help. Her heels click as she goes. As usual, not a hair out of place. What would it be like to have a normal life? I'll never know.

She returns with a phone and hands it to me. "They had to get you a new one. The other one was lost in the scuffle, I suppose."

I take it from her, but I don't miss the guilty way she avoids my gaze and presses on her pearls. She left me with Nate and never gave that vulnerability a second thought. She's why I'm here. She's why I'll always wear a scar from that day.

"Do you have anything to say to me?"

She freezes, her perfectly sculpted brows pinching into a frown. "What do you mean?"

"How could you leave me alone with him?"

She straightens the blanket one last time, her lips tight. No apologies will pass through them, I'm sure of it.

"Get some rest, Charlotte."

As she turns to leave, my father enters the room. If I hadn't seen him, I could have sensed him. Everyone is on high alert. The staff with their attentive smiles. Even my mother adjusts her ramrod straight spine at the sight of him. He commands a reverent kind of attention. He is the very definition of power.

"Can I have a moment with my daughter?"

Everyone smiles politely and leaves us alone. When the door clicks shut, he comes toward me.

He sits on the edge of the bed and takes my hand. "How are you feeling?"

The smallest gesture of affection threatens to send me into a fit of sobs, but I manage to keep it together. "I'm better. Thanks, Dad."

"I didn't want to burden you with this right away, but I figure it's best to let you know where things stand. I'm aware of the photos Nate had in his possession before all of this happened."

I bite down on the inside of my lip. It doesn't matter how much I love Zane or how little I regret every moment of being with him. Being exposed so explicitly to my father is still embarrassing.

"I'm sorry," I mutter quietly.

He pats my hand. "I know. It's okay. I've taken care of everything."

"Thank you." My chest falls on an exhale. The relief is undeniable.

But what about Zane? He's been absent since the shooting. I desperately want to see him.

"What about Zane?"

My father's expression reveals nothing, as if this is the most normal conversation he's ever had. "He's been reassigned. We felt that was best under the circumstances. He made no objections. Doesn't much matter because I've been thinking about the whole Georgetown situation. Things have been moving quickly since the election and maybe asking you to uproot from New York so soon was rash. I spoke with your mother and we're both in agreement that you should resume your coursework there for the time being."

"But..."

My jaw falls. Not only because of my father's sudden change of heart, but because I'd stopped mourning my life in New York the second Zane found his way into my heart. With him is the only place I truly want to be.

Before I can speak, my father pats my hand again. The gesture is losing significance. I'm feeling less like a daughter he cares about and more like a pet he's trying to appease so it trots off and leaves him alone.

"Chester will arrange to have your things moved from View 17. As soon as you feel well enough to travel, he and a team will accompany you. Security has been increased, obviously. Nothing like this will ever happen again."

I sense the sentiment is half reassurance and half warning. But it doesn't stop me from trying to figure out how I can reconnect with Zane as quickly as possible.

My father ends the conversation with a kiss on my forehead and a swift retreat toward the door. With his hand on the knob, he turns. "And Charlotte. You're not to have any further contact with Agent Parker. If you do, I can assure you there will be serious consequences. He'll suffer far more than you will."

My heart is racing as the door slams behind him. My blood boils. A scream threatens to tear its way up my throat. Anger claws at my frayed nerves and wears down my already waning energy. Immediately, I reach for my phone and scroll through my contacts. But the phone is empty. No photos. No texts. No contacts.

Zane has effectively been erased from my life.

ZANE

I stand in the center of Charlotte's apartment. Chester let me know the movers would be coming by in the morning. I'd never have a chance to say goodbye to her, so this would have to do.

For now, the place still feels lived in. Our dishes in the sink. My shirt on the floor. This is how she'd left it the morning of the shooting. The morning I left her for the last time.

Being here is salt on the festering wound of missing her. It's been weeks with no contact, but the hole in my chest only seems to be growing wider and deeper. How could a woman carve out so much of me in so little time?

But falling in love with her happened long before I lured her into bed. How long would it take to fall out of love? I had no idea. I had no frame of reference for this kind of pain.

My heart tugs me toward her bedroom, because I'm a glutton for punishment. The sheet she wore around herself that morning is still in a pile on the floor. I pick it up and bring it to my face. When I inhale, I take her scent into me. Her hair, her skin, her pussy.

I should stop. I should get the hell out of here and never look back. Instead, I walk to the bed and drop down onto it, taking the sheet with me. I graze my palm over the ripples in the silky sheet. I remember her body and the hours we spent in this very place. I relive the way her back arched off the bed when I plunged into her over and over. The way she clung to me like she'd die if she let me go. The way she said my name, her lips falling open like she wanted to tell me more. Like she wanted to confess that she loved me the way she did in our last moments together.

I close my eyes tightly and bury my face in the sheet again.

I'll never have her. Never again.

I have to learn to accept it. I have to learn how to live without my heart.

Charlotte Daley was a mistake. But she was the best goddamn mistake of my life.

CHAPTER TEN

CHARLOTTE

I shiver at the frigid sensation of the metal stethoscope pressing against my back.

"Okay, Charlotte, take a deep breath in for me and hold it." Dr. Holden's voice is gentle and measured behind me.

I draw a deep breath of air into my lungs and stare ahead at the poster hanging on the wall. For the past five weekly checkups, I've done this exact same routine. This time, though, I'm fixated on the poster—a black and white portrait of a couple embracing in the rain—in a way unlike before. Was the couple saying goodbye? Were they reuniting? In my mind, it is the latter. Maybe that's because I'm desperate for a reunion with Zane. Even though it's been almost seven weeks since he was ripped out of my life, I still hold out hope that he will somehow find a way back to me.

The doctor moves the stethoscope to another location on my back. "Excellent. Now, slowly release your breath."

I blow out the breath I've been holding, aware of the slight burn that it leaves in my chest.

Dr. Holden smiles at me as he wraps the stethoscope back

around his neck. "Your lungs sound perfect, Charlotte. I can tell you've been working on your breathing exercises. Just be sure to keep doing those several times a day. As I've told you before, it will take several months to get your full lung capacity back."

"When do you think I can go back to exercising?"

"I think you can safely resume most of your exercise routines, as long as you don't push yourself too hard. Be sure to start out with something slow and low impact, and then work your way up. If you feel any shortness of breath or pain, I want you to stop immediately and contact me."

I nod, relief washing over me. Something as simple as walking on the treadmill will give me something to look forward to every day. Zane is all I can think about anymore. I need all the distractions I can get now.

Dr. Holden retrieves some examination gloves from a box. "Let's have a look at your incision, shall we?" Using his fingertips, he gently applies pressure on my scar. "Have you been experiencing any pain or discomfort since I last saw you?"

That's a loaded question. Pain stabs at my heart every day. But it's not the pain he's talking about. Unfortunately, no magic pill will alleviate that.

I shake my head. "I haven't had to take any of the pain medication for a while now."

"Very good. I must say, I'm very pleased with your recovery, Charlotte." He removes the gloves, tosses them in the nearby bin, and reaches for my file. After making a few notes, he closes the chart, and tucks it beneath his arm. "I feel confident enough in your progress to go ahead and release you from my care. Since your mother informed me that you'll be moving to New York City soon, I have a colleague there that I will be referring you to. I don't foresee you having any future complications or problems, but if something were to arise, Dr. Lang will take excellent care of you. Once you get dressed, I'll have my nurse bring you her contact information."

Suddenly the reality of everything that has passed and the anticipation of the transitions ahead bear down on me. I owe my life to this man. If it hadn't been for his quick thinking and skilled hands in the operating room, I wouldn't be alive today. Now, my life is taking me back to a city I love, many miles away from the man I love.

"Thank you for everything, Dr. Holden." I try to hold back the emotion in my voice, but I can't.

He gives me a gentle pat on the back, his smile soft and sincere. "You are most welcome. I wish you the best of luck in New York."

A few minutes later, I meet Chester in the reception area. "All set to go, Charley girl?"

"All set." I try to smile, but my heart is heavy. Maybe once I get to New York this roller coaster will end and I can get my life back on track.

I walk by his side toward the bank of elevators. We wait, and my thoughts drift until Chester's grip tightens on my arm. His gaze is pinned ahead of us, and when I follow it, I am leveled by the gray eyes staring back at me.

"Zane." His name falls from my lips in a painful whisper.

I stand frozen, too afraid to blink for fear he will disappear like some sort of mirage. I notice the dark circles that rest below his eyes. They make his handsome face look gaunt and tired. His broad shoulders lack the confident lines I remember, his once tailored suit seemingly a size looser on his body. Every part of him appears to reflect just how much of a toll these past seven weeks have taken on him.

Zane steps off the elevator toward us, but Chester pulls me back, as if being this close to Zane would put me in grave danger. My heart flies into a rapid rhythm. He's so close. Close enough to touch, if only Chester weren't here to keep us apart.

"What are you doing here, Parker? You know you aren't allowed anywhere near her."

Zane's eyes never break away from mine as he speaks. "The department scheduled my physical at this clinic. I had no idea she would even be here." His voice is hollow, lacking the sharpness he always had around me, when he was protecting me...or dominating me.

"Fine. We were just leaving anyway." Chester urges me toward the elevator.

His heart is in the right place, but I don't move. I glance up at him, offering my best pleading expression—the one he can't often resist when it comes to giving me my way. "Can I just have a minute with him?"

His brows shoot up onto his forehead. "What? No, Charlotte. Absolutely not."

"Chester, please. I'm moving to New York next week. All I want is to tell him goodbye." I speak loud enough so that Zane can hear me. If this is my only chance to see him before I leave, I have to let him know where I'll be if he decides to come looking for me.

"You're moving back to New York?" The pain in Zane's voice now matches the pain in his eyes. His gaze slides back to Chester, his eyes pleading as he speaks. "Just give me one minute with her."

"You know I can't do that, son."

Zane takes a tentative step forward. "I'm begging you. One minute. That's all I'm asking."

Chester's jaw is tight. "Stop it, Parker. You're only making this situation worse for her, and you know it."

Zane stares at his old friend, the pain draining from his expression until all I can see is desolation. He steps aside wordlessly, allowing Chester to pull me into the elevator with him.

Panic sets in. I have to do something to convince Chester to change his mind. "Don't do this, please, Chester." I fight to free myself from his hold, but Zane's voice stops me.

"Don't fight him, Charlotte. He's right. I'm only making this worse."

Tears sting my eyes, and the panic tightening my throat doesn't wane. I meet his stare, realizing our next few seconds together before the doors close will be our last. I'll never see him again.

As the elevator doors draw closed, dividing us, I mouth the words that will forever be etched in my heart.

"I love you."

Downtown traffic is at a complete standstill.

I stare out my window at a couple holding hands as they pass by on the sidewalk. My heart is breaking into a thousand pieces, yet everyone around me seems so happy. Why is the universe so determined to destroy my happiness?

Chester finally breaks the silence. "Do you plan on talking to me anytime soon? If not, it looks like this is going to be a long car ride."

I wipe the tears from my cheeks. "Why did you have to do that to me? To Zane? All I wanted was a minute with him to tell him goodbye."

"You know I couldn't allow that. Your minute alone could cost me my job, not to mention what would happen to him. It's bad enough that the two of you even saw each other today."

I narrow my eyes at him. "I thought you of all people would understand how hard this has been for me. I thought you cared."

The lines around his eyes soften. "I do care, Charley. More than you will ever know. I've watched you mope around in that house for weeks now. You're holding out hope for something that isn't going to happen. No matter how much you want things to be different, they're not going to be. I know it's hard, but you've got to let him go."

His words hit me like a slap across the face.

"Let him go? How am I supposed to do that? I'm in love with him."

He frowns back at me in the rearview mirror. "After everything you've been through, you're finally getting your life back. Isn't that what you wanted months ago? You're young. You have a bright future ahead of you in New York. It's time you realize that Zane isn't going to be a part of that. He can't be. It's that simple."

"Because my parents say so?" When he doesn't answer, I stare out the window. "Someone's been deciding my life for me since the day I was born. My mother is in New York choosing an apartment for me as we speak. Giving me a choice in the matter has never been a consideration, because that's how it's always been. Tell me, Chester. When do I get to make the decisions in my own life?"

I hear him blow out a heavy sigh. "I don't have an answer for you, Charley. God knows I wish I did. Maybe one day things will be different."

I trace my fingertip down the inside of the tinted glass. "I used to live every day with that hope. But now I think that hope has run out."

ZANE

She's moving back to New York.

I still can't wrap my head around it. New York City is a four-hour drive from DC, but she may as well be moving to Mars. Once she leaves town, she'll be impossible to reach. This is it. The end.

The thought of losing her forever is unbearable.

Closing my eyes, I turn up the bottle of tequila and welcome the burning sensation as the liquid trickles down my throat. Desperate to numb the pain, I waste no time turning the bottle back up for another swig. The sooner I'm drunk, the faster I can forget how much I hate my life without Charlotte in it. Between my degrading transfer in the Secret Service and losing contact with her for the foreseeable future, I have plenty of reasons to stay intoxicated.

Soon, the effects of the booze start to kick in. I collapse onto the couch and swipe the picture frame off the side table beside me. The picture is of Charlotte and a friend standing in front of some sort of art exhibit. I stole it from her apartment the day I did my final walk-through. Seeing her smiling face in the photo offers glimmers of solace on rough nights like these.

I roll onto my back and hold the picture above me, staring at her until my eyelids grow too heavy to keep open. Soon the world drifts away and sleep overtakes me, leaving me holding on to the only part of her I have left.

◆ ◆ ◆ ◆

The sound of my front door slamming shut jolts me awake. Either my sister has finally remembered her keys or someone is here to put me out of my misery.

"Zane?"

I sigh. Lauren's voice isn't enough of a reason for me to lift my head up off the couch. My body aches and my head throbs, so lying face down into the cushions is how I'll stay. I can ignore my miserable life much better this way.

"You're hungover? Un-fucking-believable."

My head snaps up when I hear glass bottles being tossed into a garbage can across the room.

Jesus Fucking Christ. Does she have to be so loud?

"It's Saturday." I ease myself up to a sitting position and cradle my pounding head in my hands. Maybe I overdid it just a touch on the tequila pity party last night. Then again, maybe

I underdid it.

"How are you even living in this mess? This place is a complete pigsty."

"You can keep your opinions to yourself, Lauren." I reach for the tequila bottle sitting on the coffee table in front of me, twist off the cap, and turn up the bottle.

Just as the alcohol touches my lips, Lauren swipes it out of my hand, drenching me in tequila.

"What the fuck did you do that for?"

She cocks her hip, propping her hand on it. "If you think I'm going to stand by and allow you to self-destruct, you have another think coming."

She's got fire in her eyes. The kind I used to have back when I had a purpose. I can't even muster enough anger to yell at her. "If you don't like what you see, you should leave," I say, my voice flat. *Please leave*, I beg silently in my head. I just want to be alone with my misery and anything that will numb it for a while.

She holds up the bottle of tequila like she's ready to make a point. "I'm not going anywhere. And *this* isn't a solution to your problems. It's the cowardly way out. The Zane I know wouldn't choose this way. He'd fight."

I glare back at her. "The Zane you knew doesn't exist anymore. You should know that by now."

Her eyes soften. She eases herself onto the wooden coffee table in front of me, setting the bottle beside her. Leaning forward, she places her hand tenderly on my chest. "You're wrong. He's still in there, buried beneath all the pain and hurt. I've tried for years to get through to you, to knock down those walls you keeping building around your heart. I couldn't do it, but someone you care deeply for did. She broke through that invisible shield somehow, and now you're scared shitless." Lauren points to the tequila bottle. "You're hiding behind that bottle because it's easier to numb the pain than it is to face it."

"I'm not hiding behind anything," I snap, pushing off the couch to stand. The room starts to spin for a second, but I manage to steady my balance.

"It's okay to feel, Zane. I don't care what the military taught you, you're not a fucking robot. You're a human being. Get angry. Be sad." She throws her hands up in the air. "For God's sake, just feel *something*."

I brace my hands on the back of my head and walk toward the long window that overlooks the city. The dark ominous sky outside matches my mood.

"Talk to me, Zane. Let me help you." Her tone is softer now, pleading.

"Talking isn't going to solve this. Nothing is."

"Drinking yourself to death isn't going to solve it either."

I let out a chuckle. "Trust me, if you knew what was going on in my life, you'd understand."

"I'm not stupid, Zane. I know you're in love with Charlotte Daley."

I spin on my heel to face her, my eyes wide.

A smirk tugs at her lips. "Don't look so surprised, big brother. It doesn't take a genius to figure that one out." She crosses her arms. "I had my suspicions the day she showed up here at your apartment. The way she reacted when I opened your door told me everything I needed to know."

"Why didn't you mention it?"

She shrugs. "What's the point? I knew if I confronted you, you would've just denied it. Besides, it's not like you ever pick up the phone. I had to hear about you getting shot over the national news, for heaven's sake. You and I both know that if I didn't stop by here on my layovers, I wouldn't see you at all."

The hurt in her voice slices right through me. How could I have been so callous and cruel to alienate my own sister? Despite everything I've done to her, she still fights for me, still believes in me.

I step forward and pull her into my arms. She tenses for a second, then wraps her arms around me and relaxes. I can't remember the last time I'd hugged her, which makes me feel even worse.

"I'm so sorry, Lauren. I know those words don't make up for what I've done, or how I've treated you. I don't like the man I've become. I thought I was protecting you by pushing you away."

She breaks our embrace, and then takes my hand into hers. "When are you ever going to learn? I'm your sister. Good or bad, I'll always be here for you."

I give her a weak smile. "Thank you. I mean it. But the situation with Charlotte is impossible. There's no hope."

"Oh, yeah? Try me."

I tense, sensing the walls creeping up again. Could I really tell her about this? When I think about all the hurt I've brought into her life and the great pains I'd taken to keep her from getting too close, the walls slide back down. There may not be hope for Charlotte and me, but I have to believe there's hope for Lauren and me.

"You might want to sit down for this."

CHAPTER ELEVEN

The cab driver pulls up in front of Crave and parks next to the curb. Grabbing hold of the door handle, I hesitate and look over at my sister. "Are you sure this is going to work?"

Lauren had spent her entire layover at my apartment listening to the mess I'd made with Charlotte and then helping me figure out a way to get her back. Three hours and two pots of strong coffee later, Lauren had somehow managed to put all the pieces together. The plan she's devised is the first thing that's given me hope in weeks. If this works, she is a fucking genius.

"From everything you told me, it sounds like this Katherine girl is your only key to seeing Charlotte."

"But what if she doesn't want to get involved? This is dangerous territory. I wouldn't blame her for saying no."

Lauren smiles and takes my hand into hers. "Just trust me, all right? She's Charlotte's best friend. She's going to want to help. It's a girl code."

When I step out of the car, she scoots toward the door and pokes her head out the window. She looks up at the old abandoned building behind me and grimaces. "This is the place?"

I grin. If she only knew the luxurious sex club that lurks just below these streets.

"Looks can be deceiving."

"Well, I wish I could stay longer and help, but I've got to fly out in a couple of hours. Promise me you'll call me later to give me an update, okay?"

"I will. I promise. Thank you for everything, sis. Really."

She winks. "That's what I'm here for. Now, go get your girl."

◆ ◆ ◆ ◆

Like most Saturday nights, Crave is complete mayhem, full of explosive sexual energy and half-naked bodies. One step into the club and the women are on me like flies on honey. I'm not affected by it the way I used to be, which doesn't surprise me. My spirit's been broken, and I'm struggling to find enough spark to fight and get Charlotte back.

The VIP lounge is located above the club floor. I spot Demitri sitting in his normal booth in the center of the lounge. Normally, he is surrounded by beautiful women, all hoping for the chance to be his submissive for the night. However, tonight he sits with his arm possessively wrapped around only one very familiar brunette.

Katherine.

The gentle way he is looking at her takes me by surprise. In all the time I've known him, I've never once seen him look at a woman that way. I'll be damned. Could the beautiful troublemaker Katherine Harrison have won him over?

The bouncer at the foot of the stairs recognizes me and steps aside wordlessly, allowing me access to the glass staircase. Demitri waves me over to his table.

"It's good to see you again, my friend."

"Same." I shake his meaty hand and take Katherine in. She's dressed in a barely there lace minidress.

"So, tell me, what brings you here? Looking for a new pet?"

I wince, and Katherine's cool assessing stare collapses into a glare. First toward me, then to Demitri. All humor flees his expression when their gazes lock.

"Kitten? What's wrong?" His tone is surprisingly tender, making his accent less evident.

She hesitates and places her hand on his cheek. "Nothing's wrong. I'm just going to get some air. I'll let the two of you visit."

When she starts to scoot out of the booth, I hold up my hand to stop her. "No, wait. Don't go. You're actually the reason I came here tonight."

She pauses. "Me? Why?"

I swallow hard, pleading with my eyes. "Because you're the only one in the world who can help me."

CHARLOTTE

After a long night of tossing and turning, I had just managed to fall asleep when the landline phone beside my bed begins to ring. With my head buried in the pillow, I blindly pat the nightstand next to me until I feel the phone beneath my fingertips. Even though I'm half-asleep, I manage to somehow lift the receiver up to my face.

"Hello." My voice comes out in a low croak.

"I'm sorry to wake you this early, Miss Daley, but Miss Katherine Harrison is here downstairs. She says it's urgent that she speak with you this morning."

I look over at the clock. It's just after five in the morning. What can possibly be so fucking urgent this early?

"It's fine. Send her up."

I hang up the phone and let out a loud groan, throwing the covers back up over my head. If Kat wants to talk to me, she'll have to do it while I'm lying here. I don't think I have the energy to crawl out of bed right now.

I've almost drifted back to sleep when my bedroom door opens and slams. Seconds later, Katherine is switching on the lamp beside my bed, blinding me instantly.

"We need to talk."

I've always hated hearing those words, especially when they come out of my best friend's mouth. No good can ever come from them.

I sit up in bed and hold up my hand to shield my eyes from the brightness of the lamp. Once my eyes focus, I notice she's still wearing a tight short black dress.

"Did you come from the club?"

"Yeah." Katherine tosses an envelope onto my lap. "Here."

I rub the sleep out of my eyes and open the flap of the envelope. I pull out a rectangular card and read it. "This is your urgent news? You came here at five in the morning to tell me you're throwing me a going away party?"

Mischief glints in her eyes. "Yep."

Shaking my head, I hand the invitation back to her. "Look, Kat, it's really sweet of you to think about me, but no thanks. I really don't feel like a party."

Katherine plops herself down at the foot of my bed. "Good, because there's not going to be a party."

"What? Look, I don't know what this is all about, Kat, but you're confusing the hell out of me. I just want to get some sleep."

"The invitation is just a cover, Charlotte."

"A cover for what?"

Her lips twist into a coy smile. "For you to see Zane."

The mere mention of his name hits me like a triple shot of espresso. I rise up to my knees, placing my hands on her shoulders. "You've seen Zane? When? Where?"

"He came into Crave."

My heart plummets into my stomach and I sink back onto the bed. "Oh."

The thought of him being there to look for another woman makes me sick.

As if she's read my thoughts, Kat grabs my hand. "No, no, nothing like that. Zane wasn't there to pick up a woman. He came there to see me. With everyone watching him so closely, he knew the club was the only place we could talk privately. We came up with a plan for him to see you before you leave for New York." She eyes the invitation. "While everyone thinks you're at a going away party, you'll be alone in a hotel room with Zane."

I run her plan through my head, almost too overwhelmed with the prospect of seeing Zane to doubt we can pull it off. I throw my arms around her neck and give her a breathless hug. "Oh, Kat. Do you think it will really work?"

She hugs me back tightly. "You bet your sweet ass it will. Now, get out of bed. We've got some planning to do."

I lay the short red dress across my bed. The last time I'd worn it was the first night I'd gone to Crave with Katherine. That night had changed everything between Zane and me. I skim my fingertips across the fabric, blushing at the memories. I'm hoping to get the same reaction from him tonight as I did the first time he saw me in it. With any luck, the dress will be on the floor within seconds of me entering the room.

I'm just about to step into the shower when my phone begins to ring. My mother's name on the screen instantly dampens my good mood. Sliding my finger across the screen, I force myself to answer with a pleasant tone.

"Hello, Mother. How is everything in New York?"

"It's been very busy. Between your father's appearances and apartment shopping, I haven't had a moment to spare." She pauses for a second. "I trust you've been packing?"

I glance across my room at the stack of empty boxes sitting in the corner. All of them should be full by now, but I haven't been able to bring myself to pack a thing. I simply can't deal with the reality of moving.

"I've been sorting through things that I'm taking with me. I'll have everything done before I have to leave next week."

"That's actually why I'm calling. Everything went much quicker than I anticipated with finalizing the apartment. With your father and I leaving for London in a few days, I see no need to wait until next weekend to move you in. I've made arrangements for you to fly to New York this evening. We will begin moving you in first thing tomorrow morning. The sooner we get you settled, the better."

A wave of panic hits me. I can't leave without seeing Zane one last time.

"I'm not packed though."

"We can have someone pack the rest of your things. Don't worry about that."

"But there's no way I'll be able to leave today. Katherine is hosting a going away party for me at the Fairmont tonight."

My mother huffs into the phone. "Why must you make things so difficult, Charlotte?"

"She's gone through so much trouble getting everything together," I lie. "I can't cancel on her on such short notice."

I hold my breath as I await her response. If she says no, I don't know what I will do.

"Fine. I'll have a pilot waiting at the airport on standby. But the instant this party is over, you will immediately head to the airport. Is that understood?"

My head is spinning. How can all of this be happening so quickly?

"Charlotte? Did you hear me?" My mother's harsh tone snaps me out of my panicked thoughts.

"Yes, Mother. I heard you. I'll be there."

"Very well. We'll see you tonight then."

When I end the phone call, I'm shaking so badly that I have to sit down. This can't be happening. Not now. Not after

I'm finally getting the chance to be with him.

I glance at the clock on the wall. I have a little over an hour and a half before I leave for the hotel. I can't fall apart now. I refuse to let anything ruin this evening for us. Even if tonight means goodbye.

♦ ♦ ♦ ♦

As the hotel comes into view, I find myself smiling from ear to ear. In just a matter of minutes, I will be back in Zane's arms again. I've thought of little else for weeks.

"I've missed that smile." Chester's voice startles me out of my thoughts.

I catch his reflection in the rearview mirror. Sometimes I think he can see right through me. Can he see the real reason behind my smile?

"It just feels good to be out of the house for a change, even if it is for a going away party. I'm sure I'll be crying after I have to say goodbye to everyone."

The truth is, I will likely be in hysterics, but I can't think about that right now.

"Goodbyes are always hard, especially when it's someone you care about. But you'll be back with your old friends in New York soon. You'll be fine," he says as he parks the car in front of the hotel.

Chester circles the car, opens my door, and follows behind me as we enter the hotel.

As planned, Katherine is waiting for me in the lobby and dressed for the party we're not really attending. She greets me with open arms. "There's my guest of honor. I'm glad I caught you. I was just checking with the front desk about having some more champagne sent up to the suite. We can ride back up together."

She looks over my shoulder. "That is, if it's okay with you, Chester."

I turn around to look at Chester, pleading with my eyes. "Do you think you can take your post down here instead of upstairs? I just want one night to be normal with my friends."

Chester frowns. "The last time I agreed to that, the two of you snuck off."

I place my hand on his arm. "I think I learned my lesson, Chester."

He purses his lips, looking back and forth between Katherine and me.

I hold my breath, knowing the fate of my night now rests in his hands. "I won't leave the hotel, Chester. I swear."

He knits his brows together. "Don't make me regret this, Charley. I mean it."

Relief barrels into me like a freight train. Thank God.

"I won't, Chester. Thank you." I give him a quick kiss on the cheek, and without another word I follow Katherine to the elevator.

Once the metal doors close, she blows out a long breath. "Jesus Christ, that was close. For a second there, I thought he was going to say no." She hands me a room key card out of her jeweled clasp. "You're in suite twelve seventy-eight. Zane's already upstairs waiting for you."

I look down at the key card in my hand. Just holding it makes everything become so real, so final.

Katherine nudges me. "Cheer up. Tonight will be amazing."

I look up, tears stinging my eyes. "I know it will be. But it's going to be our last. I leave for New York tonight. My mother is insisting on it."

Katherine's eyes widen. "Shit. Why?"

The elevator climbs and I take in a deep breath, forcing myself to hold it together. I can't cry. Zane can't see me upset. Tonight has to be perfect.

"Doesn't matter. But Zane can't know until I'm gone."

She turns me to face her and gives my arms a gentle squeeze, as if reading my troubled thoughts. "Just focus on making every moment with him a memorable one."

The elevator chimes as it reaches my floor. I straighten my dress and step out into the hallway. I'm surprised when Katherine follows behind me.

"I'll meet you back here at ten," she says, retrieving another room key card out of her clasp.

I blink a few times before she winks.

"Let's just say you're not the only one who will be having a good time tonight."

With a laugh, we part ways and move in opposite directions down the hall. I count down each door that I pass until I'm finally standing in front of the suite. I tap my foot on the ornate carpeted floor, determined to put tonight's flight to New York out of my mind until our time is up.

My hand trembles as I slide the key card into the door. It beeps and opens, and I step inside, letting the door glide shut behind me. Zane stands on the other end of the room. He's dressed in dark jeans and a thin navy blue sweater that hugs his muscular chest. In one breathless moment, I'm leveled by his presence, his intense gaze, and the love that radiates there.

It doesn't last long, because he crosses the distance between us in a few long strides. Then I'm engulfed in his embrace, held close by his strong arms. I melt into him, pressing my nose into his chest to breathe him in. The urge to cry hits me hard, but I fight it.

Zane pulls back and cradles my face. Before I can take my next breath or tell him how much I truly love him, his lips are sealed over mine. His smoky flavor hits me with a rush of memories I've relived a thousand times since Nate's death ripped us apart. Tonight we'll make new ones I'll carry with me forever.

My hands find his hair, and I tug him closer to me, deepening our kiss. Zane moans into my mouth as he begins walking us back into the room. He turns us and my back hits the wall. He breaks our passionate kiss, leaving me breathless as he feverishly begins working his mouth down the side of my neck. I can feel the moisture gathering in my panties. I haven't even been through the door a full minute.

"I've missed you. So fucking much," Zane pants against my ear. "I told myself I would be gentle with you, that I would take things slow. But I don't think I can."

His erection presses into my stomach, making my pussy ache with need. I tug off his sweater and drop my hands between us, working to unfasten the front of his jeans. "It's been too long. I need you inside me, Zane. Don't make me wait."

His eyes darken when I push his jeans past his hips, causing his cock to spring free. I reach for him but he hoists me up, and I wrap my legs around his waist. I hear a rip as he tears my panties free. Never breaking his intense stare, he aligns himself beneath me. As he lowers me onto his length, I search his eyes, slave to the delicious way he stretches me. We both let out a simultaneous sigh when he's joined us completely. I'm so sensitive that I already feel myself tightening around his cock.

His first thrusts are slow and careful, but that doesn't slow down the rush of my orgasm. He's barely gotten inside me and I'm ready to scream out in ecstasy.

"It's too good, Zane. I'm so close. Please, let me come."

Bracing his hands beneath my ass, Zane begins pumping in and out of me. Each drive of his body into mine is more desperate, more forceful than the one before.

"I'll give you anything, Charlotte," he rasps.

My heart breaks a little more with his words. I wrap my arms around his neck, needing to be as close to him as possible.

"Look at me, baby. I want to see you when you let go."

I'm afraid to show him what hides behind my eyes, but once we lock in, I'm overwhelmed. The connection between us soars past the physical. Our hearts are joined, and I've never known anything like it. With one forceful push of his cock, I surrender. The blissful climax takes me under, and I lose myself in his gray eyes and the love I see reflected there.

We may not have forever together, but tonight I'm going to pretend we do.

ZANE

After all this time, watching Charlotte come in my arms levels me. I've never experienced anything like it. Everything about our connection reinforces the desperate way I've felt without her.

As eager as I am to continue fucking her against this wall, that's not how I want our first night back together to be. Tightening my grip on her ass, I pull her in for a kiss and carry her toward the king-size bed.

I slip out of her and ease her down until she is standing. I recognize her dress as the one she wore to Crave. I rest my forehead against hers as I now reach for its zipper.

"Charlotte... God, you're so beautiful. You owned me the minute you walked into that club wearing this dress," I say as I inch the zipper down her back. The fabric loosens at the top, allowing me to pull the straps down the sides of her arms. My heart stops when I see the scar across her chest. I bring my fingertips tenderly across it, pain heavy in my heart.

"I'm so sorry." My voice is hoarse and low with unfathomable regret. "I should have been quicker. I should have protected you better." My mind flashes back to the image of her bleeding on the ground. Blinking out of the thought, I look at her with tears in my eyes. "I almost lost you."

She reaches for my face, skimming her palms along my clean-shaven jaw. "I'm alive because of you. You saved me." She moves her hands to touch the scar on my shoulder. "This connects us. It always will."

I drag in a painful breath. "I love you, Charlotte." The

words fall effortlessly from my lips. For all the time I'd agonized over telling her, I know now the sentiment lingered in my heart for far longer.

"I love you too." She blinks up at me, her gaze seeming to say more. "I'll always love you," she whispers tearfully.

I can't watch her cry. Not tonight. Tonight is for us, for her. I push her dress down to the floor, lower my lips to hers, and ease her backward onto the bed. Her long blond waves spill across the dark bedding, creating a halo of gold. She looks so beautiful that it takes my breath away. I position myself between her legs and pause just as the tip of my cock reaches her opening. Our eyes never waver as I push into her. Once I'm fully inside, I pause, savoring the way she tightens around me.

"Nothing has ever felt as perfect as you, as this," I breathe across her ear as I thrust again.

Charlotte slides her hands to my ass, urging me to go deeper, faster. I quicken my pace, giving her exactly what she wants. She's already close. I know I won't be able to hold out much longer.

I grab her thigh and lift it against her chest, sinking deeper into her body. The simple change of angle is enough to send her over. Charlotte throws her head back and cries out. I can't hold on any longer. Her orgasm triggers my own release. I wrap my arms around her waist and thrust into her body one last time with a feral groan—the sound of all the weeks of longing for her and not knowing if we could ever be together again.

Sated physically and so high on the intense love I carry for this woman, I roll onto my back and pull her into my arms. She rests her head against my chest and we lie there trying to catch our breath. Our time together is so limited. There is so much I want to say to her, so much I want to do.

"I'm going to fix this, Charlotte. No matter what it takes. I promise you, I'm going to find a way we can be together."

Charlotte raises her head and places a finger over my lips to silence me. "We're together right now. Let's not waste a single second of it."

Silently, she brings her body over mine, straddling me until my cock slides against her folds. Even though we've just had an explosive round of sex, my cock is already hard for her again. She inches herself down onto my length, her eyes closing with a soft sigh.

She's beautiful, sexy, and perfect. I want to revel in all of it, but something's changed between us. Each thrust, each touch feels as if she is somehow saying goodbye.

◆ ◆ ◆ ◆

I shrug into my jacket and get ready to head back to View 17. My body hums with the memory of our incredible night together. It's the only thing keeping my heart in one piece right now. Saying goodbye to her, if only for now, was far from easy. I promised her more nights like this, but not knowing when I'll see her next already has me ready to climb the walls.

I reach for my keys when I hear a light knock on the door. I look through the peephole and recognize Katherine standing in the hallway. The moment I open the door and catch the solemn look on her face, dread washes over me.

"What's wrong?"

She glances up and down the hallway. "Can I come in for

a second?"

"Yeah, sure." I step back and allow her into the room.

"Charlotte wanted me to give this to you." She holds out a long ivory envelope. I take it from her and rip it open. The folded handwritten note is long, but I only have to read the first line to understand its purpose.

I shoot her a desperate look. "She's leaving for New York tonight? Why didn't she tell me?"

Katherine gives me a tight smile. "Her mother called and demanded that she leave tonight. Charlotte didn't tell you because she didn't want to ruin your last night together."

My instinct is to argue with Katherine, but she's only the messenger. I step away from her, my shaking hands making it hard to read the rest of the note. I start from the beginning, Charlotte's voice clear in my head.

Dear Zane,

By the time you read this, I'll be on my way to New York, back to a life I thought I'd always wanted. You and I will have spent another incredible night together—one I'll never forget.

For those on the outside looking in, mine seems to be a charmed life. You've always known better. No one will truly understand my world the way you have.

Despite everything I've been through, spending the last two months apart from you has been the most painful time of my life. Sometimes I can't believe that getting shot isn't penance enough to be with you the way I desperately want to be. Instead, it's a wound that will never heal because the rest of the world and circumstances beyond our control will never let us be together.

If you come after me, my parents will punish me, but they'll stop at nothing to ruin you. I just can't live with that.

You saved my life, Zane. You've taught me what real love can feel like. You don't deserve to suffer for their ignorance. Neither of us do. But this is my life. It's the one I've always known, and I have to believe that I'm stronger for the lessons it's taught me and the experiences it's given me. After all, this crazy life brought me to you...

I will never stop loving you, Zane. Know that, in my heart, I'm kneeling for you, craving your touch, never far from the memories of us. I will always hold them close. Always...

All my love,

Charlotte

I crumple the letter in my hand as the door clicks shut, leaving me alone with her goodbye.

Every path to Charlotte is closed. Every crack in my heart is jagged and broad, bleeding with the love I hold for her. I'm raw. I've just held her, made love to her, recommitted to finding a way to be together. Every instinct tells me to run and find her and make this right, but the letter in my hand keeps me still, paralyzed by her wish.

CHAPTER TWELVE

One year later...

Happiness bubbles through me like the champagne fizzing in my glass. Leianna, the posh art director at the King Gallery prattles on with Katherine about the success of the night. I can't disagree. In addition to a host of prominent artists and New York elite, several friends I've made between New York and DC and the private schools I'd attended in New England have come out to see my first show. Having so many eyes on my work is humbling and a little terrifying, but the response has been overwhelmingly positive.

Being who I am, carrying the label of the President's daughter despite the life I've worked hard to carve out in New York, I'd prepared myself to face criticism. The collection I'd titled "A Life in Gray" was edgier than anything I'd done before. Raw and vulnerable, the pieces had been inspired by a particularly progressive NYU art professor who'd encouraged me to release myself from everything that was holding me back: the constant pressure of my parents—notably and mercifully absent opening tonight—and everything else brought on by one of the most emotionally challenging years of my life.

The result was a series of paintings that had helped me process the years I'd spent in the pressure cooker of political life. Of course, among those experiences, nothing had hit me harder than losing Zane. Letting him go had been selfless in some ways, selfish in others. I wanted him for myself, at nearly any cost. But I couldn't live with the guilt of knowing he might sacrifice his career for us—a career earned through years of harrowing military service. I refused to accept that he would lose it all for me.

"I'm just so proud of you!" Katherine's smile can't be contained. She throws her arm around my shoulder and squeezes me against her, nearly splashing her champagne out of her glass as she does.

"They were simply head over heels for the collection, darling," Leianna says. "Even the critics. Just wait for the features that will come. This is only the beginning, trust me." She waves gracefully as her assistant comes up and whispers something in her ear, drawing her attention away from us. "Oh?" Her thinly plucked brows wrinkle into a frown.

"Is everything okay?" I glance around. The crowd has thinned out and the show is coming to a close. The entrance to the gallery is guarded by security, my usual team among them.

"Someone's insisting on seeing you. He tried to come in through the back, but our security stopped him," the young girl says.

"Who is it?"

Leianna shakes her head. "It's fine. We'll take care of it. You shouldn't have to worry about these sorts of things, tonight of all nights." She waves off her assistant.

I watch the girl dressed in all black disappear toward the offices in the back of the gallery. I'll never be the same since the shooting. Paranoia and concern about my safety hang over me like a cloud on a daily basis, reinforced by the ever-present team of Secret Service agents who shadow my every move. But what I feel now isn't that same unsettling threat of danger I'm used to.

"Excuse me for a moment," I force a smile and leave Katherine and Leianna, tracing the steps of her assistant toward the back.

I hear the girl's voice after she turns the corner, slipping out of sight. "I've spoken with my boss. I'm sorry, but the event is for approved guests only. There are no exceptions."

"Will you just tell her I'm here? I only want a moment of her time," a male voice answers. A voice that vibrates over my skin like nothing ever has. Or nothing since...

"Zane?" I turn the corner, his name on my lips the second he comes into view. He's dressed in a black suit over a black collared shirt that's unbuttoned at the neck. A simple but sophisticated look that nearly knocks me breathless.

Two men in suits flank the doorway, their postures defensive. When Zane takes a step toward me, they raise their arms in unison to push him back.

"Stop," I say, pushing between them. "He's a friend. It's fine."

The agents look at me and then each other before stepping back to let Zane pass. He reaches out for me but stops, lets his hands drop to his sides, and balls them into tight fists that match his tense jaw. "I'm sorry," he says. "I just wanted—"

"Come with me."

Without another word, I take his hand and lead him into the gallery's green room where I'd left my personal things. I shut the door behind us and turn to face him. He's still gorgeous, but there's something different about him. His hair is longer, and he seems even bigger than I remember. Who is he now? A year has gone by. I've changed... Has he?

He licks his lips, a sensual motion that sends a sudden rush of heat over my skin. His gaze journeys up and down my body, before settling on the floor. "I'm sorry, Charlotte. I didn't mean to upset your night. I heard about the opening. I didn't want to cause a scene or get you in any trouble. I just wanted to tell you how proud I am of you."

His words twist my heart, but the danger he's put himself in for me can't be ignored.

"Thank you, but you didn't have to."

He nods. A few seconds pass in silence before he speaks. "I'll go." He reaches for the doorknob.

"No, don't go." I take a step closer and rest my hand on his arm. So warm, impenetrable. The memory of how those arms once felt around me hits me like a shockwave. "Stay. Please."

The intensity in his eyes nearly brings me to my knees. My grasp falls away, only for our hands to find one another, weave together and draw us closer to each other. I rest my back against the door and he's right there, the heat of his body only a hair's breadth away.

Slowly he pins both wrists above me. When he adds pressure, his hold transforms into something dominant, something painfully arousing. I'm pulsing with it. I weaken against him, intoxicated by his touch and his presence. The second his lips brush against my neck, I whimper and bow against him.

"Zane." My breaths come fast. I'm slipping. A year has gone by, but nothing's changed. I'm still his... So completely his.

"I can't keep torturing myself like this." He runs his nose along the column of my neck. "I see you on the street and I ache to touch you this way. I don't know how to stop wanting you. Tell me to disappear forever. Tell me you hate me. Tell me you've fallen in love with someone else. God, Charlotte, break the rest of my heart and save us both."

I swallow over the knot in my throat. "I can't. I still love you. Nothing will ever change that."

The paintings that hang outside these walls prove that, evidence of what he still means to me, my heart—raw and bleeding—on display. Red is my submission, splashed onto dozens of canvases of moody grays, brush strokes of Zane and his memory creating the backdrop of every day. This was my year of obsession disguised as healing. If he only knew... If only we could find a way to be together.

"I want to be with you, Zane. But I can't ask you to risk everything for me. It's not fair after everything you've been through."

He lifts his head to stare into my eyes. "I've got nothing to lose."

I wince. "What do you mean? Your job..."

"I left. I wasn't about to spend my life at the service of

your family after they took you away from me." He releases his hold on me and takes a step back. "I moved to New York six months ago. I joined a private security company. The hours are better, and I don't have to answer to anyone but the partners."

I gasp. "You've been in New York all this time? Why didn't you reach out to me?"

He shrugs. "I wanted to give you your space. You told me to stay away, so I did. I shouldn't have come tonight. If your father finds out—"

"I don't care what my father thinks. The day I left DC was the day I started living my life again. That's what this show was about. A fresh start. Something that was truly and unapologetically me. Why do you think they didn't come?"

Sadness softens his features. "They didn't come?"

I shake my head. "My mother said the pieces were shameful. Tasteless." The echo of her words hurts, but not enough to cast a shadow on this incredible night. "I'm glad they didn't come, because nothing's going to stop me from living my life the way I want to now."

He's silent, his eyes searching, every muscle taut like he's standing on the edge of a dangerous cliff, unable to step away. "What are you saying, Charlotte?"

I take in a deep breath and straighten as I close the small space between us. "I'm saying that *you* are what I want. And I'm not going to hide or apologize for it."

"They'll be furious."

"So what?"

"They'll want to keep us apart at any cost."

I smile. "I'm America's sweetheart, Zane. People want to

see me happy and in love. If I walk out of this gallery with you by my side, that's the beginning of a love story that even my parents won't be able to make disappear."

He shakes his head slightly. "I've never met anyone like you."

I laugh. "Oh really? And why is that?"

"You're as beautiful as you are stubborn. You're passionate and willful. You've been a total handful ever since the day I met you."

I wind my arms around his neck and bring my chest to his. "Thankfully, I know just the man to get me under control."

For the first time in a year, I see Zane smile, and it's the most incredible moment of my night. Knowing I still have his love, believing we have a future where it seemed impossible before.

He brushes his lips tenderly over mine. "Oh, I'll get you under control, beautiful girl."

His words disappear into our kiss—raw and real and filled with a year's worth of missed opportunities. I know there's so much more to come, and we'll have all the time in the world for it.

Keep reading for

The Dom
a companion novella

by Meredith Wild and Mia Michelle

The Dom

BY MEREDITH WILD & MIA MICHELLE

CHAPTER ONE

KATHERINE

I've been to Crave a dozen times, but I've never been as overwhelmed as I am right now. I've seen him here before, but I've always avoided his gaze. I certainly never knew his name. Now that I do, it suits him. Demitri Nicoloff is enormous. His presence…everything about him. He's one of the most intimidating people I've ever met, which is saying a lot.

All my life I've lived in DC, a city that thrums with power and influence. My best friend's father happens to be the President of the United States. Mine is the Attorney General. If either of our fathers were to find out about tonight at the club or the rules we love breaking all too often, we wouldn't be able to see through the Secret Service agents assigned to keep us out of trouble.

And the only thing standing between us and a massive amount of trouble is Charlotte's bodyguard. The very one who's whisked her away to talk, leaving me here alone with this man who's looking at me like he wants to eat me.

We're tucked into a private sitting area in the back of

the club. Demitri sits on the adjacent couch and leans back as a server brings him a glass—a lowball filled with amber liquid.

"Can I get you something?" His accent rolls off his tongue and skitters across my bare skin, a hot pulse like the one at his neck as he slides his gaze over me.

"I'm fine," I say, though a shot of anything would certainly take the edge off.

The server disappears, and Demitri brings the drink to his lips, taking a small swallow.

"Make yourself comfortable."

I cross my legs and then my arms, the most defensive position I can muster.

He cocks his head a mere centimeter. "I've seen you here before."

"And I've seen you. So what?" My presence couldn't have been that remarkable, but part of me preens a little that he recognizes me.

"What are you frightened of?"

His bold question throws me more than his domineering presence.

"I'm not afraid of anything," I snap.

He doesn't know me. He doesn't know anything about me...

"If you're not afraid, why don't you uncross your arms? I won't bite."

I tense my jaw and contemplate his request. I've just met him, and I've hardly been warm. After a moment, I relent. I exhale a sigh, unfold my arms, and convince myself to lighten up. Charlotte should only be another minute, and then we can get out of here before anyone finds out we sneaked away.

"And your legs."

My jaw falls open at Demitri's last request, which is undeniably laced with sexual innuendo.

I cross my arms tightly again. "I don't think so."

He stares, and my God, it's a look made of blue-eyed steel. Strong, impenetrable, unequivocally dominant. It's all I can do to keep my body's reactions contained, schooled to appear unaffected, when everything he's doing is affecting me. His thumb collecting a stroke of dew on his glass. The deep, rhythmic breathing that ripples the suit that I have no doubt was tailored to accent every obscene muscle in this powerful man's body. But it's his stare that's pulling me apart at the seams.

When I come to the club, I watch, and it thrills me. I'm propositioned, and even the refusal gives me a buzz I've never experienced. But for all the highs I come here for, nothing measures up to this moment under his gaze.

The music transitions to another song and seems to pull his attention away. He turns his head toward the crowded club and the half a dozen scenes playing out. I've lost him.

My heart does something—a half beat, a pause, and then a panicked rush of fast ticks. It hurts. Something about his lack of attention causes physical pain in my chest. So much that I'm uncrossing my arms . . . and my legs.

"Take off your panties." His eyes meet mine again briefly. "No one here cares if you bare yourself to me."

I should tell him to go to hell, but that quickly his attention is somewhere else. Somewhere deep in the crowd, away from me. I bite my lip, hard. I can't believe what I'm doing, but I can't seem to stop myself. I'm trailing my hands up the edges of my dress. Reaching under, I hook my thumbs over the thin straps of my thong and, slowly, drag it down.

Every inch the garment drags down my legs is a prayer . . .

. . . answered when his gaze flickers back to me.

A breath of relief rushes past my lips. Then my panties are on the floor, dangling off one of my ankles, while my pussy throbs like it never has before.

His eyes hold me there. He's not undressing me. He's undoing me, a tractor beam of intensity right to the heart of me. I can barely breathe.

"You like attention." He lifts his glass to his lips and takes a slow swallow.

I nod. Because, yeah, I like it.

"When it comes from you," I admit, immediately regretting my honesty. This club is wall to wall with Dominants looking to play, and no one else has affected me this way.

A slight squint in his left eye. "Will you entertain me, then? Will you show me something worth watching, kitten?"

Kitten? My whole body heats. Why do I want to purr at this man's feet when he says it? I should be outraged and walk out of here, with or without Charlotte.

But I can't. My knees tremble even as they begin to part. For him. For his steely will that I want to bend to for reasons I can't comprehend.

His tongue takes a seductive sweep across his bottom lip. "*Krásná,*" he murmurs.

CHAPTER TWO

KATHERINE

One year later…

I'm fire starved of oxygen. A rosebud locked in frost.

I've spent my life in a cage, cloistered by politics and social maneuvering. A prisoner to expectation. Yet I'd give anything to be a certain man's slave. I can't breathe, can't bloom until he makes me his.

My breath fogs the car window. I slash lines through the condensation, the freezing air outside seeping into my fingertip. Details of the world beyond flicker through. I'm almost there.

A year ago I wouldn't have recognized the woman I've become. That was before I discovered Crave. Before Demitri ripped the inhibitions clean off my body the first time he undressed me with his icy-blue eyes in the club that fateful night.

My skin heats with the mere thought of staring into them. The cab slows to a stop in front of the hotel entrance. He's only steps away now. Waiting for me with a plan. He always has a plan.

I pay my fare and hurry toward the entrance as quickly as I can in my stilettos. Thick snowflakes have begun to coat the sidewalk. Holiday bells ring faintly in the distance, and warm white lights wrap around the trees lining the busy street. The ambience tugs at my nostalgia for something more intimate. Someone to share a little of that magic with. But Demitri is too calculating for fairy tales. He's far too focused to let anything as superficial as a holiday distract him from getting what he wants. All I can do is hope it's me he wants tonight.

I take the elevator up and pause in front of the hotel room he reserved for tonight. I lift my hand, resting it silently against the door.

"Tonight," I whisper with a short nod.

Tonight will be the night. It has to be.

I exhale and hover the keycard over the sensor. It flashes green with a beep, and my heart does a hard thump as I open the door. Darkness fills the hallway leading into the suite. I walk toward the light inside.

Demitri paces into view. His tall, broad frame makes a daunting shadow on the opposite wall. His physical strength doesn't frighten me because he's never used it against me. If anything, I ache to know how he could.

He speaks into his phone, disrupting my budding fantasy. His tone is loud and brusque. I have no idea what he's saying, but the conversation sounds tense.

The door closes loudly behind me, and he halts his pacing. His gaze travels up and down the length of my body, warming me from the inside out. He rattles off more of his conversation in his native Czech, his tone a little less angry.

My focus is trained on his expression as he continues to pace. His light skin and hair, his chiseled features. A jaw that could cut through ice . . . and his lips. Full and framed with the promise of unimaginable pleasure.

I slip my heels off, one at a time. He lowers himself into the chair in the corner of the room. He doesn't have to say a word. One look and I know what he wants.

I walk toward him and kneel, ensuring my knees are a few inches apart and my mini dress is pulled high and taut. I place my palms on my thighs the way he likes. I resist the urge to stare up at him like a puppy and instead focus on the floor. At his dark leather shoes. The peek of gray socks that's shadowed by the deep-blue suit pants he's wearing. I've only ever seen him in a suit. He runs Crave, and while it might be a sex club, he's professional as hell as about it.

"*Čau*," he finally says before hanging up. He closes his eyes, sighs, and opens them again. "Kitten."

I smile. "Sir."

He runs his thumb back and forth over his lower lip, looking more pensive than hungry suddenly. "I didn't know if you'd come."

"It's just a little snow. It'll take more than that to keep me from our lessons."

His brows wrinkle. I'm not sure what it means, so I look down again. This time I focus on the pattern on the chair's ruffled upholstery. Gold and blue. Expensive. Not like the red leather at the club. There's no thumping beats here either. No depraved acts on display. Just us. The sound of our breathing. My heart beating in time to the pulse between my thighs. My thoughts drift to the first time I set eyes on Demitri there. He had no less effect on me then.

"What are you thinking about, *krásná*?" Demitri's voice is gentle, like a caress. I close my eyes and feel it skitter across my skin. *Beautiful.*

"I'm not allowed to say," I murmur.

We've been meeting this way for nearly a year. Every few weeks he arranges for lessons I've come to live for, anticipating each one like a child waits for Christmas. He's claimed damn near every spot on my body with his thick fingers and his gifted mouth. Without a doubt I've enjoyed every minute, but I'm teetering on the edge of desperation now. He won't tolerate begging, otherwise I'd chain myself to the bed until he took the last of me, giving me the ultimate gift.

He's silent a moment. "You can tell me your thoughts without begging."

I open my mouth to speak, but my lips are trembling and I fear my voice will too. My thoughts are an avalanche threatening everything I wish tonight could be.

He glides his foot over the carpet, between my knees, adding pressure to one side so I spread a little more for him. Then he lifts the toe of his shoe to touch my sex through my panties. The contact is blunt, the perfect amount of pressure to send a hard hit of desire through my veins. I inhale sharply.

"Answer me." His voice hardens with the command, which only makes me crazier.

I curl my hands into fists. I'm so wound up. It's been too long like this. What more do I need to do to show him my dedication? My commitment to being his and only his?

"I—I can't sleep, Demitri."

"Excuse me?"

I swallow hard and wince at the disapproval in his tone. "Sir." *Fuck.* Always with the rules. "This is torture."

"Is it? Do you think you know what torture feels like, kitten?"

For me, that's the only word that can sum up this agonizing journey to pure submission.

"All I can think about is what it's going to feel like. I'm obsessed with it. I can't think straight. I can't hold a conversation with someone without fantasizing about it."

He shifts forward so he's resting his forearms on his thighs. I fix on the sexy way his arms look under the rolled-up sleeves. His skin is a peachy white, his blond hair too light to compete with the corded muscles that run over his incredible body—the body I've yet to fully see and appreciate.

"What do you fantasize about?"

I blink out of my lusty appraisal of his physical attributes and cast my gaze down again. What if he'd taken me that first night at Crave? What if Charlotte hadn't interrupted us to take me home? Would I still be here, feeling as desperate as I do?

He tilts my chin until I'm staring straight into his hard gaze. "Use your words."

My lips thin, and I struggle to harness the pent-up frustration that's ready to bubble over. "I want you to fuck me, *Sir*. Is that clear enough for you?"

He pauses a beat. "Are you sure that's what you want?"

"Positive." A flutter of hope blossoms somewhere deep inside me that he's even asking.

"Are you sure you don't want me to make love to you instead?"

My jaw falls open before I snap it shut quickly. Our conversations always revolve around the mechanics of this relationship. My training. His expectations. My routine insubordination. Love never comes up, but one mention of it tonight drains me of my complaints. Love is a frame I'm too afraid to see this relationship through.

"I want what you want," I say, barely hearing myself.

"No." He draws his hand lower, cuffing the column of my throat gently. "No, you don't."

"I want to please you."

He purses his lips slightly and leans back in the chair, taking the gift of his touch with him. "You crave the pleasure I give you."

"What's wrong with that?"

He has the audacity to smirk. How can he be so impossibly gorgeous and infuriating at once?

"This isn't about pleasure."

I throw my arms up, breaking my pose. "Then what is this about?"

He chuckles softly before the smile fades. He seems thoughtful and suddenly distracted. He brushes a dot of lint from his pants, absently stroking his thumb over the place where his obscene thigh muscle meets his knee. God, how

I ache to touch him, to discover him in all the ways he's discovered me. Run my tongue over every inch—

"Peace."

"Huh?" I lift my gaze from the fantastic bulge between his legs to his eyes.

"This." He gestures between us. "You on your knees. Me here, expecting you to be without having to say a word. This isn't about your pleasure or your orgasms, though you have no idea the satisfaction they bring me. This is about your submission. The peace it gives you. The emptiness it creates in your thoughts. The trust it demands. Submission is the main course. The orgasm is just dessert, kitten."

I sigh and slump my shoulders in defeat. I get it. At least I think I do, but I'm too frustrated right now to detach from the physical longing he's inspired and get my head in the right place. If he would just take me, make me his once and for all, I could finally be the good girl he wants. The best little sex slave he's ever had.

And he's had them. Before I'd been introduced to Demitri, I'd seen the other girls from the shadows of Crave, kneeling at his feet, staring up at him with doe eyes and wet pussies, worshiping him like a king the way I am now. How could I blame them?

"Submitting to me means I'll fuck you with my mind before you'll ever feel my cock." He says the words almost absently. Almost like he's said them before to someone else who was once begging at his feet.

I'm jealous and furious and aching. I'm a fucking mess, and it's entirely his doing.

"Then fuck my mind, Demitri. I don't care what you do. Tie me up. Flog me. Mark me. Just . . . *take me*. I'd beg you all night for it, but you hate when I do."

He *tsks*, his gaze melting over me like warm chocolate. "You have so much to learn, kitten. I don't play that way. And for the record, your begging satisfies me deeply. I just don't want you to waste your air when it won't sway me right now. You'll have lots of time to beg, and I'll enjoy it thoroughly when the time is right."

That's it. I can't take a minute more. I push to my feet and turn to get my shoes. I hear him rise from the chair behind me.

"Where are you going?"

Steadying myself on the bureau, I hook on one of my stilettos. "Home. I have a perfectly good vibrator that will get me off if you don't want to."

Without warning, he lassos his arm around my waist and tosses me onto the bed. I bounce with the force of it and open my mouth, ready to tell him to go to hell, until he starts unbuttoning his shirt, a different kind of fire in his eyes.

"You want me to fuck you?"

The way he says it, the question feels more like a threat. I sink back onto the bedspread, cautiously hopeful. My heart races. He's pissed off, but I'm not sure if it's enough for me to stop him if he's finally ready to give me what I want.

I trap my lower lip between my teeth and nod, unwilling to let my smartass mouth screw this up.

He yanks the crisp white shirt off, revealing his massive shoulders and chiseled abdomen. I bite my lip harder. He climbs over me, and I fall back. Then his lips come down hard on mine. I lace my arms around his neck and draw him closer. He settles between my thighs, and it's divine—the pressure of his body pushing me into the mattress, the hard ridge of his erection teasing me through our clothes. I sigh. Every time he touches me, it's bliss. Water in the desert. But it's never enough to truly quench my thirst.

I lift my hips and add to the friction between us. His groan rumbles through me. I feel it in a rush to my clit before he finds his way there, pushing my panties aside. I arch against him, urging him on. More, more, more…

Then he shoves two fingers deep inside me, deeper than he's ever gone.

"Ow!" I widen my eyes at the sudden sting.

"What about this, kitten?"

He doesn't pull away. He adds more pressure, enough that I almost give in to the urge to scoot away and ease it.

"Did you think I didn't know? Did you think I couldn't feel it when I was making you come all those times?"

I bite my lip so hard it might bleed. I've never made a point to advertise my virginity. Charlotte doesn't even know. It's always been easier to find friends to get into trouble with when they didn't think I was so innocent. But for all my thrill-seeking, I could never bring myself to go through with it. At least not with the blue bloods who were prowling DC for their next hookup. Not until Demitri seduced me with a look. The first command off his lips, and I was his.

But now he seems even more pissed than before, and I wish like hell I'd told him.

"I wasn't trying to keep it from you," I lie.

He pushes harder, and I wince at the discomfort.

"You want me to break it with my fingers or my cock?"

"Your cock," I whisper.

"Then tell me the truth when I ask you a question."

I take a few shaky breaths and fight tears. I'm so angry with myself. "I didn't want to scare you away."

"Do I look like someone who's easily intimidated?"

He withdraws from my tender tissues, which is both a relief and its own kind of agony.

"I'm not like the other girls. The subs you usually go for."

He manages a dry laugh. "You have no idea what you're talking about."

I wilt. Having Demitri this close, pinning me to the bed, I feel so exposed, unable to escape the truth he now knows. I turn my head and squeeze my eyes closed.

His lips are a warm whisper along my neck, and I relax a little at the tender touch.

"I can't wait to break you, *krásná*. And when I do, you're going to bleed for me. I'm not going to slow down. I'm going to kiss your tears and fuck you harder. Your mind and your body. Until you can't tell the difference between the pain and the pleasure."

He sinks his teeth into my neck, and I shudder. His promise is electricity lighting up under my skin, willing me closer, tighter, seeking his mouth again. We're deep in another kiss when a shrill sound severs the contact. My purse vibrates once, then twice. He lifts himself up and hands it to me. I check it quickly. It's a text from Charlotte.

> *Can't wait for you to visit! I'm working*
> *on plans for New Year's Eve. Let me*
> *know if you want to bring a date.*
> *Zane's already in bodyguard mode*
> *about it,*
> *so a distraction would be great!*

She appends the message with an eye-roll emoji. A weak smile tugs at my lips. I toss the phone down. The little spark of excitement I feel about seeing my best friend in New York is quickly replaced with my own frustration for not silencing my phone. Because now the moment is gone.

Demitri has his shirt on and is buttoning it up again. "I should go."

I frown. "Why?"

"I have work to do."

"One night away from the club isn't going to kill you."

He shrugs into his suit coat and comes to me. "Something came up that needs my attention."

I refrain from reiterating how much *I* need his attention, because I can tell it's not enough to make him stay. I stand, wishing I had my heels on. He's so much taller, but he brings his arms around me and pulls me to him. Lifting me off my toes, he finds my mouth once more and kisses me with the passion I'm desperate to know more of. I never want it to end, and then it does.

"Good night, kitten. I'll call you for your next lesson, okay?"

I sigh and nod, trying not to show him how hard it is to say goodbye.

CHAPTER THREE

Master.

That's what they call me. Plenty of submissives have surrendered to me over the years. Never once have I been completely consumed by one... My kitten.

From the moment Katherine Harrison stepped into my world, she's been the exception to every rule, a very sexy distraction that I didn't need. Choosing her as my new plaything was about as safe as playing a game of Russian Roulette with a fully loaded gun.

Her father holds enough political power to crush any man he doesn't approve of. I'm certain he wouldn't approve of anything I've been doing to his only daughter. I'm dancing with danger. A little bit of danger never stopped me before, though. Especially now that I want Katherine in a way that would terrify most... in a way that should terrify her.

Leaving her in the hotel room was far from easy. She wears me down a little more every time we're together. Her virginity should deter me more than anything, but the circumstance only makes me obsess more over what I can't have. What I refuse to take.

I've held back for months, feeding her hopes and desires just enough to keep her coming back for more. And as long as she keeps entertaining our little lessons, she stays away from Crave, which keeps both of us out of trouble with her father. Because she's too spirited to take no for an answer.

I don't want to turn her away either. I've come to love this game of *Cat and Mouse* that we're playing—even if the current heavy ache in my balls suggests otherwise.

I approach Crave's private back entrance, slide my access card into the reader, and turn the handle on the door. The smell of pussy and sex greets me. My cock instantly hardens, and I fight to compose myself. Being here tonight is going to be torture.

Of course, I have the power to do something about it. Crave is literally crawling with willing subs. With one snap of my fingers, I can have my pick of any one of a dozen women, a few of which are already eye-fucking me as I pass through the club's main floor.

There's just one problem. None of them are Katherine. I've been fantasizing about training her sinfully sweet mouth all day. I would have, too, except Ronan called and shot that plan all to hell.

Relieved to reach my office, I open the door to find a man sitting behind my desk. Ronan Lockhart is tilted back in my expensive leather chair with his feet propped up on the edge of the mahogany. He's staring at the security monitor that hangs on the adjacent wall like it's some sort of porn video. In his right hand is a half-drained glass of my most expensive bourbon. The nine-hundred-and-seventy-five-dollar bottle of Parker's Heritage is uncorked on my desk. Friend or not, he seriously needs to learn his place.

I walk around to where he is sitting and knock his feet off my desk, causing him to spill some of his drink.

"What the hell, D? This shit's expensive." He wipes the bourbon off his arm with his shirt sleeve.

"Yeah, I know. I'm the one who fucking bought it." I snatch the glass out of his hand. "Get the hell out of my chair."

Ronan stands, glowering. His six-foot-three frame matches mine in height, but my thirty extra pounds of muscle give me quite an advantage over him. He can challenge me all he wants, but he knows how a showdown between us will shake out.

"What crawled up your ass?"

As he walks off, I turn the glass up, finishing it in one gulp. "I had important plans tonight before you ruined them. If I'd known you were coming here to drink up all my booze, I would've stayed where I was. I left a beautiful, needy woman for this meeting."

"Well, excuse me for interrupting your fuck fest with the precious feline. But this meeting is more important."

"It better be."

Ronan's expression turns solemn. "It's Lennox."

Lennox Novak.

One name. That's all it takes for my blood to boil. The monster inside me rises to the surface—one that's capable of unspeakable things. The version of me that Katherine's never seen and never will.

I slam the empty tumbler down so hard on the desk, I'm shocked when the glass doesn't shatter. "What about him?"

"My sources are telling me he's here … in DC."

"The Czech government is watching him like a hawk. He's not even allowed to leave the country."

"*How* he got here shouldn't be your concern. It's the *why* part."

My eyes narrow. "You and I both know why he's here."

He nods. "It's just a matter of time before he tries to make contact. And when he does, I need you to accept a meeting with him. If we plan this out well, the agency can bring him down and we can put him away for good."

I shake my head. "That's not going to happen. I won't agree to any meeting."

Ronan gives me an incredulous look. "The man murdered your parents and left your sister for dead. He's been untouchable for years. And now that he's practically in our backyard, you don't want to do something about it? Are you insane?"

Ronan's eagerness to bring Lennox down is fueled by more than a desire to help avenge my family. Eliminating one of Eastern Europe's largest criminals would be the ultimate career boost for him. Ronan might be my most trusted friend, but he values his career with the CIA just as much as his alliance with me. The intel I've been feeding him over the years has already helped him rise in the ranks at the agency. I've never minded helping him on other cases. But this one is personal.

Very fucking personal.

"I can't be in the same room with him and not put a bullet in his head, Ronan. There's no way I can meet with him and not lose control. And if I lose control, I'll start a war that puts people I care about at risk. I left that life behind for a reason. Adriana has paid enough for my sins."

I'm not about to bring danger to my sister's front door. Not after everything she's been through. She's been happy here in DC for a long time, and I plan to keep it that way.

"Don't you think I want that too? I would never put Addi in danger. I would never let anything happen to her."

Ronan drops down into the chair across from my desk. Calling her "Addi" is a bit too personal for my liking. I'm ready to press him on it when my phone chimes with an incoming text from Katherine.

*Can't sleep. Thinking of stopping
by the club for a while.*

As much as I'd love to pick back up where we left off on her training lesson, I'm too amped up over Ronan's news. And I don't want her anywhere near Crave. Not tonight. Not ever.

I exhale a regretful sigh and type my reply.

Not tonight, kitten.

When I look up from my phone, Ronan is studying me hard.

I narrow my gaze. "Is there a problem?"

"You've gotten too close to her."

"I don't remember asking your opinion."

Ronan doesn't back down. "I'm not giving you my opinion, D. I'm simply stating facts. You've got feelings for her. Admit it."

I set my phone on the desk, trying my best to appear impassive. Except Ronan is exactly right. From the first time I laid eyes on Katherine Harrison, I knew she'd be different. Her curiosity drew me in—the way she'd watch the club from the dark corners. Always watching, never playing . . . until I tempted her to play with me.

I had to seek her out after that first encounter. I couldn't resist. I couldn't stop feeding the infatuation. Now I'm every bit as preoccupied as she is with the things we haven't done. I want to discover all her insecurities, test all her limits. I want to fucking break her. The only problem is I'm afraid she's going to break me first.

"She's a submissive in training, nothing more," I say in a clipped tone. I don't know who I'm trying to fool. Even I don't believe my own words.

Ronan straightens in his chair, a smug smile spreading across his face. "Oh, yeah? Prove it. Pick a girl from the floor and take her to one of the playrooms."

I glare at him. "I don't have to prove a fucking thing to you."

Ronan shoots me a triumphant smirk and leans back in his chair. "You just did, *kamaráde*."

CHAPTER FOUR

Buzz. Buzz. Buzz.

Letting out a loud groan, I blindly pat my hand next to me in search for my vibrating phone. I open my eyes, and the time displayed on the bright screen slowly comes into focus.

9:02 a.m.

Shit.

I snooze the alarm and sink into my pillow long enough to feel the fatigue pull me back under. I only caught a few hours of sleep last night. Thoughts of other subs satisfying Demitri's needs kept me up to the point of exhaustion. I have no right to be jealous, but I am. He had to be needing a release. He was still hard when he left me, going to the one place where he'd be surrounded by horny, willing subs. He can't possibly be satisfied from what little I give him.

My heart twists. Just the thought of him with another woman makes me sick. Why won't he treat me like the others?

Because I'm still a virgin.

His rejections make sense now. I thought I could hide

my inconvenient secret, but I should have known someone like him would know instantly that I've never been with a man. No one knows my body better than he does. But no matter how hard I try to please him, he won't take me the way I want him to.

The alarm goes off again. God, how does ten minutes pass so damn fast?

I turn twenty-two today, and I'm running out of time to make it to the restaurant in time to meet my parents. I throw off the covers, bolt up out of the bed, and quickly get dressed. I cinch my hair into a low bun, slip on the diamond earrings my grandmother gifted me for my sixteenth birthday, and quickly check my appearance in the mirror to ensure I'll pass inspection.

Satisfied, I grab my cherry-red peacoat and take the elevator down.

"Good morning, Miss Harrison." Derrick, the building's young doorman, winks as I pass by him in the lobby.

I smirk and raise my hand to hail a cab. "Morning, Derrick."

I praise the taxi gods when a car slows at the curb. Derrick opens the door for me and ushers me in, his hand firm at the base of my spine.

"Thanks," I say tightly.

By some miracle, I make it to the restaurant with a minute to spare. In my father's desperate attempt at trying to make us appear to be a normal family, my presence at our monthly Sunday brunches has become mandatory. Of course, nothing about our lives is remotely normal.

My father's rising legal and political career destroyed any semblance of normalcy years ago. Now my parents pencil in quality time with me on their calendar like a routine dental appointment. Except these fake attempts to appear to be something we aren't make me resent them that much more. I'm so tired of pretending, tired of acting.

As the host leads me to the table, I run my palm down my navy-blue shift dress and plaster my best fake smile on my face—the one that often fools even me into believing I can be the perfect daughter in a perfect family. But we're not perfect. We are far from it.

My father stands to greet me and leans in for a brief hug. I wait for him to acknowledge my birthday, but he doesn't. I give him a quick kiss on the cheek and glance over to the empty seat beside him where my mother normally sits. Her customary mimosa is also missing from the table.

I carefully situate myself into the chair across from him. "Where's Mom?"

My father gives me a smile that doesn't reach his eyes. "Your mother decided to stay a few extra days in Naples. I guess she doesn't want to give up the sunrays yet. She sends her love, of course."

Swallowing down the hurt, I nod and reach for the tall menu in front of me.

I can't believe it. They forgot my birthday. Again.

I quietly berate myself for getting my hopes up. I've learned to shoulder the disappointment so many times before. I don't know why I thought this time would be any different.

The waiter takes our order, and then my father and I resume our awkward silence.

He takes a sip of his coffee, studying me hard. "How's school going?"

"Fine," I say. "I really enjoyed my classes this semester."

It's not a lie, but his face wrinkles with a faint grimace.

"You know, when your mother and I agreed to lease you that apartment, it came with the understanding that you would act responsibly and keep your grades up in school."

A defensive knot forms in my stomach. "I have been. Grades from finals haven't all come in yet, but my grade point average has been a perfect 4.0 all term."

He leans back in his chair and crosses his arms. "Do you expect me to believe that you can maintain that kind of average with the late hours you've been keeping?"

My stomach drops. Has he had one of his men following me? If he ever were to find out about my relationship with Demitri, there's no telling what he would do.

"Where is all of this coming from? I don't understand."

"Let's just say that the doorman at your building has proven to be very informative."

Anger surges through me. "Are you kidding me? You have the doorman spying on me now?"

My father matches my glare but doesn't acknowledge the accusation. The waiter arrives, sets our food down on the table, and quickly leaves us alone. With my appetite now gone, I push the plate of French toast away from me.

"Since when did you start caring about my whereabouts? You and Mom are never home."

The vein in his temple protrudes the way it always does when he gets riled up about something. "I didn't bust my ass to get where I am to have you tarnish this family's name with your wild-child behavior. Either it stops immediately or you can figure out how to pay rent on your own. Is that understood?"

"But—"

He raises his hand to stop me. "From now on, you are to be home by midnight. No exceptions."

"Midnight?" My voice comes out in a loud shriek. "You can't do this to me. I'm an adult."

"Then start acting like one instead of a spoiled brat. You want to live in one of the nicest apartments in the city and enjoy the expense account we allow you, then you play by my rules."

I clench my teeth so hard I worry I might crack one. I'd do almost anything for a mimosa, but the last thing I need are more criticisms. So I pick at my breakfast, sip my tea, and listen patiently while my father tells me about his travel plans for the week, as if they have any bearing on my life whatsoever.

Twenty minutes later, he signals the waiter for the check, and I begin to count the seconds until I can escape his presence. Finally, after we hug goodbye, I excuse myself to the ladies room instead of walking him out.

At the marble bathroom counter, I stare at myself in the mirror, disheartened at the girl staring back at me. I've lived under his thumb all my life. Him threatening the small amount of freedom I've been able to negotiate is nothing short of devastating. And humiliating. Twenty-two years of life, and I'm this pathetic.

My eyes water. I reach for a Kleenex, determined to pull myself together and not let my father's ultimatum ruin my whole day. I freeze at the sound of heels coming across the room, suddenly aware that I haven't been alone. I glance up in the mirror and lock eyes with a beautiful tall blonde. Her expression is soft with concern as she approaches the counter.

I avert my eyes and begin dabbing the tissue at the puffy circles, thankful my makeup isn't a wreck from all this upset.

She gently places her hand on my shoulder. "Are you okay?"

I relax when I hear Demitri's accent in her voice. I've never shared my feelings about my parents with him, but for some reason I wish I could now. Even as I think it, I berate myself for wanting something more meaningful with him. Something he may not be capable of giving me.

I manage a nod. "Yes, I'm fine. Just having a bad day. Bad birthday, actually," I finish with a dry laugh.

The woman gives me a sympathetic look. "I'm sorry. Boy trouble?"

I don't feel like touching that topic, so I opt for the truth. "My parents forgot my birthday. It's no big deal."

The concern in her expression deepens. "That's horrible."

I shrug. "It stings. But it's not the first time. I'm sure it won't be the last. Really, I'm fine."

She bites down on her plump bottom lip and then

glances down at her watch. When she looks back up, her eyes brighten. "My brother is supposed to meet me at the bar for some drinks. How about you join us? His treat, of course." She winks.

I tuck my hair behind my ear and shake my head. "Oh, no. Thank you, but—"

"I insist. It's your birthday. We have to celebrate."

"I don't know…"

Before I can argue with her, she hooks her arm into mine and leads me out of the bathroom.

"Just one drink," she says with a wink.

I don't know why I'm accepting her offer, except that I could really use a drink…and a friend. Even if we've only just met, I'm already attracted to her warmth and energy. I tell myself it has nothing to do with the accent that haunts my dreams.

We bypass the main restaurant and enter into a quieter and darker bar area of the establishment. She leads me past the slick mahogany bar, and we settle into one of the wraparound booths. We order drinks. A cranberry vodka for her. A bourbon neat for me.

"My name's Adriana, by the way." She extends a perfectly manicured hand across to me. Even though she is a complete stranger, I find myself at total ease around her.

I shake her hand and smile back at her. "I'm Ka—"

"Oh!"

Adriana's expression brightens, and as it does, goose bumps break out across my skin. As if on command, my attention is drawn to the front of the bar. I lock on to

Demitri's icy-blue stare.

God, what those eyes do to me.

The rest of my body reacts as he strolls toward us. Confident. Commanding, even from this distance. Every cell in my body immediately acknowledges his presence in the room. I pulse and tighten and quietly ache to feel every inch of his dominance.

I squirm in my seat, feeling the delicious heaviness growing deep in my core. Dropping my gaze down his body, I take in his startling transformation. Instead of his normal expensive designer suit, he's wearing a formfitting black shirt and dark denim jeans. I can't get over how different he looks. But why is he here?

"*Bratr!*" Adriana scoots out of the booth and throws her arms around Demitri's neck. He returns her embrace, keeping his eyes firmly fixed on me the entire time.

Shit. The accent. The fair features. Adriana is Demitri's sister. I ignore the pang in my chest that comes with the realization that we know so little about each other still. After all this time...

Adriana places her hand on Demitri's chest, following his tractor-beam gaze to me. "I hope you don't mind, but I invited my new friend to join us."

"Hello, Katherine," he says in his sexy deep voice.

Adriana's mouth gapes open. "Wait a minute. You mean you two already know each other?"

I bite my lip and try to school my features and all the ways this man turns me inside out. "You could say that," I say, my voice faltering.

CHAPTER FIVE

On any given day, I exist in two worlds—two very different worlds. Crave, and the real world. They rarely intersect.

As much as Katherine suddenly being within arm's reach is a welcome development, seeing her beside my sister is unsettling. I've always made sure Adriana knew nothing about Crave or my lifestyle. And Katherine was never supposed to know anything about me outside this club. Yet here I am, sitting in a booth across from both of them. In this moment, it's become painfully obvious that I have never been more fucked.

"How did you two meet?" Adriana looks expectantly between Katherine and me.

"I was about to ask you the same question," I respond, hoping by the time my sister hits the bottom of her drink, she'll forget to ask me again.

Adriana's enthusiasm dims a fraction. "Well…"

"I was having kind of a rough morning. She took pity on me in the ladies room," Katherine says, her voice taking on a sad quality that stabs at my insides. "And here we are."

Adriana nudges her shoulder gently. "Stop it. Everyone should be able to toast to their birthday. How old are you anyway?"

I swallow hard. Her birthday… I feel like a bastard for not knowing. No, I feel like possibly the worst scum of the earth. Especially considering the way I brushed her off last night. I'd left us both unsatisfied. Both needing so much more.

"I'm twenty-two," she answers, not meeting my eyes.

"Cheers to that." Adriana lifts her glass, clinks it with Katherine's, and polishes off the last of her drink as the server returns.

She asks for another round, and I order the same as Katherine, resolved to end this party as soon as I finish. I have shit to do and a business to run, but having Katherine this close overwhelms everything else. I'm already itching to haul her into my lap and kiss her breathless.

She looks different. A little tired but polished and expensive. Like a politician's daughter. Someone who shouldn't be spending her nights with the likes of me.

"If you weren't so young, I'd totally set you up with Demitri. But he's old and serious. No fun at all. He's obsessed with work. Isn't that right?" Adriana juts her elbow into my ribs.

I sigh. Jesus, what kind of Pandora's box have I opened with these two?

"What do you do for work?" Katherine licks her bottom lip.

My cock notices.

"Imports and exports," Adriana says with a hiccup. "What about you?"

"I'm an undergraduate student at George Washington University. One more semester, and I'm a free woman," she answers with a tense smile, making me wonder about the truth beneath her words. Everything she's not saying out loud.

For the next hour, I listen as the two women interview each other on everything from Katherine's classes to their favorite nail polish colors. If I were a passing stranger, I'd guess they were best friends. Because of what my sister endured with Lennox, she's never trusted many people enough to let them into her life. I couldn't have been more blown away to see her chatting with another woman when I stepped into the bar. And not just any woman. My kitten.

"I just can't believe the two of you know each other. That is crazy. Wait . . . You never told me how you two met," Adriana says as she finishes off her third cranberry vodka.

Three is always her limit. Anything past that, and I know I will be carrying her up to her apartment. No way that is happening today. I'd already shot a quick text to Ronan to pick Adriana up and get her home safe so I can get Katherine alone.

Except she's downed the rest of her bourbon and is ordering another. I shoot her a look of disapproval, but she doesn't seem to notice.

"Maybe you should take it easy on those," I warn. Another night I would have made every excuse to get back to the club for work, but after watching her talk and laugh and just *be* . . . Now I have other plans. And I want her sober for all of it. Her birthday might have started out shitty, but I'm about to make up for it.

"Maybe you shouldn't worry about it," Katherine shoots back.

Adriana giggles. She has no idea the game we're playing.

My cock hardens at the thought of making Katherine pay for that comment later. But the more alcohol she drinks, the darker her mood becomes. I'm not sure I like this version of her.

"D, what's up?" Like clockwork, Ronan plunks into the remaining space in the booth beside me. He lifts his chin to Adriana. "Addi."

She smiles, and I swear new color rises to her cheeks. I tell myself it's the alcohol and try to ignore the way Ronan's looking at her like he wants to do more than get her home safe. I've been fantasizing about all the ways I want to scandalize Katherine for over an hour. I've got sex on the brain, and I'm probably just projecting.

"What are you doing here?" Adriana plays with a loose wisp of hair.

"I was in the neighborhood. Do you need a ride home?"

She glances to Katherine as if she's unsure.

"I'm fine," Katherine says. "This was possibly the best birthday celebration I've had in years. Thanks."

She smiles and hugs my sister tightly.

Ronan shoots me a questioning look. Fuck, this looks awful. If he suspected I was getting too close to Katherine before, arguing otherwise is pointless now.

"Coincidence," I say quietly.

His face splits with a smile as he rises.

I inch out of the booth, and Adriana follows. We hug goodbye, and the second she and Ronan are gone, the bartender comes by with Katherine's drink. I fish a couple hundreds out of my wallet and drop them on his tray.

"That should cover it."

"Yes, sir." He thanks me a couple times before doubling back, leaving us alone again.

I extend my hand to Katherine. "Time to go."

"I'm not done." She leans back and crosses her arms.

"Yes, you are. Get up, or I'm carrying you out of here."

"Where are we going?"

"My place," I say. I pull into the garage under my building and park.

She hesitates long enough for me to open the door for her. She stares up at me, confusion plain in her eyes. "Your place?"

"You didn't think I lived at Crave, did you?"

"No, but..." She shakes her head like she doesn't understand and gets out.

We take the elevator to the penthouse, and she walks in slowly. Several minutes pass in silence as she assesses the apartment. I follow her gaze, wondering what details she's taking in. I've owned the condo for a few years, and while I enjoy the space, I've kept it purposely bare. White walls and surfaces. Natural wood and sparse decor. I wanted my time away from work to be just that … A departure from the business I've lived and breathed for so long.

She approaches the granite island in the kitchen. "I don't feel like I'm supposed to be here for some reason."

I laugh softly. "I don't bring girls here. That's what the club is for." I take a bottle of water out of the fridge and hand it to her. "Here, drink."

Darkness passes over her eyes. She snatches the water bottle out of my hand and twists off the top before guzzling a few gulps down.

I cross my arms and lean against the refrigerator. "Is there a problem, kitten? Or does the bourbon bring your claws out?"

She regards me for a moment. I brace myself for one of her sarcastic comments. I'm not prepared for what comes next.

"What do I mean to you?"

Her question is a swift punch to the gut. *Fuck me.*

I push off and pace into the living room. She follows me. When I turn to face her, she's a few inches away. I'm aching to haul her against me and kiss away this conversation. Make her come until the question that lingers between us fades into the background. But deep down I know she deserves an answer. She's not inherently clingy. She's not as desperate as half the subs who would crawl for me at Crave. She's the Attorney General's daughter, and I've been feeding my obsession with her for far too long.

"You're too good for this life, kitten." I brush my hand over her cheek and touch the sparkling diamonds decorating her ears. "Too beautiful for the things I want to do to you."

"You think because I'm wearing my grandmother's diamonds that I can't kneel for you?"

The visual those words give me is almost more than I handle.

"Crave is an escape. It's not who you are, which is why I've kept you away from there. But this thing between us . . . It doesn't need a name because it's . . ." Folly. Impermanent. Doomed to end.

She stares, her gaze searching mine a moment until it seems like she finally understands. Then she turns and heads for the door.

I follow her and take her arm, spinning her toward me.

"You're not leaving like this."

Her jaw sets tightly. "Really? It's my birthday, and I can spend it how I'd like."

I cinch her closer to me and run my palms along the expensive fabric of her dress. She looks like she should be going to a charity luncheon, but all I can think about is how I can dirty her up.

I brush my lips over hers and move to her neck. "I haven't given you your present yet."

She inhales and releases a few shallow breaths, her body melting into me a little more. I slide my hand under her dress, unable to stop myself from seeking evidence of her arousal, even though I can already smell her. Feel her heat. Sense that she's on fire for me, ready to give me everything.

"Demitri . . . don't."

I can sense her curling into herself, untangling her

emotions from me even as her body says something else. I stare down at her, needing to read her face for everything she's not saying.

She blinks up at me from under her soft lashes, a sad defiance swimming behind her eyes. "There's only one gift I want from you."

I tense inside. I could satisfy her a thousand ways, but not the way she wants.

She seems to know this. Placing her hand gently against my chest, she steps back and reaches for her purse.

"Kitten. Don't go."

She shakes her head, her expression tight. "I can't stay. Not like this. Not anymore."

Suddenly I'm stricken with panic. Because this doesn't feel like she's saying *until next time.* It feels like she's saying *never again.*

I catch up to her at the door. "Katherine."

She pauses at the command in my voice. If she only knew how much desperation is behind it.

"Look at me."

She has one hand on the door, the other wrapped defensively around her midsection. All of it is killing me. Her back to me. All the body language that's telling me—screaming at me—that she's done with this game.

"If I look at you, what am I going to see?"

I release an agonizing breath. "A man who doesn't want to watch you leave."

She shakes her head.

"Kitten," I whisper. I lean down and brush a kiss to her

neck, shamelessly breathing her in as I do.

Then she's turning the knob. "You don't want it enough."

CHAPTER SIX

Somewhere between Demitri's place and mine, I sober. The bourbon may have brought my emotions a little too close to the surface, but I don't regret the strength it gave me to leave. I may have been slowly falling in love with the dominant side of him all these months, but I'm done letting him pretend to master a relationship that's going nowhere. After today, I realize that my heart just can't take it.

The cab pulls up to the entrance of my building. The relief I should feel is swallowed up when I see Derrick's face. His crooked smile is directed at another resident passing through the front doors. He holds the door open as I approach him.

"Miss Harrison."

"You have real nerve."

His smile slips. "I'm sorry. I don't understand—"

"Tipping my father off when I come home late? Really?"

He opens his mouth to speak but shuts it again before any words can slip out. The guilt on his face unmistakable. All this time I thought he was a harmless flirt. I never pegged him for a snitch.

"I hope whatever he's paying you to keep tabs on me is enough to keep you afloat when I tell your boss that you're sharing personal information about residents."

He presses his lips together tightly. I move past him, satisfied I've landed my blow. Except I can hear him on my heels. I mash the elevator button and try to ignore his presence. Except he's too close. I can hear him breathing a couple of feet away. I can feel the force of his stare on me.

Finally I meet it with a glare. "Can I help you?"

"You should think very carefully about the threats you're making." His voice is low.

I let out a laugh. "You're kidding, right?"

"Your dad's not the only one who might be interested to know about your comings and goings. That's all I'm saying."

My jaw feels like it might unhinge. "Are you actually threatening me?"

"Not at all. I'm just giving you some friendly advice, Miss Harrison. We've always been friendly, haven't we?"

I'm two seconds from slapping the condescending look off his face when the elevator dings and the doors slide open. I step through and hit the button for my floor. I can't get away from this conversation fast enough. Away from this slimeball my father's entrusted to follow my every move. Somehow I'm not entirely surprised that he's managed to plant a spy—a disloyal one at that—in my building.

Back in my apartment, I toss my coat and purse on the designer bench in the entryway. I love this apartment. I love most everything in it too. But in this moment, it hardly feels like home.

I go to my bedroom and undress, trying not to think about how naked and satisfied I could be right now if I hadn't left Demitri's the way I did. The thought of exploring more of his apartment, getting tangled in his sheets, and learning a little more about the man behind the cold exterior is both intoxicating and heartbreaking. Now I'll never know.

I turn on the shower and step in when the spray turns warm. The water pelts me, creating an endless assault of heat and steam. Some of the tension begins to release from my muscles. In its place comes something worse, though. Sadness. Disappointment. Despair.

I'm twenty-two. I'm in love with a Dominant who doesn't love me. My parents have no idea who I really am. Worse, they don't seem to care. But they've raised me to eat from their palms in exchange for obedience. Obedience I'm not sure I can offer anymore. Not when I'm this restless. This unsure.

The sting of emotion starts in my throat, but the tears disappear in the shower's stream. God, I'm such a mess.

When the water turns cold, I dry off and collapse into my bed. I check my phone, a little more heartbroken to see no new messages from Demitri. Fresh tears threaten just as the phone begins to vibrate with an incoming Facetime call. Charlotte.

I think about ignoring it, but right now, I need to hear my best friend's voice.

"Hey, Charlotte." I muster a smile that I hope seems genuine.

"Happy, happy birthday!" she sings through her phone. "I'm at an opening tonight, but I wanted to make sure I saw your gorgeous face before things got too hectic here." The fact that she remembered my birthday—when my own parents had not—is too overwhelming. The tears finally spill over.

Charlotte's sweet smile falls. "Kat? What's wrong? Why are you crying?"

I take a couple more tissues off the bedside table and try to explain through the sobs I'm trying to swallow. "Everything is a mess right now. My parents forgot my birthday. Again."

"What is wrong with them?" Charlotte huffs.

"I don't know. I honestly thought that was why they had scheduled brunch for today. My mom didn't even come, and my dad basically threatened to take away my apartment unless I stop going out at night. He's imposing a strict curfew."

"A curfew? But you're twenty-two!"

"That doesn't seem to matter to him. He's got the doorman to my building watching me like a hawk."

"God, I hate so much that I'm not there with you right now. I'll see you soon, though. A couple more weeks."

I nod sadly. "I know. I got your text."

"Are you thinking of bringing anyone?"

I shake my head, biting my lower lip to keep from saying anything more.

"Kat."

"What?"

She tilts her head. "I know that look."

"What look?"

"You're thinking about Demitri again. You get this look on your face every time. Something between dreamy and totally gutted."

I laugh. "That's . . . strangely accurate." My mouth turns into a sad smile. "He's just a dream of something I thought might be able to take me away from all this. My dad's world. This life. You know how it goes."

She nods. If anyone knows, she does. Except she found her prince. Somehow they found a life outside this rat race. They found love.

"Maybe you should see him," she presses.

There's so much she doesn't know. The last update I gave her was that Demitri and I had exchanged a few texts, toying with the idea of meeting up. But once the lessons started, I never told her about them. She kept asking about him, so I kept talking about him. I just left out all the details. The thousand little moments that are weighing so heavily on me now.

Charlotte frowns when the room she's in suddenly grows too loud to continue our conversation. "Listen, honey, I've got to go, but I promise to call you back later. Don't let them ruin your day. I love you!"

"Love you, too." I barely have time to say the words before our call is disconnected. Hearing her voice will probably be the highlight of my day, but somehow I feel lonelier now than I did before.

CHAPTER SEVEN

I'm going to be here all night. I don't even care, because there's nothing waiting for me at my apartment. Not solace. Certainly not Katherine. Even though a few minutes with her in the space made me want to keep her there. For a lot longer than I had the right to ask for.

I should let her go. I *did* let her go. Something I should have done a long time ago, instead of stringing her along. I've been fooling myself too. I thought I had things under control, but the more time goes by without seeing her, the deeper her absence affects me. We've spent days apart before. Weeks even. Nothing I couldn't handle, because I knew I'd see her again. Now I'm not sure.

I should have reached out to her by now. But the bastard in me keeps rationalizing that if she's feeling half the devastation I am, the heartbreak will be enough to keep her away from Crave. Out of trouble.

I sift through the massive pile of paperwork on my desk, trying to stay focused on the shit that really needs my attention. As I sort through the new membership requests and purchasing invoices, I grow more frustrated. Most of this should have been dealt with weeks ago. Obviously my priorities have shifted.

Ronan's words echo in my mind. I have to get myself in check. Only, I have no idea how I'll do it when I can't stop thinking about the brunette across town.

A hard knock on my office door only detonates my anger. "What?"

"Demi."

I recognize the seductive purr of her voice before she comes into view. It's been three years since I laid eyes on Natasha Novak. I'm not sure I'm entirely prepared to see her now. Not when I've got kitten in my blood stream, monopolizing every thought and vision.

I narrow my eyes on my unexpected guest.

Natasha plumps her lips and rests her hand on her cocked hip. "Baby, you look stressed."

Her tone is heavy like her perfume permeating the room. Just one small whiff sends all the painful memories rushing at me with full force.

"How the fuck did you get in here?"

"The delivery man let me in as he was leaving." A sly smile curves her glossy red lips.

One glance over her, and I can imagine the delivery man drooling over the cleavage bursting from her tight black dress. She knows how to get exactly what she wants with her body. She was raised to master the oldest profession in the world. Once upon a time, I took pity on her for her upbringing, but now I know she only uses sex to manipulate people for her family's gain.

"Then you can let yourself back out. I have nothing to say to you."

"Now, now, is that any way to greet an old friend?" Undeterred, she circles my desk.

I take a step back, determined to keep as much space between us as possible. Natasha may be luscious in her own way, but she's no less devious than her brother.

"Lennox wants to meet with you." Facing me, she rests her ass on the edge of the desk, parting her knees slightly. An offering. An invitation.

"So what? You're his messenger now? I figured that was beneath you."

She doesn't flinch at the insult. She knows she's not beneath anyone. *Even when she was beneath me, she was using me. Playing her games…*

"I volunteered to come. I've missed you, Demi," she murmurs softly.

Except I know she's anything but soft and demure. I cringe at the nickname she gave me so many years ago. She extends her index finger, trailing it down the front of my chest, her lacquered nail ticking every button on my Oxford shirt.

"Don't you remember how good it felt when we were together?"

"It's easy to forget the forgettable, especially when there are plenty of better options."

She purses her lips, her dark eyes seeming to study me a moment. "Then maybe I need to remind you."

As if in slow motion, she drops to her knees. She places her hands on my thighs and slowly drags them up to my crotch, unzipping my pants.

I knock her hands away. I used to love making her kneel for me. Everything about her would drive me wild. But that was a history I would never repeat. Ever.

"Your charms don't work on me anymore, Natasha. Now get out of my club. And tell your brother that my answer is no."

She doesn't move. "You and I both know Lennox isn't going to accept that answer."

"Other than a bullet between the eyes, I don't owe him a goddamn thing."

She frowns up at me. "He won't stop until he gets what he wants, Demi. And you know how he gets his way. Think of Adriana."

"Don't you dare threaten my sister." The words are a mere whisper, the quietest promise of destruction if anyone dares get near her again.

Her frown deepens. "She was my best friend, Demi. I don't want to see her get hurt again. But if you don't give Lennox what he wants—"

I grab her long auburn hair by the roots and tug her head back. She has the nerve to smile, her lips parting with a lusty sigh. I ignore it and loosen my grip ever so slightly, unwilling to allow her to turn my anger into anything akin to sexual satisfaction. I lean down and deliver my next words low and clear.

"Maybe *he* needs to be brought to his knees, Natasha.

An eye for an eye and all."

She stares up at me, her gaze cold and confident. "You wouldn't hurt me. You're still in love with me."

"Wrong again."

She searches my eyes, the evolution of her thoughts flitting across her expression before finally landing on something that has her pushing away from me. "You're in love with someone else."

I swallow hard and wince. "You're being ridiculous."

She gets to her feet with less grace. "No. I know that look. I know it because you loved me once. You can deny it all you want, but you loved me. I . . ." Her eyes glimmer with emotion. "I guess I thought there'd be another chance for us."

I take long strides to the door and open it. The bass from the club downstairs is a little louder now. Maybe I should take some pity on the woman, but I can't bring myself to. I don't want her here. And I sure as hell don't want her here at her brother's bidding. I grip the edge of the door tightly, wishing I could break anything right now. Crumble something into dust.

Natasha follows my lead. She pauses close to me, too close, and pulls a business card out of the top of her dress. Holding it between two fingers, she offers it to me.

"Set up the meeting, Demi. Before you lose everything."

CHAPTER EIGHT

I hit mute on the rom-com I'm watching. After only a half hour in, I'm annoyed by their simple problems and bad jokes. I go to the window of my apartment and stare out into the night sky. DC is lit up for miles. Alive with possibility, but I'm locked here in my tower. Waiting for freedom. Waiting for my prince.

I couldn't have explained why I'd held on to my virginity for so long before. But once I discovered Crave, I knew. Deep down, I desired something different than a sweet romance. Something darker. Something only a man like Demitri could give me. Domination.

But Demitri doesn't want me. And I'm done playing his games.

That's what I keep reminding myself when the doubts creep in. It's only been a couple of days, but our text thread has been radio silent. He's done with me. He's probably relieved that I walked away. It's easy for him. Crave is his second home. A place where no desire is too dark or daunting. A place that, according to him, he needed to keep me from.

Of course, I am too inexperienced and temperamental to risk bringing further into his sex den. The more I think of it, the angrier I am. He gets to satisfy his every need inside those walls. Meanwhile, I'm here, wishing he could be the one to satisfy mine.

I go to my bedroom closet. Fresh determination makes my movements jerky and fast. I hastily begin shoving away dresses that I'd tossed away when I was getting ready for our last lesson together. I was sure that night would be special. Different. Worth the wait.

I'm done waiting.

My focus lands on the red dress draped messily on a hanger. The dress I wore the night we first met. I honestly never thought I would have the need to wear it again. Because even if Demitri hasn't taken me, I've always felt like I was his, inherently.

I hold the smooth fabric against my body and turn to examine my reflection in the full-length mirror on the wall. I could pick out a dozen things to hate about what I see staring back at me. My tired eyes, the sad line of my lips. The unflattering pajamas partially hidden by the sexy dress. But I know that once I clean myself up and slip into it, I'll be someone else. Someone free to choose a Master who truly wants her.

◆ ◆ ◆ ◆

I get past the security check, relieved when my pass lets me into the club I haven't stepped into for months. A familiar energy skitters over me. Anticipation. Excitement. And, yes, an unmistakable urge to embrace the things about this place that are unlike any other—namely, a shameless appreciation for sex. The music creates a beat that seems to echo my heartbeat, never mind the throb I can already sense growing between my thighs. I check my coat and make my way to the dance floor.

I used to cling to the edges, watching from the periphery. Tonight is different. I'm not afraid anymore. I know what I want. What I need . . .

There are half a dozen scenes playing out on different stages around the main level. Deep red and slashes of colored light pass over the crowd. The lighting is dark and moody but bright enough that I can see the faces of others staring me down as I work my way onto the dance floor. Mostly men but some women too. Heat in their eyes. Hands sliding over their visible arousal. There's no shame in that here.

The beat of the next song is fast and rhythmic, infecting me immediately. I close my eyes and sway to the sound. I let my hands roam over my curves, an invitation to be touched. Seconds later, I feel the invitation met. A small touch at my hip. Confident without being aggressive. I keep my eyes closed and pretend it's him, even though I know it's not.

I can tell immediately. He doesn't smell like Demitri, doesn't sound like him when he whispers in my ear.

"Do you want to play?"

I don't answer right away. We dance and touch until my skin is covered with a fine sheen of sweat and I've decided to stop fighting the war in my mind. The battle over my heart.

I've kept it locked away for too long. I need to move on. It's time to come out and play.

CHAPTER NINE

DEMITRI

I'm not in love with Katherine Harrison. She might be the most tempting woman I've ever entertained taking to bed, but that doesn't mean I love her. Doesn't mean watching her walk away from me carved a crater in my soul or anything. No. Natasha is being the same manipulative bitch she always was. She's just trying to get under my skin.

I tip the lowball to my lips and wait for the buzz of liquor to wipe out thoughts of her and Lennox, but most of all, Katherine. I need to get her out of my system. I should take Ronan's advice and pick a sub from the floor. I could have any one of a dozen bent over for my hand and my cock in less than five minutes.

Maybe that's part of the problem, though. Katherine's always been a challenge. She's a difficult sub. She's a dangerous conquest. She's complicated. And ever since she walked into my club, I've become a big fan of complicated, insubordinate subs.

I glare at the loud knock on the door. Everyone who works here knows not to bother me while I'm in my office.

I've been ready to snap all day. Now I just want to be alone.

The door slowly opens. Brock, one of my security men, hesitantly steps inside.

"I don't want to be bothered," I bark.

"I understand, but we have a problem, boss."

I follow his gaze to the security monitor screen on the wall. Then I see the problem.

A five-foot-seven-bombshell problem.

Kitten.

The problem isn't that she's here at the club. The problem is the sinfully tight red dress she's wearing.

Red. Crave's signature color for an available submissive. It's painting my vision with every second that passes.

I thought we were through. Maybe we are. This is either a loud-and-clear act of defiance, or she's delusional enough to think I'm going to let someone else claim her. Not on my watch. Not in my club.

I charge past Brock and out of my office, unable and unwilling to temper the flare of possession coursing through my veins. When I reach the main floor, wide-eyed club members quickly move aside to let me through. As the crowd parts, I see her on the dance floor, moving seductively.

She's already attracted plenty of admirers, a couple of whom think they can put their hands on her. I resist the urge to break their arms. It's bad for business, but I also can't fault them. I've purposefully kept Katherine away from this place. Only a select few actually know what she means to me. That she's *mine.*

I cross the distance between us, catch her by the arm,

and spin her toward me. "What do you think you're doing?" My voice booms over the loud music.

The room seems to still as people stop and stare.

Her eyes are practically glowing with anger. "Get your hands off me."

When I don't budge, her cheeks bloom red. I'm humiliating her, and I'm past caring.

"I don't take orders from you anymore, Demitri. The lessons are over."

"I don't think so." I pivot and lead her away from the hungry and curious looks on the dance floor.

"Let me go, Demitri. Damn it, just let me go!"

Not in the cards. Not tonight. Maybe not ever.

Once we're shrouded in the darkened hallway leading to the playrooms, I stop abruptly. I grab her wrists, push her against the wall, and pin her hands above her head. Our gazes lock. I'm already growing hard being this close to her.

Her eyelids lower, but her jaw is still tight with anger. "I'm tired of your games, Demitri. Fucking with my head and making me crave things I'll never have. Just admit that you don't want me, and let me find someone who does."

I press into her, making her feel the length of me and all my strength. "Does that feel like I don't want you?"

Her breathing grows shallow. Affecting her is my favorite addiction. After toying with her for so long, I know all the buttons to press. All the notes to play to get her writhing and whimpering. Begging. Yes, I think I'm finally ready to make her truly beg for it.

I lean in and drag my lips over hers, capturing the

smallest hint of her taste. "Do you have any idea how much trouble you're in, kitten?"

"How can I know if you don't show me?" she whispers.

The last of my control disintegrates. I crash my mouth against hers, growling when her tongue begins moving hungrily against mine. My God. This woman can work me up and break me down like no other. The taste of her is almost enough to melt my anger … Almost.

I release her and spin her around, pushing the front of her body against the rough concrete wall. I use my shoe to kick her feet apart, urging her stance wider. My hand slides between her legs, discovering the slickness of her inner thighs.

Always so fucking responsive.

"This belongs to me, kitten. Me and *only* me. Do you understand?"

She drops her head back against my chest and moans when my fingertips brush against the swollen wet folds of her pussy.

"Answer me." I lean in closer and clip her earlobe between my teeth. I'm desperate to get more of her scent into my lungs.

"I would have given you everything," she says. I can already hear the agony in her words. "You come here every night and take what you need from the other girls. I need more … I need a Master."

I can barely breathe. For the moment, I'm glad she can't see my face, because her words are blasting through me like heavy artillery. She thinks I'm fucking my way through the club every night. That stings, no doubt. But her honesty... the depth of her need... That's what's ripping me open right now.

Suddenly I can see how terribly I've failed her. People come to Crave to shed their skin and be whoever they need to be without the bullshit rules and expectations of the outside world. The second I found out who her father was, I refused to see her as anyone else. I forced myself to keep her in a box, entertaining our lessons together but never giving her the space to learn. To bloom.

I wrap my arms around her, binding our torsos tightly. "There are no other girls," I murmur as I brush my lips across her shoulder. I reach for the zipper of her dress and guide the metal tab down the track, watching as the bright-red fabric separates from her gorgeous curvaceous body. So beautiful.

"You're lying." It comes out a broken sob.

"I don't need to lie. I do what I want. What I want is you, *krásná.*"

She softens against me. Her hands have unfurled from their tight fists. I exhale my own sigh of relief. To have her here. Safe with me. In my arms. Under my command. Now I need her to know what that means.

"You disobeyed me by coming here tonight," I breathe against her ear. "And then you blatantly wore a forbidden color."

I seethe on that thought.

She nods, which spurs my next move. Grabbing hold of the sides of the fabric, I rip the red dress from her body in one violent move, causing her to whimper. I toss its remnants to the floor.

"You tried to seduce another man right in front of me." I keep my tone even but firm. She needs to know punishment is due.

She nods again.

I lower my hand to unfasten my belt. In one pull, I free it from my waist. Using the tip, I tease it down the length of her exposed back before bringing the leather between her legs.

"You were going to let someone else take what belongs to me. Isn't that right?"

When she doesn't answer, I give her sex a hard pop with the end of the belt. She slaps her palm flat against the wall and lets out a pained grunt.

I want more of those sounds from her. Just not here.

I spin her around to face me. Her delicious breasts jut out, tempting me. I resist the urge to take her nipples between my teeth and coax out more tortured cries. Even in this darkened hallway, I can see the desire burning in her hooded gaze. It's threatening the last shreds of my control.

"I think I deserve an answer. You were going to let someone else fuck you tonight, weren't you?"

She casts her gaze downward. "Y-Yes."

I deliver a hard slap against her swollen sex. She cries out, an anguished mix of pleasure and pain. My emotions aren't that far away. Rage laced with intense lust. The urge to fuck and fight. A tornado of craving and destruction.

"Yes, what?" I hiss.

"Yes. Yes, Sir."

I lean in closer. "I'm more than your Sir, Katherine. I'm your Master, no matter what you might think. That means you kneel for me. You respect me. You fucking obey me. And when you do that all right, you come for me. That's what you want, isn't it?"

She exhales shakily and meets my eyes. "Yes, Master."

A shot of desire hits me at the way the last word rumbles past her lips. It holds a kind of reverence I've yet to experience from her. Then again, I've never lost control with her like this. She's never pushed me this far. The devil on my shoulder wants to know how much more she can take.

"Good. Now I'm going to make sure you never forget it."

CHAPTER TEN

I've provoked the most dominant and intimidating man I've ever met. I pushed him too far. I realize that now. Now I have to accept the consequences. Hell, somehow I ache for them more badly than ever. Whatever punishment he has in store for me, I vow to endure it.

The door to the playroom slams shut behind me. He leads me toward the black leather punishing bench in the center of the large room. My heart lurches into my throat.

"You know what to do." His voice is low. Deep and dangerous.

I've seen this kind of play, but I've never done anything like it. I'm scared and impossibly turned on. I'm almost trembling too badly to place my knees onto the side platforms. I lean forward, letting the pressure push out an anxious breath. The low tilt of the device spreads my hips open wide and positions my ass high into the air. My stomach rests on the center, and my nipples harden against the cool leather beneath.

Before I can get completely situated, my arms are

suddenly forced into the leather cuffs located on the front bar. Demitri chooses the last notch on the buckles, making the restraints as uncomfortable as possible around my wrists. Once he's secured them and given them a firm tug, he steps back and begins unbuttoning his shirt.

"You have so much to learn, kitten."

He circles the bench, slowly studying me like a predator would its prey. Ahead of me, the long mirrored wall allows me to see his every move. When he stops in front of me again, I have the ultimate view. I'm rewarded with his bared muscular chest. My hungry eyes follow the lines of his ripped stomach muscles, moving downward to the perfectly cut *V* that dips below the waistband of his navy suit pants. Then the thick outline of his erection.

I can't help but lick my lips. From head to toe, the man is perfection... an Adonis. After knowing him as long as I have, I have complete faith that he fucks like a god. And right now, he's about to teach me the lesson of a lifetime.

He trails his fingertips up my arms, down the base of my spine, and up again. The teasing touch sends an exhilarating wave of anticipation through me. Moaning, I arch my body off the table, forcing my ass higher in the air.

He groans softly and circles behind me again. Then I notice the leather belt is still in his hand. I'm terrified and exhilarated in the same moment.

"Four strikes. One for each of the ways you disrespected me tonight. Understand?"

I'm not sure I can handle four hits with his belt, but I answer quickly. "Yes, Master."

"Good girl. Now, count for me."

I grab hold of the bar in front of me and brace myself for what is about to happen.

"One."

The biting pain of the leather nearly takes my breath away. Tears instantly form in my eyes. I push them back and force my focus on the mirrored wall across from me. Tightening my grip on the bar of the bench, I prepare myself for the next blow. When I'm brave enough to speak, I resume the count.

"Two."

The second strike lands across the opposite ass cheek, and a strangled cry tears from me. My body seems to absorb the pain faster, though, because the next thing I notice is an unexpected rush of wetness gathering between my legs. I stare at my reflection—my flushed face and dilated eyes—all signs that Demitri's punishment is doing more than testing the limits of my pain tolerance.

How could this possibly turn me on?

I punctuate the thought with another request. "Three," I rasp, almost welcoming the next blow as it comes and the mixture of pleasure and pain it brings.

As the sensation fades, I know I'm on my way to becoming addicted. I silently wonder how much of the blissful torture I can take if tested.

"Four."

The belt drops to the floor abruptly.

"Enough," he murmurs.

In seconds, he strips the rest of his clothes and rolls on

a condom. Coming close, he drags the tip of his cock along my soaked tissues.

His lips part, and I attempt to shift my hips back and join us. I'm mourning the end of my punishment, but we've never been this close to actually fucking before. Between the two, my head is buzzing. I grip the bar with a tortured moan. Part of me wishes I could move and coax him into me, but the restraint is its own kind of perfection, keeping all that desire lit up under my skin with no place to go.

"Please," I beg, the sheer desperation evident in my voice. "Take me."

I meet his smoldering gaze in the mirror. I've never seen such a dark look grace his features. His sculpted chest is heaving, and I know he's fighting to stay in control.

"Like this, kitten? Here?"

I move my hips back and forth, trying to urge him on. Wrapping a fistful of my hair around his hand, he tugs my head back. The bite of pain and his hot breath against my ear trigger a desperate whimper to leave my lips.

"Say it. Beg."

"Please, Demitri," I whisper. "Make me yours."

He notches his cock at my entrance, thrusts forward, and enters me with such force that it steals my breath. His second thrust is just as unforgiving as he pushes himself deeper still, past the place inside me that his fingers tormented days ago.

A painful cry tears up my throat. "Oh God!"

The piercing sting of being torn inside brings tears to my eyes. They spill over as I suck in a few rapid breaths. It's so much more intense than the whip of the belt on my skin. He's so deep, invading the untried places inside of me. I need a moment to adjust to him, but he doesn't allow it. Instead, he pulls out and slams back into me, this time forcing his massive length even deeper into my core. He curses something in his native Czech tongue.

"You're so deep." I close my eyes and try to process the overwhelming sensation.

When he moves again, I can't help but wince at the soreness.

"You have a safe word, *krásná.*"

I shake my head, an almost imperceptible motion. He's tearing me apart. It's everything I wanted. Except I've never seen him this unleashed. We're playing without limits.

I meet Demitri's eyes in the mirror once more.

"Don't stop," I say.

I tighten my grip on the bar, but he goes still. He slides his palms lower, spreading me as he gazes down at the place where we're joined. "You're bleeding for me." His lips part and his chest heaves.

Something inside me gives way. It feels like surrender. It rumbles deep in my bones. It tightens like a knot deep in my belly as he proceeds to fuck me. Slowly at first, then faster and harder. The fierce drives of his body into mine stirs new sensations. My inner walls tighten down on him, making every invasion more intense. I'm gasping for breath and reaching for more.

He must feel it too, because he slams into me with a growl. Hard and incredibly deep. He slips his fingers around to my clit, delivering urgent strokes designed to bring me to the edge. Again and again until the orgasm rips through me like a violent storm. Bowing my back up off the bench, I scream out his name. His last drives vault me even higher, into more pleasure than I've ever experienced.

"Fuck!" Demitri lets out a feral growl, digging his nails deep into my flesh as he buries himself to the hilt.

He stays there, pulsing someplace deep inside me, a place that's his now. Even with the condom between us, I feel utterly claimed. I'm shaking. More tears spill down my cheeks. Not from the pain, which is a distant memory now. But from the raw intensity of the moment.

I'm still turned completely inside out as he slips out of me and circles the bench. He removes my wrists from the cuffs. But before I can come down off the euphoric high, I'm being lifted up into his strong arms. Wordlessly he carries me toward the king-size bed on the other side of the playroom, where he lays me down. The aftershocks of the orgasms are still working their way through my system when he crawls over me and pins my hands above my head.

I look into his eyes, trying to read his thoughts. Possession, hunger, and something else I'm afraid to name.

"You belong to me, kitten. And we're not leaving this room until you know it."

CHAPTER ELEVEN

DEMITRI

Fine snow flurries kiss the window of my office. The sky is growing dark with impending dusk, which means a new day is beginning for me. I'd slept late after spending all night and a better part of the morning with Katherine. Fucking her. Teasing her. Tasting her. Feeling her . . .

Once that last boundary between us was taken away, I was a man possessed. Utterly obsessed. The hours we spent together weren't enough, even though we both should have been beyond sated after the first round on the bench. Those memories are burned in my mind for eternity now.

She's mine. Truly mine. She'll feel me for days because of it. I've been waiting for the guilt to hit. The worry that I've well and truly fucked up this time, but all I can think about is when I'll be able to see her again.

Soon, I promised, as I sent her home in a private car when morning light began to dawn.

In the meantime, I have business to take care of . . .

I flip Natasha's card around and around. It's blank white except for the ten-digit phone number printed in the middle. Lennox's number. I can't imagine what he wants, but I'm confident it's nothing that will interest me. Our business abruptly concluded the second he destroyed my family in the name of money and personal gain. Not the kind of wealth that piles up in overseas accounts and sets families up for years. No. Just enough money to slip through his fingers so fast, all he could do was set up his next racket.

I'd been young, and we'd been friends. Partners. Close enough that I looked the other way too often, ignoring his mean streak and bad decisions. I liked the money too. I was determined to crawl out of the poverty we'd grown up in. He was always the brains, and me... One look at me would scare most of his enemies into submission. Sometimes my fists extinguished all doubt. I'd been loyal to a fault.

Shame flows through me. My life before coming to the States was one horrific black mark that I'd never be able to erase. I could build a better life for myself and Adriana here, but I couldn't bring my parents back. I'd give anything if I could. For a few bleak moments, I move through the grief that's hung like a dark cloud over me since their death. I can see the sadness in Adriana's eyes. The weight of the guilt that's only mine to bear. None of it was her fault.

I drop the card and pinch the bridge of my nose until it hurts. Anger is so much more potent when it's laced with regret. I've lived with it for so long and tried like hell to bury the person it made me. If I think I can ignore Lennox and pretend we're safe—that *Addi* is safe—then I'm signing up for a lifetime of sorrow. I can't risk him getting to her. I *can't* lose her. Natasha's threat wasn't an empty one. No one knows better than me what that bastard brother of hers is capable of.

I pick up my phone and swipe my thumb over the screen. I have to end this. End *him*. In this moment, I'm certain I'm the only one who can.

The shipyard by the harbor is dark. Quiet of activity save the waves crashing against the sea wall and the occasional groan from a moored ship. If I were anyone else, I'd be worried about meeting here. But I'm confident that if Lennox only wanted to kill me, he wouldn't have sent me such a bold invitation first. Truth is I don't think he really wants me dead at all. At least not the way I've wanted him dead.

I hear the clip of footsteps ahead of me. The shadows of several bodies break off from the darkness, and I can soon recognize Lennox's signature swagger among the other men flanking him. He always carried himself in an exaggerated way, like he had something to prove. He's dressed in a gray suit. His hair is slicked back. Light glints off his large watch.

"Nicoloff. Old friend. I was beginning to wonder if you'd ignore me forever." He smirks and lifts his chin to meet my stony stare. "You look good. Hell, I'd say we almost make a pair."

He might be right. We've come a long way from the streets we grew up on. Still... "We're nothing alike."

"I don't know. I'm still in the game, but we're both moving up, aren't we?"

"What do you want, Lennox?" Enough with the bullshit.

Last thing I want to do is intrigue him with my business affairs. I already know he's a perverted fuck.

He exhales through his nose, eyeing me quietly. "We used to be a good team, you know?"

My instinct to beat the life out of him is almost blinding. I force myself to stay focused. To be smarter than the brute he'd once bent to his will so successfully.

"You raped my sister and killed my parents when they went to the police about it."

"Listen, you know how things go. Sometimes there are bumps in the road. Things are smooth now. They're about to get smoother." He rubs his fingers together with a sly grin. "And greener."

I work my jaw and force the fantasy of smashing him into the pavement out of my brain. "Good for you. Do your business and get the fuck out of my neighborhood."

"I need your help before I can do that. I heard you've got a nice little underground operation going. Some decent cash flow too."

"My business is legitimate. Discreet, but everything is on the books." I'd given up breaking the rules a long time ago.

"See, that's why this is perfect. I need to do some housecleaning. I have some important purchases to make here in DC, but I need the money cleaned in your little sex house first."

I laugh, both at his description and the offer.

"A few thousand dollars here and there getting charged to the club is nothing. You need a bigger front than I can offer you."

"Then you're going to have to take some risks. Won't be without rewards, though."

"I've got white-collar membership requests a mile long. Senators, ambassadors, you name it. A waiting list for months. Anyone gets a whiff of scandal, and it's all over."

He nods and stares down at his shoes. I can see they're shined to perfection even in the moonlight. "I saw Adriana the other day. God..." He smiles broadly. "She's beautiful, isn't she?"

The rush of murderous thoughts starts flooding me again. I have to stay in control... "You would know," I say, my voice dangerously low.

"She was special. Still is. I wanted her for a long time, but you never knew it. It was our friendship that always held me back. I still regret everything that happened between us. I really do. She was just..." He sighs loudly into the air, the puff visible in the cool air. "We never asked, you and me. We just took. For years, we took whatever the fuck we wanted, and look at us now. We won't die like our families did. Poor, miserable, stuck in the same place always."

You'll die with my hand around your throat, begging for forgiveness that I'll never give you.

I clench my fists, the thin thread of my self-control too taut for comfort. One wrong move, and one of his men will put a bullet in me. I have to get out of here. Have to get my head straight and figure out a game plan now that I know his.

"I'll think about it," I say, even though I never will. "On one condition."

His eyes brighten, and I hate the satisfaction I've just given him.

"Name it."

"Stay away from Adriana and stay away from the club. If I find out you or anyone get near either, the deal is off the table completely."

He stares at me in silence. "When do I get my answer?"

"You'll know when you have it."

He chuckles. "You're not making this easy for me."

"Then find another business partner."

"What if you don't give me the answer I want?"

"You know where to find me," I say. The words are out of my mouth before I can stop them. A challenge I'm all too eager to offer.

Only he doesn't know the deal is impossible. That the challenge is a promise—an inevitable declaration of war.

CHAPTER TWELVE

Adriana greets me with her megawatt smile as I enter the small coffee shop.

"Katherine! I'm so glad you could make it!" She gives me a quick hug, and we make our way to the counter, where a cute male barista takes our orders. I pull out my card to pay, but Adriana waves me off, pushing her card into his hand.

"My treat. I invited you, remember?" She winks over her shoulder at me.

I smile and put my card back into my wallet. "Thanks, but next time it's on me."

"Deal."

Once we have our drinks, we decide on a table near a large window. I shiver into my coat, waiting for the chill outside to leave my bones. As I settle into my seat, Adriana studies me with her dark-brown eyes.

"You look exhausted."

I give her a shy smile and nod. "I was up pretty late the other night." I raise my latte in the air. "Caffeine is my hero right now."

"You should have told me. We could have done this coffee date another day."

"No, I'm glad you called. I wanted to thank you again for what you did for my birthday."

She waves her hand at me. "You don't have to thank me for that. I just hate that my brother had to cut our fun short."

I try to suppress my smile. She has no idea just how much *fun* her brother and I have had since that night. It's been a couple of days since we met at the club, but I can't stop replaying every moment in mind.

"So, tell me. How did things go with Ronan after you left?"

Adriana shifts nervously in her seat and tucks a strand of her long blond hair behind her ear. "What do you mean?"

Cute. She's being coy.

Smirking, I take a sip of my drink "I *mean* the way you were looking at him at the bar the other day. I didn't think the two of you would make it to the car without tearing each other's clothes off."

Adriana's eyes widen "Was it that obvious?"

Unsure of what to say, I give her a hesitant nod. "Were you trying not to be?"

She lets out a long sigh, playing with the label on her cup. "It's just a really, *really* complicated situation. I'm sure you probably don't want to hear about it."

"Believe me, I know all about complicated. I'm like the poster child for it. Lay it on me."

She's silent for a moment, and I wonder if maybe I'm pushing too hard. After all, we barely know each other, even if it feels like we've been friends for ages.

"It's just that my brother and I have been through a lot together. When our parents were killed, he brought me here with him to the United States to have a fresh start." She winces as if she's remembering a painful memory. "Demitri met Ronan not long after we moved to DC. He seemed to trust him enough to become friends, which is not something my brother does with anyone. The first time he introduced me to Ronan…" She closes her eyes briefly. "There was this insane chemistry between the two of us. At first, we both tried to fight it. But the attraction only grew more intense until neither of us could resist it. When we're alone, everything is perfect. It's like nothing else in the world matters but us. But when we're out in public or around my brother, Ronan acts like we're just friends. And that's so hard because…" She drops her gaze to her lap. "Because I'm in love with him."

Her confession hits me hard because I can relate. Even before my incredible night with Demitri launched my heart and my body into euphoric bliss, deeper feelings had already taken root. Undeniably, I'm in love with Demitri. I have been for a long time. Now I'm scared to death that he might not be able to return those feelings… ever. After what Adriana's just shared about their parents' death, I have no idea what kind of demons might come between us having a real relationship.

I reach out and touch her hand. "I'm so sorry about your parents."

"Thank you."

"Have you told Ronan how you feel?"

She shakes her head. "No, but it doesn't matter how I feel. Ronan is my brother's best friend. He's never going to risk jeopardizing their friendship over me." She's quiet a moment. "I'm seeing him tonight. Every time I try to be smart about this, I just fall back into being with him. I'm probably nothing to him but a dirty little secret."

"Are you sure? Because that's not at all how it looked to me. I really think you should tell him. You can't let your brother stand in the way of your happiness, Adriana."

"Ha! That's easy for you to say. You don't know my brother."

My hand nervously slips from hers to my cup, and its contents spill onto the table.

"Shit!" I shoot up out of my chair and frantically begin blotting the table with napkins. From the corner of my eye, I see the cute male barista rushing over to our table to help.

"I'm so sorry."

My apology earns a warm boyish smile. "Don't worry. I got it. How about I get you another one . . . on the house?"

"No, I think I've finally reached my limit of caffeine, but thank you," I joke, trying to mask my embarrassment.

When he leaves, Adriana leans in and diverts her gaze from me to the barista. "He's totally into you."

"Not my type."

"Okay, then tell me. What is your type?"

Tall. Blond. Icy-blue eyes . . . Your brother.

As if I've just sent out a psychic message, my phone chimes with a text from Demitri.

Are you sore?

I feel my cheeks heat. I bite my lip and type my reply.

> *Yes, Master. I can't wait*
> *for our next lesson.*

When I glance up from my phone, Adriana is smirking.
"That must have been some text. Your face is flushed."
I touch my cheek with my hand and smile.
"So?" She wiggles her brows. "Tell me about him."
I shrug. "There isn't much to say, really. It's nothing serious."
Even though I desperately want it to be. Even though it never can be because of what he does and who my family is.
I try not to let the reality of my situation change my mood on the outside. Thankfully Derrick wasn't on shift when I got home the morning after Demitri and I spent the night together, but I'm still waiting to catch hell from my father about it. Once he remembers I exist.
"How long have you been seeing each other?" Adriana pushes.
Long enough to fall in love with him. "On and off for about a year. We've kept things really casual, though."
She raises her brow. "A year? That sounds serious to me. Do you have feelings for him?"
Yes.
I shift in my seat, noting the unmistakable soreness from Demitri's merciless fucking. I bite my lip and clench

my thighs together as those memories wash over me.

"He and I don't exactly have the typical kind of relationship, if you know what I mean?"

"Oh, I see. So, it's just physical between you two?"

"Basically," I lie. "This way it's easier to walk away when you're ready to move on."

Just saying the words sends spikes of pain through my chest. How am I supposed to walk away from Demitri now that I've given him so much of myself? How will I survive when he wants to move on?

Adriana's thoughtful sigh breaks up my panicked thoughts. "Believe me, I know all about that. It's easy enough at the beginning. It's just sex until you can't get them out of your head. Then it turns into more. You fall in love with them, and there's always the danger of getting hurt."

She's not buying the "no strings" way I'm painting this relationship, so I give up on it too. Who am I kidding? I'm falling hard and fast for Demitri. The more I admit it to myself, the scarier all this seems.

"I guess all we can do is hope it's worth risking the heartbreak."

She smiles. "If you really love someone, it's always worth risking the heartbreak."

She looks wistfully out the window, and I know Ronan is consuming her thoughts. Just the way Demitri consumes mine. Everything about him. The way he fucked me like nothing could keep him from taking what was truly his. The tender look in his eyes when we should have been satisfied but he couldn't stop touching me. The little whispers uttered in a tongue I didn't recognize but felt somewhere in my soul. If only I could repeat them and make Adriana tell me what he said . . .

But that would feel like a violation. He'll show me his heart when he wants to, if he ever does.

Suddenly Adriana's face falls. Her skin grows too pale.

"Is everything okay?"

She jerks her stare to the table. "It . . . It can't be him," she says, her breath hitching. "It's not possible."

"Adriana, you're scaring me. Talk to me."

She reaches into her purse, her hands shaking badly. "I need Ronan." But she's trembling too hard to hit the right buttons.

I take the phone from her quickly and open her contacts to make the call. I hold her hand as I push Call.

"Hey, sexy," Ronan answers.

"Ronan, it's Katherine." I try to remain calm for Adriana, but Ronan immediately picks up on the fear in my voice.

Adriana is frantically searching the street now, like she just saw a ghost.

"Katherine? What's wrong?"

"It's Adriana. I think she saw something . . . or someone."

"Fuck. Where are you?"

"We're at the coffee shop across from her apartment."

"Whatever you do, don't let her leave. Put her on the phone."

I immediately comply and turn the phone toward her.

I feel helpless as she tries to calm her breathing.

"R-Ronan. I. Can't."

Ronan's words are loud enough to make out across the small space. "Yes, you can. Just focus on my voice, baby. Relax your chest and slowly blow out your breath. I'm on my way to you. I'm close. Just stay put, okay?"

Several minutes pass that way. Her breathing through the panic and his reassurances. I follow her gaze to the street, as if maybe I can spot the phantom terror that's sent her into an emotional tailspin. But all I can see are pedestrians passing by. Nothing out of the ordinary.

Moments later, Ronan bursts through the door of the café and rushes toward us. "It's okay, baby. I'm here." He's out of breath but pulls her into a tight embrace.

"I saw him," she whispers. "I know it was him. But it can't be, right?"

He pulls back, cups her face in his hands, and places a soft kiss to her forehead. The tender act only solidifies what I'd already known to be true. He's in love with her too.

"Let me take care of it. I promise, it's going to be okay."

She rears back, fresh tears in her eyes. "Ronan, what aren't you telling me?"

He glances to me briefly, then back to her.

Before I can excuse myself to leave them alone, Adriana begins speaking rapidly in Czech. When he replies back to her, I'm shocked to find that he also speaks the language fluently.

Even though I can't understand a word they are saying, it still feels awkward to listen in on their conversation. When her tears start to flow heavier, I stand to leave. She's falling

apart in Ronan's arms, and I have no idea why.
All I know is I'm powerless to help my friend.

CHAPTER THIRTEEN

DEMITRI

I wish I could erase every horrific memory of my past. But I don't deserve to forget. I deserve every ounce of pain and torture that comes with those memories. I'm the one who brought hell straight onto my family's doorstep. If I had been half the man I should have been, my parents would still be alive and my sister wouldn't be haunted by a monster who took her innocence.

A shuffling noise behind me startles me out of my thoughts. Ronan walks silently through the hall and turns into my sister's kitchen. A couple of minutes later, he remerges carrying two tumblers full of what looks to be Scotch. Walking over to where I'm sitting, he extends his hand out and offers me one of the glasses.

"How is she?" I ask before taking a sip. I'd come straight to Adriana's apartment once I'd gotten his voicemail. In between consoling my sister, he'd managed to fill me in on some of what had happened. But I still don't know enough of the story.

Ronan sinks into the oversize leather chair across from

me. "She's sleeping. Or at least she's pretending to be." He takes a long swig of his drink and then rests the tumbler on his knee. "I don't think I've ever seen her in this bad shape, D."

I study his worried expression over the rim of my glass. I know he cares about my sister, but this is a different kind of worry . . . a deeper kind of worry.

"I still don't understand why she asked for you instead of me." I can't mask the irritation in my voice. The fact that my sister had reached out to Ronan first is a hard blow—even harder to accept once I arrived and she asked for him to sit with her until she fell asleep. She's always needed me when she was frightened. I've nursed her through dozens of panic attacks. What's suddenly changed?

Keeping his focus on the tumbler in front of him, he shrugs. "I don't know. I guess because I live closer to her than you do."

He's lying.

"Besides, you didn't exactly answer your phone when I called you earlier."

I grit my teeth as I speak. "I came as quickly as I could. I had important business to take care of."

"Since when did you start choosing business over your sister?"

"You know I always put her first. This wasn't ordinary club business that I was dealing with. I was trying to figure out this bullshit with Lennox."

Ronan shoots forward in his chair. "You met him?"

"The other night at the docks. He wants to use the club

to scrub money for some local business he has here."

Ronan bolts up straight. "You met with the motherfucker without talking to me first? Are you insane?"

His reaction is exactly why I didn't tell him until now.

"He sent Natasha to my office. I only agreed to the meeting because I wanted to make sure he knew better than to come anywhere near Adriana or the club. That was before I knew he'd cross that line anyway. He's always been good at sending messages."

Ronan's jaw tenses. "We need to figure this out, D. He can't get away with this."

"He won't. I have a plan."

"Then perhaps you should fill me on it, because you're not doing this alone."

There's no way I can risk telling him my true intentions of this partnership with Lennox. If he knew the goal was to kill Lennox, he'd never let me go through with it. Ronan took an oath with the government to serve and protect. Our definitions of justice are too far apart on this. And I plan to get retribution, even if it costs me my life and freedom in the process.

"The less you know about this plan, the better. Let's just say the agency won't approve of what I have in store for Mr. Novak's future."

"Fuck the agency. This is personal."

I narrow my gaze on my friend. "I know you care about Adriana, but she's *my* sister. She's not your responsibility."

"Care about her? Is that really how you think I feel?"

"Do you want to enlighten me?"

"Ever since the day I met your sister, I've watched her get stronger, braver. And in one instant, that fucking monster puts all of that fear back into her eyes. I can't stand back and pretend to just be her friend any longer, especially now." He takes a few short breaths. "I'm in love with her. And don't act like you're fucking surprised about it either."

I clench my jaw and stand, staring him down. "You *love* her?"

"Is that a problem?" His challenge catches me off guard.

Is it a problem? Is there someone else I'd rather care for her? Even if the thought of them sharing a bed isn't one I want to imagine, I can't deny that she's safer with him than anyone else. Maybe even safer than she'd be with me, which is something I have to consider now that Lennox has her in his sights.

"And what about her? How does she feel about this?" I ask.

"Demitri." We both turn to find my sister standing in the hallway. The men's T-shirt she's wearing hangs off her petite frame, hitting her just mid-thigh. Her long blond waves are a tangled mess. She looks so tired and broken, everything that I fought so hard to keep her from. "Please don't fight over this. You're my blood. But Ronan is… He's everything to me."

Ronan moves past me toward her. He stops in front of her and brushes her hair away from her face. "No more pretending," he says before kissing her gently on the lips.

A strange feeling of envy grows inside me. Somewhere deep, I yearn for that kind of closeness with Katherine, but

I don't deserve it. She deserves to be cherished by someone who isn't consumed with dark secrets and demons from an ugly past. And that someone would never be me.

Adriana wraps her arm around Ronan's midsection, and they move into the living room together. I know from the anxious look on her face that she is preparing for my reaction. There is a lot I want to say, but now isn't the time to get into all of that. I believe in actions, not words. If Ronan loves my sister as much as he says he does, then he'll have to prove it.

"I want you to take Adriana and leave town," I say.

Adriana objects first, tears glimmering in her eyes. "No, I'm not leaving. You're the only family I have left, Demitri. Lennox has taken enough from me. I won't lose you to him too."

"I don't need reminding of what we've lost, Adriana. I see it every night when I close my eyes. I thought I was protecting you when I brought you here to the States. I thought by starting a new life, we could put the past behind us. But as long as Lennox breathes, neither one of us will ever be free. I have to end this . . . For the both of us."

"Then we do it together," Ronan says. The vengeance in his eyes reminds me that he's in this fight. For his own reasons but for ours too. This *is* personal for him now.

"No," I say firmly. "Adriana can't be alone."

"We can keep her close and still keep her safe. Think about it. Lennox will expect you to send her away. He won't expect her to be right underneath his nose."

I let his words sink in. As much as I hate to admit it, he

might be right.

"She can stay with me at my place," Ronan offers, pulling her against him.

I shake my head. "If either of you have been sleeping over at each other's places—which I'm sure you have been—that's not going to be safe. I don't know how long he's been watching her. It's got to be somewhere she's never been."

"I can stay with Katherine," Adriana suggests.

No way that's going to happen. "Out of the question. Her father is the Attorney General. The last thing I need is for him to be asking questions about why you're staying there."

Ronan suddenly pales. "Shit."

The way he says it sends chills up my spine.

"What?"

He pushes up from the couch and paces to the other side of the room. "Katherine was at the coffee shop when this all happened. I was so focused on calming Addi down, I didn't think about—"

I bolt straight up and take threatening steps forward. "You didn't think about what it might mean to send Katherine out there unprotected?" I jerk my thumb toward the door, fresh panic sliding into my veins. "Fucking hell. If they've been watching this place, they've been watching mine too."

Adriana's voice is a small reminder that Ronan and I aren't alone in this conversation. "She's a friend, but we just met. I don't know why they'd go after her."

The silence becomes thick between us. She's staring at

me like only a sister does. Like she's about to call me on my bullshit. All my lies.

"Demitri, how do you know her? You never gave me a straight answer that first day I met her."

I run a tense hand over my face and exhale heavily. "We've been . . . seeing each other."

Her jaw falls slightly. "For how long?"

"A while."

"Like a year?"

I work my jaw, not liking the look on her face now any better. It's full of accusation, and somehow I just know Katherine's talked about us. God knows what she's said. All I know is I deserve every ounce of blame and all the venom my sister's sending my way.

"You're an idiot, *bratr*."

I nod tightly. "I know. I need to make some things right between us, and I will," I promise. "But first I have to find her before Lennox does."

CHAPTER FOURTEEN

KATHERINE

A strong winter wind slams into me as I step out of the department store, my arms heavy with shopping bags. With Christmas a few days away, I decided to pick up a few small things for Charlotte and my parents. Adriana too. Even though I know Ronan is taking care of her after the incident this afternoon, I feel bad for leaving her so upset. I can't imagine what would send her into such turmoil. Then again, I haven't known her very long.

I'm ready to hail a cab when a familiar sweet aroma makes its way to me—the bakery across the street. I tug my coat close to my body and quickly cross over. I'm not sure when I'll see Demitri next, but when I think about what he might like from the massive sugary display, I let myself go overboard and leave with plenty of selections.

The large bronze clock hanging in my building's lobby strikes six o'clock just as I step through the front doors.

"Evening, Cinderella."

I halt at the sound of Derrick's voice. Clenching my jaw, I shoot him a narrow look.

"Don't ever call me that again. You may be on my father's payroll, but that doesn't mean I'm going to take your shit."

He smirks. "You know I'm not the bad guy here, right?" Derrick steps closer, raking his eyes down my body before settling his gaze on my chest. "If you want to stay out late, like I heard you did the other night when I was off shift, I'm more than willing to keep quiet about it." He caresses his fingers along my exposed collarbone. "For a price, of course."

I slap his hand away. "Get your hands off me. I'm not paying you a dime. Hit my dad up for cash if you need it so badly."

A wicked grin spreads across his face. "I wasn't talking about money, sweetheart. I'm more interested in another form of payment." Dropping his hand, he adjusts his crotch.

I avert my gaze, feeling sick to my stomach suddenly. "Stay the hell away from me." I stagger backward and head for the elevators.

His laugh echoes in the lobby. "Think about it, Katherine. It's a win-win. I get what I want, and you get what you want. Besides, you might just like it."

I'm relieved to get to my apartment, away from Derrick's prying eyes and indecent proposals. I drop the bags in the entryway and tug off my coat. One look at the pastries, and I remember Demitri. We don't call each other a lot, but things feel different now. Like there might be a path forward. I take the box to the kitchen and pour a glass of wine, hoping to ease a little of the tension of the day before I brave a call.

A faint bang near the front of the apartment yanks me

out of my thoughts. I set my glass down and listen. Footsteps. My heart starts beating wildly. So loudly I can hardly hear the steps as they get closer. My phone. It's still in my purse.

Then I hear them. The voices of two men. I can't understand what they're saying, but I recognize the accents. Could they be friends of Demitri's? The prospect doesn't make me feel any better about intruders. I take a deep breath, forcing myself to stay focused. I could hide out and wait for them to leave, but the apartment isn't that big. My phone is near the door. I can run for it and get out the door quickly. Maybe before they notice.

I'm shaking, but the prospect of waiting to see what they want is worse than making a run for it. So I do. I duck around the corner and sprint for the door. In my periphery, I see one of them coming out of my bedroom.

"She's here!" he shouts.

I have to get out of here. Fast.

I trip over the shopping bags and scramble for my purse. The second I get my hand around the phone I feel myself being pulled back by the collar on my shirt, then my hair. I scream. The phone flies out of my grasp as I struggle to break free. The man swings me around, sending me stumbling deeper into the apartment. I straighten just enough to have him give me another shove onto the living room couch.

"Stay," he barks.

There's laughter behind him. Then another man's face comes into view. He's shorter and better-looking than the other one. Well-dressed in a crisp suit. My guess is he's not the henchman but the boss. But who on earth are they?

"What do you want?" I can't help the faltering in my voice.

My adrenaline is pumping so hard. I've never been this terrified in my life.

The boss saunters closer and takes a seat adjacent to me.

"What's your name?"

I frown. If he doesn't know who I am, he doesn't know who my father is either.

"Katherine."

He nods, his gaze traveling over me. "Pretty. Do you play at Nicoloff's little club?"

I'm getting lightheaded, so I force my breathing to slow down. I shake my head.

"No? Why not?"

"He doesn't want me there."

He tilts his head to the side as if he's genuinely intrigued. "Interesting. You must be special to him."

I lock my jaw tight. I have no idea what I truly mean to Demitri, but even if I did, I wouldn't tell this intruder.

"Who are you?"

"I'm an old friend of his. Name is Lennox." An impish grin curves his lips. "I was hoping to find a way to work together, but I worry Nicoloff is going to drag his feet. I just don't have a lot of time to play games. I came to see if you might send him a message for me."

I swallow hard. "What kind of message?"

He licks his lips, his gaze wandering over me again. He takes his time, letting the silence hang awkwardly between us. "I was going to have you give him a little reminder. Tick tock. But now that I've met you, I wonder if he might need a stronger message."

"I... I can call him if you want." The possibility of getting Demitri on the phone...of letting him know I'm in danger and badly in need of his help is overwhelming to think about.

The panic is turning into something else. Desperation. It's tightening my throat and burning at the backs of my eyes.

The henchman hands Lennox my phone. He takes it and casually flicks his finger over the screen.

"He's called you. Many times." He smiles again. "He must be worried."

He tosses the phone aside, and I feel the tears threatening harder now. Why the hell did I have my phone on silent? Did he try to warn me? Did he know Lennox would come here?

"He'll come for me," I warn. I pray he will. He has to.

"I think he will. Not before we have some fun, though, all right? I want him to know I'm serious. Serious as I was last time his family tried to fuck with me."

His family... Demitri's parents. Adriana.

Everything clicks together. But it's too late. He nods toward the henchman, who lunges for me.

I scream, but he's not deterred. He flattens me onto the couch, holding me down with his knee on my chest. I can barely breathe but manage another feeble scream when I feel tugging at my jeans.

"No!"

I claw at anything I can reach, but the knee on my chest feels like a kiss once my wrists are wrenched into his viselike grip.

I can't even pull enough air into my lungs to cry out, but I try. I beg for help and for Demitri. Hot, angry tears slip down my cheeks and pool in my ears. I kick against the man I can't see, whose hands are tearing at my clothes and grabbing at my flesh.

"Please," I beg. "Please don't."

A loud bang pierces the air. My ears ring, but I can suddenly breathe. The weight is gone. The furious clawing at my body has stopped. Then I see the blood. The henchman's hands are drenched in it seconds before he drops onto my carpet. First on his knees. Then the rest of him collapses into an unmoving heap.

"Nothing happened." Lennox is at the foot of the couch, hands in the air.

I scramble to a seated position. That's when I see Demitri and he sees me. His muscles are coiled tight, but his face is ashen.

"Katherine."

Ronan pushes forward, a handgun tight in his grasp. "On your knees, Lennox."

"We can work this out," the man says, dropping to his knees on command.

Ronan laughs roughly. "Don't worry. I'm not going to kill you. Even though you fucking deserve it."

Demitri's gaze darkens. He moves past Ronan, gaining on the man who nearly raped me. If they hadn't gotten here in time . . .

I can't finish the thought before Demitri takes him by the throat and slams him against the wall. "You vile piece of shit. I should crush your throat. Watch you fight for air. Watch you fucking die."

"Nothing happened. I didn't hurt her," Lennox rasps, barely able to get the words out.

"D, don't. He's not worth it. I've got agents on the way. He's done anyway."

"He needs to pay," Demitri growls. "This needs to end."

Ronan glances between me and the scene playing out before us, his eyes betraying his worry. Demitri wants to end Lennox. But he can't. I won't let him ruin his life for vengeance.

"Demitri . . . please. You'll have justice."

His nostrils flare, but he never takes his eyes off Lennox. I worry he can't hear me through his hatred. His rage. He dwarfs the other man with his size and strength. Any second this could be over for Lennox. Over for me if it means losing the man I love too.

"Please . . . I need you." A sob rocks me. "I need you."

I press my hand to my lips, another sob ripping through me. I've never needed anything more. I close my eyes against the torrent of tears. The agony of what's happening. The pain in my chest. The sickness of knowing how close they were to taking advantage of me.

Then I feel him. His arms fold around me. A massive cocoon of warmth. Safety. He hushes me softly.

I blink my eyes open. Through the blur of emotion, I

can see Ronan has moved to where Demitri was. He's with Lennox, shoving him roughly to the ground and cuffing his hands behind his back. Moments later, agents are spilling into my apartment. Guns raised. Reading Lennox his rights. Interrogating Ronan with smiles on their faces and slaps on the back like they've just caught a prize fish.

A couple of agents come up to me looking more concerned than celebratory.

"Are you all right? Do you need a medic?"

I shake my head and turn into Demitri's strong chest. He's all I need.

"Demitri…"

He tugs me tighter. "I'm sorry," he whispers against my ear. "So sorry. This is all my fault. I'll never forgive myself for not getting to you sooner."

"Don't leave me," I beg.

"I'm never leaving you. You're mine to protect, and I'll never stop. For as long as I live, kitten."

I fist my fingers into his shirt and burrow closer, wishing I could find a way to crawl inside and hide from everything. Everything except him.

"I was so scared."

"I know. I came for you as soon as I knew he could be watching you. He paid off the doorman for a spare key to get in here. Don't worry. He's going to pay for it too."

The added betrayal is a twist of the knife inside me.

"I don't feel safe here anymore. I don't know what I'm going to do. My parents control everything. They'll make this my fault—"

"You'll come home with me. No one's going to keep you safer than I will."

"What about my parents? They'll find out about us…"

He pauses, and I worry that's the one circumstance we'll never be able to get around. "Your father knows a lot of important people who could make trouble for me. I haven't gotten this far without making a few friends of my own. We'll just have to cross that bridge when we get to it. In the meantime, you're staying with me."

I weaken against him, intoxicated by the thought of his protection. But for how long? I'll have to move on eventually.

I look up at him. "I don't want to be a burden."

"There hasn't been a single moment I've spent with you that's ever been a burden." A line forms between his brows as he lifts his hand to touch my cheek. "I love you, Katherine." He closes his eyes briefly before opening them to me again. "I'm not good at this. I know I haven't been fair to you."

My heart clenches at his admission. I'm not sure if I've ever wanted to hear those words more from anyone.

"You were just trying to protect me. I get that now."

"I was worried about what your father would do if he ever found out you were coming to Crave. But I couldn't let you go either. I was selfish." He brushes tangled strands of hair from my face. I must look terrible, but the adoration in his eyes says something else. Like maybe what he sees is deeper.

"I love you too, Demitri. Every moment we spent together, I fell a little bit more. I wanted you to be my Master, but I wanted to be in your heart too."

He grasps my hand gently and presses it to the place on his chest where his heartbeat can be felt. "You're already here."

I fight back tears until he takes my mouth in a tender kiss. When we part, he whispers against my lips, "Come home with me, kitten. And stay."

CHAPTER FIFTEEN

"A white Christmas. How lucky is that?" I marvel at the winter weather swirling outside Demitri's living room window.

"Not as lucky as me," he murmurs, sinking his teeth gently into my neck. "Come kneel for me, kitten. Master has a present for you."

I moan and lean back into him, pleased to find him as turned-on as I feel. We haven't had sex since I moved in. He insists I need time to recover from what happened with Lennox. He might be right. But every day I'm forced to endure moments like these adds to my torture.

When he steps away, creating an unwelcome chill, I turn. Even in the few days we've been together, he manages to routinely take my breath away. Maybe it's his Czech blood or his sheer size, but he seems immune to the cold. This morning he's shirtless again, with red plaid pajama pants slung low on his hips. Barefoot and totally at home. A stark contrast from the unforgiving sex club owner I've been falling in love with a little more every time he's taken me over his knee.

Watching him walk away and sink into the chair beside the tree is redefining Christmas spirit for me. I take a snapshot in my mind—my own private holiday photo card. Demitri… my Master… against the backdrop of his apartment, which I've transformed a little bit with decorations here and there. Some garland over the fireplace. A modest tree with a few ornaments dangling from its branches. I hope we're here next year, just like this, adding to them.

He crooks his finger toward me. "Crawl for me, kitten."

I set my hot cocoa down and do as he asks, never taking my eyes off him. I settle between his thighs and take my usual position.

"Good girl. Now look over here for your present and bring it to me."

My heart does a little skip. Quickly I find a small flat box wrapped in silver paper and a shimmering bow under the tree. I bring it back to him and offer it.

He shakes his head. "You open it. Go slow. Don't rip the paper."

I laugh a little and follow his instructions. The anticipation is killing me, but of course that's what he wants. Delayed gratification. But it's more than gratification I feel when I'm finally able to pop open the box, revealing a thick platinum necklace. The front joins around a circle piece made of diamonds with two sharp ears on top. I smile and look up.

He smiles too, something rare that he's giving me more of lately—vulnerability that I cherish along with all his other gifts.

"For my kitten. My lion."

My cheeks warm. He takes the collar out of the box and clasps it around my neck. I know that's what this is. More than a holiday trinket. This is an official claiming, a Master of his sub. I'm so overwhelmed I'm shaking when I bring my fingers to it.

"Thank you, Master."

He leans down, tunnels his fingers into my hair, and tugs me upward for a kiss—a deep and savage kiss that has my knees trembling too.

"I am your Master, and you are my kitten. And always *moje láska.*"

I search his eyes for a clue. I've never heard him call me that before.

"My love. My only love."

I smile so hard it nearly hurts. I've wanted these moments with him so badly for so long, to have them is pleasure and pain. A sweet and heart-wrenching satisfaction.

"Can I give you a gift?"

He regards me thoughtfully a moment. "All right."

I bite my lip and stand to slip off my nightshirt, which is actually a shirt from his drawer that I've grown attached to. But not so much that I'm not happy to leave it in a pile on the floor while I straddle the man I love. He groans, grasping my hips tightly.

"This is the gift?"

I pepper his mouth with needy kisses. "The gift that keeps on giving."

"Are you sure?" Some of the heat in his eyes melts away, replaced with concern.

"I need this. I need you, Demitri. Please." I kiss him again and grind myself against his steely erection, trying to convey the depth of my desire. "Please," I beg again.

He answers by lifting me up with him as he stands. Then he takes us to the rug, where he settles between my thighs, shoving his pants down just enough to free his thick erection.

When he joins us, I cry out from the overwhelming sensations. The relief of finally feeling him push inside me again. The hint of discomfort from the intrusion that my body is still learning to accept. The sheer pleasure of being filled and stretched and driven to the edge of reason, with every thrust, every touch, every command. And more than anything, the deep and satisfying solace of being loved by my Master.

ABOUT MEREDITH WILD

Meredith Wild is a #1 *New York Times, USA Today,* and international bestselling author of 22 novels. After self-publishing her debut novel *Hardwired* in 2013, Wild used her ten years of experience as a tech entrepreneur to form her first publishing imprint, forging relationships with major retailers, and becoming one of the first indie authors to become fully stocked in brick-and-mortar bookstore chains nationwide.

Both traditionally and self-published, Wild's books have hit No. 1 on the *New York Times* and *Wall Street Journal* bestsellers lists. She has been featured on CBS This Morning, The Today Show, the *New York Times, The Hollywood Reporter, Vanity Fair, Publishers Weekly,* and *The Examiner.* Her foreign rights have been sold in over 23 languages. She resides in Florida with her many cats.

You can find out more about her writing projects at meredithwild.com

About Mia Michelle

Mia Michelle fell in love with the world of books the very first time she stepped inside of her small hometown library. Growing up, she loved to spend time losing herself in the world of make believe by creating her own imaginative stories. The gift of a leather journal for her eighth birthday inspired her dream of one day becoming a writer. Though Mia kept most of her writing private over the years, a childhood best friend read the first draft of Rose of Thorne and encouraged her to take the leap of faith to bring her dream to life.

Mia fully admits to having a hopeless infatuation with her Kindle and suffers from a one-click book addiction. (No intervention required.) When she isn't shuttling her two kids between cheerleading and football practice, or folding a massive pile of laundry, she can be found curled up in her favorite cozy chair with a pen in one hand and an adult beverage in the other.

Mia currently resides in a quaint little southern town in Tennessee with her husband, two children, and fur baby.